Dirty Old Town

Dirty Old Town

Ted Darling crime series

'gritty gripping northern noir'

LIVRES
LEMAS

L M Krier

Published by LEMAS LIVRES
www.tottielimejuice.com

© Copyright L.M.K. Tither 2020
Cover design DMR Creative
Cover photo Neil Smith

DIRTY OLD TOWN

ISBN 978-2901773-48-1

Contents

About the Author

L M Krier is the pen name of former journalist (court reporter) and freelance copywriter, Lesley Tither, who also writes travel memoirs under the name Tottie Limejuice. Lesley also worked as a case tracker for the Crown Prosecution Service. Now retired, she lives in Central France and enjoys walking her dogs and going camping.

The Ted Darling series of crime novels comprises: *The First Time Ever, Baby's Got Blue Eyes, Two Little Boys, When I'm Old and Grey, Shut Up and Drive, Only the Lonely, Wild Thing, Walk on By, Preacher Man, Cry for the Bad Man, Every Game You Play, Where the Girls Are, Down Down Down, The Cuckoo is a Pretty Bird*

All books in the series are available in Kindle and paperback format and are also available to read free with Kindle Unlimited.

Contact Details

If you would like to get in touch, please do so at:

https://www.teddarlingcrimeseries.uk/

tottielimejuice@gmail.com

facebook.com/LMKrier

facebook.com/groups/1450797141836111/

twitter.com/tottielimejuice

For a lighter look at Ted and Trev, why not join the fun in the We Love Ted Darling group?

FREE 'Ted Darling is billirant' badge for each member.

Discover the
DI Ted Darling series

If you've enjoyed meeting Ted Darling you may like to discover the other books in the series. The First Time Ever is also now available as an audiobook. Watch out for audiobook versions of other books in the series, coming soon, as well as further books in the series:

The First Time Ever
Baby's Got Blue Eyes
Two Little Boys
When I'm Old and Grey
Shut Up and Drive
Only the Lonely
Wild Thing
Walk on By
Preacher Man
Cry for the Bad Man
Every Game You Play
Where the Girls Are
Down Down Down
The Cuckoo is a Pretty Bird
Dirty Old Town

Acknowledgements

I would just like to thank the people who have helped me bring Ted Darling to life.

Alpha and Beta readers: Jill Pennington, Kate Pill, Karen Corcoran, Jill Evans, Alan Wood, Paul Kemp, Eileen Payne, Jo Baines, Valérie Goutte.

Police consultants – The Three Karens.

Medical advisor – Jo Baines

And a very special thanks to all Ted's loyal friends in the We Love Ted Darling Facebook group. Always so supportive and full of great ideas to be incorporated into the next Ted book. FREE 'Ted Darling is billirant' badge for all members.

To Anne

with grateful thanks for her
kind help and valued friendship

Author's Note

Thank you for reading the Ted Darling Crime Series. The books are set in Stockport, and Greater Manchester in general, and the characters use local dialect and sayings.

Seemingly incorrect grammar within quotes reflects common speech patterns. For example, 'I'll do it if I get chance', without an article or determiner, is common parlance.

Ted and Trev also have an in joke between them - 'billirant' - which is a deliberate 'typo'.

If you have any queries about words or phrases used, do please feel free to get in touch, using the contact details in the book. I always try to reply promptly to any emails or Facebook messages.

Thank you.

L M Krier

Chapter One

She was on the floor of the living room now. On her hands and knees. Her head was bowed. Her long hair, escaped from its restraining band, forming a curtain of sorts around her face.

She was pawing ineffectually at his feet. A futile attempt to stem the torrent of scorn he was hurling at her.

His voice stayed quiet, never rising above low conversational pitch. It somehow accentuated the venom in his words.

She felt flecks of his spittle land on her bare arms. She kept her head down, not wanting to feel the hatred rain onto her face.

Neither did she want to look up and see the growing bulge in his trousers which she knew was inevitable. He got such a perverted thrill out of treating her like this.

Please let him seek out one of his other women to take advantage of his state of arousal.

Please god.

And make it soon.

'You're pathetic, you stupid bitch. And dangerous. You're not fit to be a mother. You're going to harm the boy one of these days.'

Her head jerked up at that, the accusation stinging her like thrown acid. She tried to say something. To deny it. All that would come out of her mouth was a sound somewhere between a whimper and a moan.

'And don't look at me like that. You might say you never would, but look at you! Can you honestly say you're in control of yourself? I don't know why you don't finally do us both a favour, me and the boy, and fuck off out of our lives. For good. Have you got some pills, and plenty of them? I'll buy you some, if not.'

The boy was sitting on the sofa nearby. Both knees drawn up to his skinny chest, his face buried against them. He had his hands over his ears, but even the quiet vehemence of the man's voice found a way to seep in through his clamped fingers. He started to shout, his voice near to screaming pitch.

'Stop it! Stop it! Stop it! Mum would never hurt me. Never.'

The man gave an exaggerated sigh.

'If the idiot boy is going to join in and take your side, as usual, I'm off out to the pub. You're welcome to one another. But you'll find out one day, lad. Find out what your precious mother is really like.

'I'm going out now, for a drink or several. I have no idea when I'll be back.'

As soon as the door of the room closed behind him, quietly but firmly, followed by the click of the front door shutting softly, the boy slid off his seat and crawled towards his mother. He wrapped his arms round her, his hot tears wetting her neck and the side of her face.

'You are a good mother, mum. You are. I know you'd never hurt me. Don't listen to him. He's just a pig and I hate him. When I grow bigger and stronger I'm going to learn how to protect you. I won't let him talk to you like that ever again. Please promise me you'd never hurt yourself. Mum? Promise me!'

She pushed herself upright, kneeling up and drawing him closer, folding protective arms around him, wiping away her tears with one hand.

'You're such a good boy. I don't deserve you. I really don't. I should protect you more. You shouldn't have to see things like that, over and over. But I'm too weak. I promise I'll try to do better. And you know I would never, ever, do anything to hurt you. I'm your mum. It's my job to protect you.'

She had more control of herself now that the immediate threat had passed. Until the next time. She stood up, took his hand, and moved to sit on the sofa, pulling him gently down beside her. He snuggled close, half lying, his head in her lap as she stroked his hair out of his eyes.

'We'll sing our song together, and make a wish. We'll wish things would get better. And then they will. You'll see. We just have to believe and to wish hard enough, the two of us. Together.'

In a soft voice, she started to sing, waiting for the boy to join in:

'When you wish upon a star ...'

* * *

'Back seat, Ted,' Detective Chief Inspector Ted Darling's driver for the day, Hector, told him firmly, as he went instinctively to slide into the front passenger place.

As Ted hesitated, his hand still holding the door open, Hector went on, his tone patient, 'Unless you're going to do things a lot differently to Big Jim, you're going to have a shitload of paperwork to deal with between visits. That means you'll need room to spread it out to work on, without the distractions of being in the front.

'It's up to you how you run things, of course. You're Head of Serious Crime now, not Jim, but I thought I'd make the suggestion.'

Ted meekly closed the front door and got in the back. It was his first official day in the role since the retirement of his

3

good friend and former boss, Detective Superintendent Jim Baker. Jim had his pension now so had taken his retirement. He was going to come back as a consultant as and when needed. Knowing Jim, it would be sooner, rather than later. But in the meantime he would be enjoying spending time in the garden he cherished and was proud of. As well as finally having the free time to take his new wife to all the places she'd been gently nagging him to visit.

'So, where to first today? Is this a routine visit to all your new teams or is there somewhere specific you want to start with?' Hector asked him, as he put the car in gear and pulled away smoothly from the steps of the Stockport police station, from which he'd picked Ted up.

'Trafford first please, 'eck,' Ted told him, polite as ever.

From the day Hector had first joined the force, more than thirty years ago, his colleagues had decided his name didn't suit him. He needed a nickname instead. The former officer, now civilian driver, had handed it to them on a plate. Whenever a swear word wasn't appropriate because of the company he was in, he always said, 'Oh, 'eck', and the name had stuck.

'I'm surprised you're not doing it all by hi-tech means from your own office. Video conferencing. Isn't that the modern trend? I know Big Jim did a lot of it that way.'

'I'm the old-fashioned sort. I like to meet people I'm going to be working with in the flesh at least once, so I can form a bit of an opinion of them. There are a couple of the teams who are lacking a DI at the moment due to illness, so I want to make sure they're on top of everything. No replacements immediately on the horizon, of course.'

'Same old, same old,' Hector responded. 'Work miracles. Get the results and keep up the statistics with fewer officers.'

'Trafford have got a suspicious death currently and I want to check that they're dealing with that with no problems and don't need any help. On the face of it, it's yet another case of domestic violence which got out of hand and went too far.'

'Husband, was it? Happens all too often,' Hector asked, changing smoothly down through the gears as they approached traffic lights. They would be turning left, but there was no filter lane so they were behind another vehicle, also slowing, which wasn't signalling to turn.

Then the driver in front of them, seeing the lights change to amber as he got nearer to them, floored the accelerator and went for it. The lights were on red before he'd crossed what was a busy intersection.

'Oh, 'eck, look at that pillock. Want me to put the blues on and go after him?'

'Tempting though it might be, you're retired and I've got a probable murder to help sort out, which trumps a road traffic violation, in my book. Radio his number in, though, so any units about can keep an eye out for him, if he makes a habit of driving like that. I'd hate to think we could have prevented a serious incident and didn't do anything.'

Hector had been a Road Patrol Officer and had retired as soon as he'd done his thirty years. Now he was back, working as a civilian. There were some rumours flying round about him and the reason for his return, but Ted tended to avoid station gossip. He'd been the subject of too much of it in his time.

No doubt Hector would tell him all the details if and when he wanted to. But it seemed that the lump sum he had commuted from his pension had been used to go into business with his brother. Unfortunately, the rock solid investment had turned out to be yet another dodgy pyramid scheme which had cost Hector a big chunk of his savings. That had in turn seen him jump at the chance to drive for senior officers on a modest but steady wage to supplement his pension for a few more years.

Hector was right about Ted needing to sit in the back. Although he'd gone over all the notes he needed for the day, now he had the chance he made good use of it with another read-through of the cases which now came under his new, extended remit. He wanted to hit the ground running and not appear to be floundering too much.

As well as his usual team, operating out of Stockport, Ted had for some time been part of a mobile unit which travelled to other divisions as necessary for Serious Crime. But he'd always been answerable to Jim Baker, constantly liaising with him and running everything past him before making critical decisions.

Now Ted was Head of Serious Crime for part of Jim's old stamping ground, and flying solo. The buck stopped with him. Jim had promised he would always be at the end of the phone to give him a steer whenever he needed help, although Ted strongly suspected Jim's wife Bella would have something to say about that.

'Nice to meet you, Ted. Good to put a face to a voice at the other end of the phone or the writer of an email. Is Ted all right for you? We're a small and informal team here.'

Detective Sergeant Sarah Jenkins came to the front desk to meet Ted when he arrived at Trafford. He didn't know any of the officers on the team he was coming to talk to, but he'd been impressed with the high standard of her written reports so far.

His own team were more formal with him. He was 'boss' or 'sir' to most of them when at work, only on first name terms in a social setting, and then not to all of them. He nodded his agreement. Things were changing. The old ways, especially the formalities, were fast disappearing.

She led him upstairs to the main office, introduced him briefly to the team members, then found a quiet corner of the open plan space where she could bring him up to speed. Putting flesh on the bones of what she'd already sent him in writing.

'At face value, an open and shut case of domestic violence ending in a death,' she told him. 'Sadly far too common these days. A row that got out of control. One slap too many, and the wife has gone down, falling backwards against the edge of a work surface with enough force to kill her.

'CSI haven't found traces of anyone other than the husband in the house, except for the next door neighbour who reported the death. Although the back door was open when the first responders arrived and looked as if it might have been kicked in.'

'Any children?'

'A boy. The neighbour thinks about ten but isn't sure. Luckily he'd gone to stay with his nan, as he apparently often does because of the rows at home. And she's happy for him to carry on staying there for now. There's an older sister, too. Eighteen, nineteen or so. She's in the Army. She's been contacted, granted compassionate leave, and is on her way back. We'll need to arrange to talk to her, and to the boy, if that's possible. Perhaps the grandmother, too.'

'Post-mortem results?'

'Not been done yet. There's a backlog at the moment. But it looks as if the head wound was what caused the fatality. We've treated it as a suspicious death from the outset, in case it wasn't accidental. There were signs of some violence on her body, some of it older, going purely on initial examination at the scene.

'Here's where it gets interesting, though. Completely conflicting witness statements from the neighbours on either side of the crime scene, if it is one. It's a mid-terrace and you can pretty much hear the neighbours chewing their cornflakes through the walls. One side, an older man on his own who says the couple were always having screaming rows. Lots of banging and crashing, doors slamming, him storming off to the pub. The other side say the exact opposite. Perfect couple. Devoted. Never a cross word, and so on.'

'What does the husband have to say for himself?' Ted asked.

Sarah made exaggerated quotation marks in the air as she replied, '*Not me, guv, I was in the pub with me mates. I kept telling the wife she had some dodgy friends. Druggies and*

7

*such, and she should steer clear of them, but she wouldn't lis-
ten.*

'He reckons one of them must have come round while he
was out, kicked the door in, argued with her over something,
then shoved her over and legged it. And to prove it, he's got
about half a dozen or more of his mates all prepared to swear
blind that at the time it happened he was having a drink and a
game of darts with them in their usual pub, where they're well
known. And the bar staff confirm he was there. It's taking us a
while to get all the witness statements, but they basically all
say the same thing. Exactly the same thing.'

'Does he work? What's his job?'

'Security work on an industrial site.'

'Does he fancy himself as a bit of a hard man? It can sometimes go with the role, though not always. What's his background?'

'Not a glowing employment record. Bits of this, bits of
that. Walks the walk for the tough guy. He works rotating
shifts. Two weeks of days, two weeks of nights.'

'So who reported the death?'

'The next-door neighbour who says things were far from
harmonious. He went out to the back garden to put something
in the bin. He noticed the neighbours' back door was wide
open and no signs of life so he stepped over the fence – it's
only low – and went to have a nosy, as he put it. You could say
he's either a good citizen or someone who likes to interfere. He
did have the presence of mind not to touch anything, when he
saw the victim lying on the floor, other than to check if she was
still alive, so we've got his DNA to eliminate from the scene.
But he confirms there was no sign of the husband in the house,
and he hadn't noticed him go out earlier. And before you ask,
he's older and quite frail, so I'm not at the moment suspecting
him.'

'Right, keep it as a suspicious for now, unless the PM
throws up anything strange. Let me know if you need any more

officers and I can draft some in as needed, but you seem to have everything well under control. I was particularly impressed with your written reports.'

She smiled at him as she said, 'Creative writing is my hobby, so I try to string sentences together to make some sort of sense.'

Once Ted had been round most of his new area and Hector had dropped him off, with a reminder he wouldn't be available the following day as he was driving the Chief Constable, he went into the station to find Inspector Kevin Turner for a catch-up before rejoining his own team.

'How's your report for the ACC coming along?' Ted asked him, taking a seat.

He and Kev were going to a meeting the following day, with other officers from various divisions, to discuss crime statistics with the Assistant Chief Constable (Crime), Russell Evans. A way to concentrate available resources where the demand was highest.

'Crime?'

From his tone, Kevin Turner was not in the best of moods. He shuffled papers round on his desk, pulled up the sheet he was looking for and brandished it in the air.

'I've been pissing about with these papers all day when I could have been doing something useful. And do you know what's come out near the top, statistically, of the so-called crime that's currently getting reported to us? Fly-tipping! Bloody fly-tipping. Our officers aren't binmen. What do the public expect us to do about it? The ACC's going to love that as a statistic.'

Then he got a grip of himself and calmed down a bit.

'What about you? What's currently top of the charts in Serious Crime? Gang stabbings? Drugs deaths?'

'Domestic violence,' Ted told him. 'Of the killings we've got on our books at the moment, the highest number relate to

9

domestic violence. So spare a thought for me having to come up with some sort of preventive strategy for that which would get the ACC's backing.'

* * *

She was lying on top of the bed clothes, spooning around her sleeping son. He smelled of soap and shampoo. He'd been so unsettled about the earlier incident he'd actually allowed her to help him with his bath and to wash his hair for him. He hadn't done that for a long time.

It had taken him some time to settle when she'd helped him into bed. Even as he dozed off, he kept twitching and thrashing about for nearly half an hour before exhaustion finally caught up with him. He was now sleeping deeply and soundly.

She felt the sudden flutterings of panic in her stomach as she heard the front door open then close again. Firmly, but quietly. Never loud. Nothing to alert the neighbours.

His tread on the stairs was heavy, measured. She heard him go first to the bedroom they shared, then give a tutting sound of annoyance not to find her there. Then he stumped along the landing to the boy's room, pushed the door open and walked in.

He didn't raise his voice as he spoke but it still chilled her.

'Get up. Stop smothering the boy. He's far too old for you to be treating him like a baby.'

When she didn't immediately react, he crossed the small room in a couple of strides, grabbed a large handful of her hair and pulled her up. The boy stirred for a moment then burrowed back down into the sanctuary of sleep.

His mouth was close to her ear, his voice still icily

quiet. His breath stank of beer and whisky, with overtones of strong curry.

'Get up, when I tell you to, you stupid bitch. Time to do your wifely duty.'

He dragged her from the room, closing the door softly behind them, his grasp on her hair so vicious she felt it being torn out by the roots. She tried to keep up with him, to stay level. Anything to stop the terrible pain in her scalp. Once again he shut the door noiselessly. She heard the key turn in the lock.

He forced her face down on the bed, his hand still grasping her hair, kneeling across her legs to immobilise them. She could barely breathe, her face pressed down as it was into the duvet.

She felt him tearing roughly at her clothes. Heard the unmistakable sound of his own trouser zip being yanked down in haste.

She let the same tune play over and over in her head on a loop the whole time it was happening to her.

'When you wish upon a star ...'

Chapter Two

'Right, boys and girls, remember what I said. Line up at attention in an orderly fashion. The Big Boss is home.'

Ted, putting his things away tidily in the hall, chuckled at Trev's words to the cats from in the kitchen.

'Not quite the Big Boss, but trying my best to fill his large shoes,' Ted replied, walking through to find his partner once he'd hung up his jacket. His tie had long since been relegated to the pocket.

Trev paused in his cooking to give him a brief kiss, then said, 'Poached salmon, okay? Fish is supposed to be good brain food and I thought yours might need refuelling after a hard first day in the new job. How was it?'

'That sounds great, thank you. What's for afters?' Ted asked hopefully, looking round for clues.

'You and your puddings,' Trev laughed. 'It's a wonder you aren't the size of a house, with that sweet tooth of yours. It's sticky toffee pudding, of course, with clotted cream. I thought that would work for whatever kind of day you'd had. So how was it?'

Ted was carefully greeting each of their cats in turn, in order of seniority. He was making young Adam wait until the end, for once, despite his protests. When he did get to him, he scooped him up for a sneaky cuddle which sent the little cat into a squirming frenzy of purrs.

'My new driver made me sit in the back like a proper Big Boss. He's got my measure. He's going to be a big help, I think. I met most but not all of the new teams. Some good ones, some might need a bit of a kick up the backside. Especially as some seemed to think, unwisely, that they might get an easier ride from me than from Big Jim.'

'Oooh, I sense a few kick-tricks coming on,' Trev told him, bringing full plates to the table and setting them down.

Ted was unbuttoning his cuffs and turning his sleeves back in readiness for the meal.

'And if you start exposing bare flesh at the dinner table, I won't be responsible for the consequences,' Trev went on teasingly as he sat down. 'So to prevent unseemly behaviour I will, just this once, permit you to talk shop in the house. Tell all.'

Ted was already tucking into his food. He vaguely remembered grabbing a sandwich at some point during the day, but it certainly hadn't made a lasting impression. He hadn't realised quite how hungry he was and the meal was as good as Trev's cooking always was.

He didn't often talk about his work at home. Certainly not at the table. Although he had shared with Trev his frustration and disappointment at not managing to arrest everyone from their last big case. He was constantly worried that those who had given them the slip would go on to start up their operations somewhere else. Which was why he'd taken the opportunity to talk to each team he'd met about the need for vigilance. Details had been circulated throughout the Force area and beyond, but Ted knew only too well that such things often got overlooked when teams were busy with other cases of their own.

'Those who don't know me, and were clearly surprised to see a skinny little short-arse turn up as Head of Serious Crime, looked ready to have me sectioned once I started telling them about our blind dwarf, who probably isn't blind at all.'

'You have to admit, if you read that in a crime fiction book, you'd be hurling it at the wall saying it was absolutely too far-fetched to be considered.'

Ted looked at him in mock offence.

'I don't hurl books against the wall. Well, at least, not very often.'

'Ted, your nose is growing into your salmon. I've seen you do it.'

Ted grinned at him, looking guilty.

'That was under extreme provocation. Nobody would make an arrest like that. And certainly not without searching the premises for evidence. The author even got the caution wording wrong, for goodness sake.'

Trev was busily grinding more black pepper over his meal. He held the grinder up in invitation. Ted shook his head.

'No, thanks, this is fine, just as it is.'

It was these mundane exchanges which helped Ted to unwind at the end of a working day. One of the reasons he didn't like to talk too much about work once he got back to the sanctuary of home.

'By the way, I've no idea what time I'll be back tomorrow, so don't wait for me. Go ahead and eat when you're hungry. I've got this meeting at Central Park, so no doubt there'll be the usual uninspiring food to tide us over.'

'What are your crime figures looking like?' Trev asked him.

Ted had mentioned fleetingly to him what the meeting was all about.

'Depressing,' Ted said frankly. 'There's a real spike in statistics related to domestic violence. There's direct correlation, too, between things which tend to keep people stuck inside the home and the numbers going up. Bad weather over a Bank Holiday weekend, for one. Sporting fixtures cancelled for whatever reason. A team losing unexpectedly. When people suddenly find themselves shut indoors together, staring at four walls. That's when it all starts to kick off.

'It's a crime that knows no boundaries, too. Classless. It's an urban myth that it's predominantly working class. No one has a clue what goes on in households, until they start looking at the kind of statistics I have been. Most towns have it. A dirty little secret people don't know about. Sometimes even people in the same household are totally unaware.'

Trev put down his knife and fork, reached across the table and took hold of one of Ted's hands. His expression was serious.

'Ted, stop it. I know what you're doing. Stop beating yourself up. About everything. You couldn't possibly have known what was going on between your parents. You were a little boy, for heaven's sake. Annie's told you it only happened when you were safely asleep in bed and they were in their own bedroom together. There's no way you could have known anything about what was happening, or even understood it, at that age.

'Stop taking everything so personally. It's what makes you a good copper and a decent person. But it makes you impossible to live with sometimes, and it could finish up destroying you. Go and see Carol. Get some more counselling sessions. Don't let it take you to a dark place again.

'Ted, I mean it. Promise me.'

Ted was saved from replying by his mobile ringing. The screen told him it was his DI, Jo Rodriguez. He made an apologetic face at Trev as he answered the call.

Trev glared at him and mouthed, 'This isn't over between us.'

'Jo, yes, what have we got?'

Ted stood up as he spoke, moving to step outside into the garden. Trev automatically rescued his plate and put it safely out of cat reach.

'Nothing for you, Ted, but I wanted to keep you in the loop,' Jo told him, informal while they were out of the office. 'An almost certain homicide. I've sent Mike Hallam initially, with uniform, because it's not too gory.'

DS Mike Hallam was not known for having a strong stomach when attending gruesome scenes of crime. But he was a good, experienced sergeant. He would do a thorough job for the initial investigation to assess the situation.

When Ted asked for detail, Jo told him, 'Man and wife arguing in a flat. She tried to leave. He's gone after her, grabbed her and thrown her over the handrail down two flights of stairs. She seems to have died instantly, from what appears to be a broken neck. At least that's what it looks like from first impressions.

'He's denying it furiously. His version is that the wife had serious mental health issues, including self-harming. He denies any argument. He says he was trying to stop her hurting herself again. Then she ran out and started to try to climb over the handrail. He grabbed her and wrestled with her but he couldn't hold onto her and she jumped.

'It's possible we might get lucky on this one, though, Ted. For once neighbours rallied round and got involved. Apparently they were getting fed up of the frequent violent shouting matches in the flat, so some of them came out. Sadly too late for the woman, but they made a citizen's arrest on the bloke, called it in, and any number of them are offering to testify that the blazing rows were a regular thing.

'With a bit of luck and a following breeze, it should be a nice straightforward one for us to wrap up quickly. Although, of course, with no eye witnesses and him offering a seemingly plausible reason for any marks we find on her body left by his hands, it's not guaranteed.

'It's only a shame no one thought to come forward sooner or it could possibly have been prevented. It really goes to show how much of this sort of thing goes on. People are always so reluctant to get involved in whatever happens inside someone else's house. The "famous behind closed doors" thing, with all the dirty little secrets that hides.'

* * *

'What's this shit?'

The clash of his knife and fork against his plate sounded so loud in the neat kitchen that she jumped involuntarily, only just managing to hold on to the glass she was washing up in the sink.

She kept her voice quiet, meek, as she replied, 'Lamb chops.'

'No they bloody aren't!'

His voice stayed low but there was barely controlled anger now in his tone.

'This is a pile of gristle and bone. You wouldn't serve that up to a dog. I'm not bloody eating it. I give you enough money to buy decent stuff. What do you do with it all that you've been buying this crap and daring to serve it to me?'

'I'm sorry. Ours were all right. Quite nice, in fact.'

She'd stopped the washing up and was drying her hands on a towel. She was trying to make light of it. Daring, for once, to contradict him.

'Do you want me to make you something else instead? I'm sorry yours wasn't as good as ours ...'

The sound of his chair scraping back on the tiles as he got to his feet made her flinch in anticipation. Her hand, as she reached out to take his plate, was trembling visibly.

'Leave it!' he barked.

His hand shot out and grabbed her wrist, his fingers biting into the flesh, deliberately letting his nails dig in. She tried to stifle the gasp it provoked.

He dragged her towards him, half across the table, bending her hand down towards her inner arm until the wrist joint was screaming as much as she wanted to.

The television was on in the next room where the boy was watching something. He hadn't yet appeared.

The man put his mouth close to the woman's ear as

he held her.

'You'll pay for this later, you bitch,' he said softly, almost gently, into her ear.

Then, keeping the tight grip on her wrist, lifting his voice to normal conversational level, he pulled her upright and moved her over to the work surface.

'How many times have I told you about cutting the fat and gristle off mine before you serve it to me?'

His tone was reasonable, patient. Explaining something, which should have been obvious, to someone who was slow on the uptake.

He reached a hand out towards the knife block, tucked away in the far corner of the work surface. He pulled out the boning knife he was looking for. Then he let go of her wrist but put his full weight up against her, pinning her there with no chance of getting away.

She was not surprised to feel how hard he was already, and she knew he had barely got going.

His free hand reached for the sharpening steel and he started to stroke the knife blade against it. Slowly to begin with, then speeding up to a faster tempo. Grinding his hips against her with each movement of his hand.

He held the knife and the steel between them. The sharp point of the knife moved perilously close to her with each movement he made, the blunt end of the steel digging viciously into her.

She was crying silently now, both from the pain of being crushed up against the handles of drawers in the units behind her, and from the revulsion of what he was doing. She kept her face averted. Anything not to have to look at the expression on his face as his thrusting movements accelerated, his hand on the knife increasing its speed all the time to keep pace.

Please don't let the boy come in and see them like that.

What programme was he watching?

Would it end soon?

He'd eaten, so he shouldn't be hungry and come looking for food.

He must have heard the man come in. He usually kept out of his way until he was sure it was safe to be in the same room.

Finally, the man gave a long, juddering sigh. His hips and his hands slowly stopped moving, in unison.

His voice, when he spoke, was once more almost conversational.

'Now, this is a beautifully sharp blade. You can easily take off any fat and sinew with it. It will slide through meat like through butter. Look, let me show you.'

He dropped the steel with a loud crash against the work surface. Then he grabbed her wrist once more, turning the vulnerable white flesh of her inner arm upwards to meet the soft kiss of the descending blade.

His mouth was close to her ear again as he said, 'Like this, you silly bitch. Remember, always lengthways, never across. And it's so much better in hot water. In the bath. When you finally do it, remember that.'

A trickle of blood appeared instantaneously where he'd opened up the skin. A flesh wound. Painful, stinging, but not serious. She couldn't stifle the cry it brought from her lips.

He flung the knife into the sink, clattering against the stainless steel, clamped his large hand over the wound, then said loudly, 'Oh, darling, what have you done, you silly thing?'

The boy came running in, alerted by the sudden loud noises. He saw the man holding his mother's arm aloft, hand gripping it tightly, blood trickling between his fingers.

'Don't worry, boy, silly mum's had a little accident with

the knife while she was seeing to my lamb chops. Don't panic, there's a good boy. I'm going to fix it. It's not serious. It looks worse than it is. Pass me a couple of clean towels, there's a good chap. Don't worry, I promise you it's going to be all right. You know how clumsy mum can be.'

The boy stood rooted to the spot, suspicion etched into his face. Then his mum spoke, choking back the tears.

'It's all right, love. Just a silly accident. It's really not serious. Get some towels, there's a good boy. It'll all be fine in a minute. You'll see.'

Warily, not convinced, the boy went to the drawer where the clean towels were, took out a handful and passed them to the man.

'I told you you weren't fit to look after the lad,' the man said, his voice low, but the words still clear to the listening boy. 'You can't even look after yourself, let alone him. You're going to hurt him one day, mark my words. Even if you don't mean to.'

She tried to smile reassuringly at her son as he stood watching, missing nothing. She couldn't find the voice or the words to reassure him, only the watery smile.

Her mind was occupied. The tune playing over and again in her head on a loop against the repeated mantra she recited deep inside her brain.

'Wish harder. It will all be all right if you wish a bit harder.'

Chapter Three

'Right, team, settle down.'

Ted started off the morning briefing in his customary way. He wanted a quick update before handing over to Jo. His DI was more than capable of running things while he was else-where. But Ted held the purse strings now, so he liked to keep an overview of what was happening with his budget, as much as anything.

'As you know, I'm off up to Central Park later, so I need bringing up to speed with what we've got on the books here, please. That way, having now met most of the other teams, I can bring extra officers in to help out as necessary.'

DS Mike Hallam spoke first.

'Boss, the fatality from yesterday. The flats in Sandstone Street. Not a husband and wife, but a couple cohabiting. Not that that makes it any better. We've got the man downstairs. I'm going to crack on with interviewing him after we've finished here but he was denying everything yesterday.'

'Gut feeling, Mike?'

'Guilty as sin, I would say,' Mike told him. 'I don't think he'll confess, though, and I don't initially see how we can make a case against him. Depending, of course, on forensics and the PM. Plenty of witnesses to say there was always a lot of shouting from the flat but there's no one who actually saw the incident on the stairs. Or not anyone we've found so far.'

'Any children?'

'A little lad of nine. Very traumatised, as you would ex-

L.M.KRIER

pect. Children's Services are looking after him for the moment, until they find a relative, if there are any. Our best bet is detailed statements from all the neighbours and anyone who knew the couple, and that's going to take a lot of time and people, boss. We'll also need the woman's medical records to check whether or not his claims about her state of mental health are true or not.'

'What does the man do for a living?' Ted asked him.

'Lead shift engineer in a manufacturing plant. In charge of a small team, keeping the production line running at full capacity. They often have to work antisocial hours so they can get access to the machinery when it's not running at full throttle.'

Ted nodded at the information, then said, 'Jo, liaise with Kevin Turner to see if he can help out with anyone from Uniform for now. Tell him I'll bring in reinforcements, too, as soon as possible.'

'Will do. It's a good time to ask him as he wants some of us to help with the big demo coming up this weekend. They would choose a Bank Holiday, of course, so we're all going to be stretched a bit thin. And it's this weekend you're on a Do Not Disturb, isn't it boss?'

'That's the theory, at least. What else?' Ted asked them.

'The Black Mould Scam, boss,' DS Rob O'Connell told him, a note of humour in his voice.

'Black Mould Scam?' Ted echoed. 'Explain, please.'

'A particularly nasty pair of individuals going round targeting older people who look like they might have some nice pieces in the house. Saleable antiques more than cash, although they take that too, of course, if they find any. Anything easy to lift that they can sell on. They tell the homeowners they're subcontractors for the council, surveying homes for signs of serious black mould infestation in kitchens and bathrooms, which is a big health risk. Usual story, one of them keeps the householder talking while the other one goes round taking anything they can pocket and making a note of anything to go back for.

'They seem to be doing their homework thoroughly as they've largely been targeting single occupant households.'

'Is there much of it going on?'

'One or two reports so far, but I suspect it might be one of those crimes which gets under- reported because people are embarrassed about it. They might feel stupid that they fell for something like that and prefer to write it off to experience.

'I've not had time to do any door-to-door yet, but I've been to one so far where the scammers met their match good and proper. An older lady, down Bramhall Lane. A widow, living alone. She let them in, because their paperwork looked genuine enough, but as soon as they separated, it made her suspicious, so she went on the offensive.

'Her late father had been in Africa during the war and brought back a load of memorabilia with him. She grabbed a weapon and started prodding one of them with it until he squealed, so they both decided to leg it fairly quickly.

'Mrs Hamer, the lady in question, is small and slight, but I can imagine her being quite fearsome armed with an *assegai*.'

'An *assegai*?' Ted queried.

'A type of spear,' Steve supplied, as Jezza added helpfully, 'Like in Zulu, boss, if you saw that film.'

The two of them often helped Jezza's younger brother Tommy in his constant searching for quiz questions and answers.

'Spear or not, she was taking one hell of a risk, going on the offensive with them. What were they like? Do we have a good description of them?' Ted asked.

'We do, boss. She's very observant. A very good witness. I'll circulate it and cross-check against known offenders. And as far as risk goes, Mrs Hamer is a retired headteacher. She started her career in approved schools with some challenging young offenders. I did have a word with her about the wisdom of having weapons lying around which could potentially be used against her by intruders. But she gave me one of those teacher looks. You know the ones. It took me right back to my schooldays, so I shut up.'

Even Ted had to smile at that. Then he looked across at Jo and said, 'When you've finished here, come over to my office and we'll talk about getting some press releases out. Some sort of a warning to potentially vulnerable people. We should talk to the council, too, work with them on getting the word out there.

'Anything else I need to know about?'

When Jo said not, Ted went back to his office. Jo joined him after a few moments, and began by asking him, 'Is Steve all right at the moment, do you know?'

'As far as I know he is,' Ted replied, as Jo sat down, nodding at Ted's suggestion of coffee. 'Have you seen something to make you think otherwise?'

'I may be overthinking, of course, but he spoke up just now in a full team briefing without calling you sir or even boss, and that doesn't happen very often.'

'Well, that's true enough. But maybe he's gaining a bit of confidence? He's finally realised none of us bite. After all, he's had some cracking ideas on recent cases. Really dug us out of a rut on a couple of occasions, and we've always been careful to let him know his input is valued.'

'He also doesn't seem very focused, to me. Not like he usually is. Other than that interaction, he seemed to be mostly staring into space. That's not the first time I've noticed it recently. A bit preoccupied by something, perhaps? I'd better keep a close eye on him, make sure he's okay. He's always so worried about saying or doing the wrong thing,' Jo went on.

'I could perhaps have a quick chat with Bill, see if he knows of anything that's worrying him more than usual,' Ted suggested. 'I can't say I've noticed, but then I've been out of the office quite a lot.'

DC Steve Ellis lodged with former sergeant, now in charge of the reception desk, Bill Baxter. At least when he wasn't spending time with his computer expert girlfriend, Océane.

'Could you perhaps have a quiet word with him, if you can find the time?' Jo asked, as Ted put drinks in front of them both and sat down.

'For some reason I seem to scare him, although I try not to. I don't think I'm a particularly scary person. Am I?'

'Honest answer or diplomacy?' Jo asked, smiling. 'But no, I wouldn't say you were scary. Although maybe I've simply never merited seeing you in scary mode. Yet.'

He took a drink of his coffee before continuing, 'I have to say he seems to have some sort of a hero worship thing going on with you.'

'D'you think so?' Ted queried, surprised by his words.

'It's obvious he thinks highly of you, and praise from you is particularly important to him. Is there anything on his files that gives a clue? Does he have any family? I've never heard him talk about himself at all, I have to be honest. I really don't know much about him. I know he lives with Bill now and before that with Maurice, but that's about as much as I do know. I can try asking Maurice, too, see if he's noticed anything unusual.'

'I honestly don't know much about his background myself. I only know that he had a bit of a rough time of things growing up. I tend not to look at files on team members. I prefer to make up my own mind about people.'

Jo's laugh was louder this time.

'I'm delighted to hear it. You'll find mine full of "spoken to about inappropriate apparent flirtation with female colleagues". It's the red-blooded Latin in me, but I hope you believe I don't mean anything by it. And I would never deliberately make anyone uncomfortable by how I behave.'

It was Ted's turn to chuckle.

'I've never got over Professor Nelson saying how much she enjoys your charm, as she puts it, when you're working together.'

Professor Elizabeth Nelson, the Home Office pathologist with whom they often worked, was not someone used to being chatted up, on her own admission. She'd confessed to Ted a fondness for Jo's style, and his flashing gold tooth.

'And if you ever got a sneak peek at mine you would doubtless find several references to "cocky little sod", but that's not for public consumption, either. Right, well, let's keep a close eye on young Steve between us. Especially if he finds himself in the front line when we have to put uniforms on to help out Kevin's officers.'

'We, Ted? Are you thinking of coming and joining us mere mortals in the thick of it? Won't you have more than enough on your plate in your new role?'

Ted threw him a conspiratorial grin.

'Why not? When I need a good excuse to escape some of the paperwork, you might find me queuing up to volunteer. But seriously, though, keep a close eye on Steve, please.'

'So statistically speaking, the most common cause of death and serous injury we're currently investigating appears to be related to domestic violence.'

Ted finished his summing up, looking towards the ACC rather than any of the assembled inspectors, chief inspectors and superintendents from around the force area. He knew most, if not all of them. A couple of them had tutted their irritation and asked him to speak up as he presented his report. Ted always spoke quietly. He found it was a good trick to get people to listen to him.

Before Russell Evans could reply to Ted, a Uniform superintendent gave a contemptuous snort and said, 'Preventive policing, Ted. That's what we're on about here. How do you propose doing anything to prevent domestic violence? Leaflets through letterboxes, asking people to play nice and stop knocking the shit out of one another?'

Evans could sense Ted's hackles rising even at a distance.

He stepped in swiftly to calm things down. They were all tense, pitching for a constantly-shrinking budget.

'All right, Vinny. Knowing Ted as well as I do, he will have done a detailed report with his proposals, which I'll take away and study, to see if any of it has legs.'

It was as near to a rebuke as anything he would say to his officers in an open meeting.

'Am I right, Ted? You've written something up for me?'

'I have, sir,' Ted told him, pulling documents in a folder out of his briefcase and sliding them up the table towards the ACC.

Then, looking directly at Superintendent Vinny Harrison, he went on, 'And I appreciate it's not the easiest of crimes to prevent. Appealing to the better nature of someone who thinks it's all right to assault their other half is a waste of time, obviously, because if they had a decent nature, they wouldn't do it.

'And I say other half advisedly, because this isn't exclusively a male on female crime, although that's the more common. I have at least one case that I know of in my area where a woman has killed her husband, seemingly after years of physical and psychological bullying of him, rather than her defending herself, according to witness statements. He'd said nothing about it because he'd clearly been conditioned to believe that men don't do that sort of thing.'

It had gone quiet around the table, all eyes on Ted. Most of them knew him, at least by reputation. Ted leaned back in his seat, folding his arms. He'd said enough. He sensed he may well have said too much. But he'd said his piece, as he'd been determined to do.

'Thank you, Ted,' the ACC told him. 'I look forward with interest to reading your proposals.'

Ted was quiet on the drive back to Stockport. He sat in the front next to Kevin Turner who was driving, their own Superintendent, Debra Caldwell – the formidable Ice Queen – in the back seat. He was worried he might have pushed things a bit far.

He was surprised when, as they walked back towards the station together, while Kevin went to park the car, the Ice Queen turned to him and said, 'Well done for standing up to Superintendent Harrison like that, Ted. He's always struck me as something of a bully himself, and after all, domestic violence is the most extreme form of bullying. Good for you.'

Ted stopped at the front desk for a quick word with Bill before he went back up to his office.

'Does Steve seem all right to you at the moment, Bill?'

'Bearing in mind I don't always see him every day, if he's off with that lass of his, then I'd say yes, he seems about as usual. He's quiet, but then he often is. Why, have you noticed anything?'

'Jo says he seems a bit distracted, and even quieter than usual. Did you ever find out any more about what you told me? About him keeping his T-shirt on in the shower?'

Bill gave him one of his old-fashioned looks over the top of the reading glasses he used for paperwork.

'Patience, Grasshopper. I'll find out if and when he's ready to talk to me, and not before. If it's anything I think you should know about, I'll tell you.'

Ted went on his way smiling to himself. The Grasshopper reference reminded him of the *Kung Fu* TV series he'd watched as a martial arts mad young boy. Repeats of a classic from the seventies.

* * *

'Mum! Why have you come to meet me? Only the babies' mums come to meet them.'

She'd hoped he might be pleased to see her waiting by the school gates for him. Instead he scowled at her in that way he had when he felt he was being shown up. It made her want to hug him. She knew he would never forgive her if she did. Not with his schoolfriends around, who might see it and tease him mercilessly about it. Not that he had many friends. He was a quiet boy who kept very much to himself. Always busy with his books or glued to his Playstation, which they'd bought him as a special Christmas present for doing well at school.

It wasn't surprising he didn't form friendships easily. He wouldn't want to bring anyone back to the toxic atmosphere which reigned in the house. She tried to shield him from it as much as she could but he wasn't stupid. Far from it. He was observant. He picked up on things. Especially when there was an atmosphere.

'It's a surprise. I thought we could go away for a day or two. Just the two of us. Look, I've brought some of our things.'

He noticed then that she was carrying a holdall. It looked new. And heavy. He hadn't seen it before.

'What about school?' he asked her.

She smiled fondly at him. He was such a good boy. Always studying hard, without needing to be chased after. He was determined to make something of himself. And he had the brains to do it.

'It's only for a day or two. And I'll send a message to your teacher to explain. You won't miss anything and you'll soon catch up anyway. You're so clever. My brainy boy.'

Her heart filled with pride as she looked at him. She couldn't resist reaching out a hand to him but he sidestepped deftly and hissed at her, 'Mum, don't.'

There were too many other pupils about. She knew she would embarrass him with any such public gesture of affection.

They turned a corner, going the opposite way to the one they would have taken to go straight home. It was only then that she became aware of a car purring along behind them. Slowly, shadowing them as they walked.

She stopped dead in her tracks, her mouth suddenly dry, her heart pounding strongly. The car stopped too, mirroring her movements. Then the passenger side window slid down.

'You're going the wrong way.'

His voice was pleasant, almost jovial. He even laughed as he went on, 'What's your mum like, eh, lad? She can't even remember her own way home. It's a good job I was just passing by when I did. Hop in the back seat, there's a good boy. Don't worry, I'll help mum with her bag. It looks heavy. She must have the Crown Jewels in there.'

The boy hesitated, looking from one to the other. His mother was still rooted to the spot, her face drained of all colour now.

'Go on, lad, chop-chop. I'll help your mum, don't worry.'

As the boy moved to the rear passenger side and got in, closing the door behind him, the man moved round the front of the car with surprising speed. His fingers bit into her arms with a vice-like grip. His mouth was against her ear as he spat the words out.

'Did you think you could leave me and take the boy with you, you silly bitch? I know every thought that runs through that pathetic head of yours. I know what you're planning even before you do. If you want to leave me, do it the way I showed you. With a good sharp knife, or a bottle of pills. The boy stays with me. Now get in.'

He made sure one of her legs was still out, her foot on the kerb, when he slammed the door shut with all his considerable force. She couldn't stop the scream of pain which escaped her lips.

Quickly, he wrenched the door open again, his face a

carefully composed study of concern.

'Oh, darling, you poor thing! Why did you pull it shut before you had both feet in, you silly thing? Here, let me have a look.'

He crouched down next to her, seeing blood already soaking through the leg of her trousers. He put both hands round her calf, his two thumbs digging into the wound with brutal strength, making her scream again.

'Oh, sweetheart, that looks so nasty. I think I should take you straight round to Casualty to get it looked at. Don't worry, lad, mum's going to be absolutely fine. We'll take her to the hospital now and get that poor old leg properly looked after.

'What a good job I was coming past when I did. Your poor mum is so hopeless at looking after herself. And you. What a good thing it wasn't you she managed to hurt, eh? I'm always saying it's only a matter of time before she does.'

Chapter Four

'I think you all know DC Graham Winters, who's come over to lend us a hand once more,' Ted began at briefing the following morning. He'd spent time before going to the Central Park meeting the previous day ringing round his new teams, the ones he'd already met, and calling in extra people to boost numbers. Concentrating on ones he knew, or felt, could be an asset and hit the ground running.

'This is Claire Spicer, a CIO, who's kindly offered to lend a hand as she lives on our doorstep and she has experience of similar scams to ours. She'll be working with you, Rob, on the Black Mould Scam. There's a good possibility that it might be the same people behind it in both areas. If you start by comparing notes you may find some common ground to go from.'

Civilian Investigation Officers could help to ease the workload on cases. Extra trained personnel for roles like statement taking from witnesses

'And these are DCs Nick Cross and Andy Green. Jo, it's up to you where you deploy people. Once I've been round the rest of the teams to get a feel for capabilities and workloads, I may be able to free up more reinforcements to send you, if necessary.'

He turned to the newcomers as he said, 'DI Jo Rodriguez will be in charge while I'm out of the office. As well as the scam which Claire will be working on, we have an ongoing possible murder case which will also need a lot of witness interviews and statement taking. DS Mike Hallam is in charge of that. What's the latest with our suspect, Mike?'

'Jo and I spoke to CPS yesterday, boss, while you were out. We're all in agreement that we haven't anything to charge him with at the moment, so we released him on pre-charge bail. That at least gives us the full twenty-eight days to see if we can make a case against him, once we have all the forensic results and the PM's been done.

'He's still singing the song of the innocent, playing the grieving new widower, and wanting the boy back in his custody. Child Protection aren't keen on that at the moment. They want to do a thorough safeguarding investigation, of course, and as the man is not his biological father and doesn't have legal custody, he can't force the issue for now.

'So we'll be very glad of the extra help with all the statements we'll need to take to build some sort of a case, at least, if there is any forensic evidence for us to take it further.'

'Right, fine. Jo, I'll be sloping off shortly so you're at the helm. I'll be on the end of the phone if you need me for any reason.'

Ted didn't want to leave immediately, although Hector would be waiting for him in five minutes or so. He wanted to sit quietly and observe for a moment, as he often did. In particular, he wanted to see what Jo had seen in Steve's behaviour to raise his concern.

He spotted it straight away. With unfamiliar faces joining the team, Steve would normally be on edge, only inputting occasionally and then hesitantly, unsure of himself in front of strangers. Now he didn't appear to be paying much attention at all to what was going on around him. He spent most of the time sitting staring into space, his gaze vacant. Occasionally he'd jerk himself back to the here and now with an obvious effort, but it didn't last long. It wasn't like him.

Once he'd seen enough, Ted went to his office to collect his things, then down to the car park where Hector had his car close by.

'Morning, Ted, where to first today?'

'Trafford again, please, 'eck,' Ted told him, climbing into the back seat without being told to this time. 'I want to see how Sarah's getting on with her possible killer with a cast-iron alibi. Although I'm sure she'll have everything well under control. She seems very competent.

'I won't be long there, I don't suppose. But long enough for you to grab a cuppa somewhere, I should think.'

Ted knew his new driver liked the opportunity to catch up with people he knew from his own days in the force.

'Then I need to explore the other far-flung corners of my new empire. I hope you've got your passport with you. We might even need to go as far as Ashton.'

Hector gave him a sideways glance at that.

'Oh, 'eck, do they even speak the same language there? Give me a quick bell when you're done and on your way back out. I've got some old friends at Trafford so it's nice to have a quick catch-up when I can.'

Ted was even more impressed when he watched the recording of DS Sarah Jenkins' initial interview with their suspect. The man was clearly a slippery character, used to police interviews. He hadn't even bothered with a solicitor. His attitude, and his sole response throughout, had been, 'Prove it.'

For the moment, he seemed fairly confident that they couldn't, and that his collection of eyewitnesses to put him elsewhere at the time of death was all he needed to avoid being charged with murder.

'What he doesn't know for the moment is that the Investigators at the crime scene have managed to get more detail out of the boot print on the door, where it was kicked open, than they initially thought they would. The boot is common enough work footwear, widely available and very popular.

'The good news for us is that the boot in question has a possibly unique pattern. There's a small nick out of one of the soles.'

'Make my day and tell me Johnson has a corresponding pair of boots,' Ted told her.

'He does indeed. He must have changed out of them when he left the house to set up his alibi at the pub because he wasn't wearing them when he was brought in for questioning. The house is still closed off as a potential crime scene and he can't get back in there. But once the results were in, one of the CSIs had a look round and found them stuffed at the back of a cupboard. At least, on a superficial look, they appear to be the same boots. We need a warrant now to seize them, and anything else which looks as if it might help us.'

'I can probably sort out a warrant before I go on to my next visit, if that helps and frees you up? One more thing I thought of, although I'm sure you're ahead of me there. The next door neighbour who reported this, and whose account of life in that household differs so much from the others. He's presumably at risk, if this bloke is as nasty a character as he appears to be.'

'Already sorted. I talked to him about it. He has a second cousin out Northwich way, so he's gone to stay there for now. Like I said, he's older and perhaps not in the very best of health so I didn't want him meeting some sort of unfortunate accident before we need him to testify, if it gets that far.'

'Excellent. You're covering all bases. You don't need me to tell you that our chances of getting a murder charge brought in the first place on this are slim, and of a conviction, even slimmer. I think the best CPS are going to agree to is a manslaughter charge. Even if we get as far as putting him at the scene at the relevant time, I imagine he's going to bluff it out and admit, at best, to having pushed her. Proving intent to kill, unless the PM throws up a miracle, is probably a pipe dream. But good work so far. You and all your team. Keep me posted.'

'Right, let's see what Ashton has to offer us,' Ted said, as Hector pulled the car up near to the main entrance at that station to drop him off. 'Big Jim warned me that some of this team might need a bit of a shake-up. One in particular. Jim never let them get away with anything, of course, but he said they might try it on with me being new.'

Hector chuckled.

'From what I've heard about you, that should be a piece of cake for you.'

Ted was gathering his papers together and stuffing them back in his briefcase as Hector spoke.

'It's a pity I have to waste my time dealing with stuff like that when we all have enough work to do as it is,' he grumbled, then headed for the entrance as Hector went to park the car.

He presented his ID to the civilian on the front desk but declined the offer of getting someone to show him the way to the CID office. He preferred to drop in unannounced here, to get a feeling for what the team members were like.

There was only one person in the office. A young woman, working away at her computer. She had short, glossy, black hair, and glasses which gave her a studious air.

She looked up as Ted entered the office and asked, 'Can I help you?'

Ted held up the ID round his neck. 'DCI Darling, from Stockport. I did send word I was coming today at some time. Are the rest of the team around?'

She stood up and held out a hand to him.

'Oh yes, it was mentioned. I'm Lee Wu, the token female, and token civilian. The rest of them are out somewhere on some sort of case conference, but I don't know where, or when they're due back.'

Ted shook her hand.

'Is there no log anywhere to tell me who's where?' he asked her, although as it was shortly after two in the afternoon, he could hazard a guess, from what he'd been told. 'And if it's a case conference, why are you not included?'

She smiled at him as she resumed her seat.

'Oh, no particular reason. Other than me being a civilian.

And a woman. And very obviously not from round here.'

She smiled again as she said it, but her words made Ted frown. He didn't like discrimination, of any kind. He looked around for the nearest chair and asked, as he pulled it closer, always aware of personal space issues, 'Do you mind if I sit down? Is this okay for you?'

She gave him a look of mild curiosity, clearly not used to such an approach.

'That's fine. Do you want me to make you some coffee? Or some tea?'

Ted hoped that didn't indicate that she was always the one who brewed up for the team.

'I want to go and find the rest of the team, before they come back.'

'I honestly don't know where they are.'

'I'll find them, don't worry. I have a good nose for finding out where coppers go at dinner time. Right now, I'm more concerned to hear that you may have experienced racist and sexist remarks from them. Is that so?'

She shrugged.

'It's nothing really. One of them calls me Chop Suey sometimes. If I react, I'm told I don't understand blokeish humour.'

'I don't find remarks like that humorous. I don't find discrimination of any kind funny. Speaking as a short, skinny, gay bloke called Darling who's encountered plenty of it in his time. Look, here's my card. If ever you want to talk to me, about anything – on or off the record – please feel free to call me, at any time.'

He stood up and put the chair away neatly before he left the office. Lee Wu was left looking after him as he left. He wasn't like any Senior Investigating Officer she'd encountered before on her short career to date as a Civilian Investigator.

Ted pulled his mobile out as he went downstairs, to call Hector.

'Can you please ask whichever copper you're with which

watering hole CID might use for their dinner break,' he asked him.

He heard 'eck relay the message, than laughter in the background as several voices supplied the name of a pub.

Hector repeated the name into the phone, in case Ted hadn't caught it, and gave him directions. It wasn't far, as Ted had suspected. He found there was generally a pub within walking distance of most police stations.

He knew the team wouldn't have dared take a pub lunch if Jim Baker was about. Nor, hopefully, when their own DI was present.

Much of the lunchtime trade had departed. There were still a few stragglers sitting at the bar, plus a group of three men at a corner table. Ted's copper's nose told him immediately they were the missing CID officers. He walked over to them. His ID was now tucked away in his pocket.

'I'm DCI Darling. Which one of you is DS Ramsay?'

The one sitting in the middle of the three of them looked guilty and got hastily to his feet.

'Sorry, guv, we were on a late meal break. Lee didn't fancy joining us, so we did a bit of shop talk over our sandwiches. Cases she's not involved with.

'I went to the office first. Your CIO didn't seem to know where you were, so I came to find you.'

'Yes, sorry again, guv, I should have told her where to find us, and to give me a bell when you arrived so we could be back to meet you. We've not been drinking. It's all soft drinks.'

Ted didn't believe the half of it. Especially not from the way the older of the two DCs avoided his gaze and busied himself stacking dirty plates, scrunching up empty crisp packets. It had clearly been a lengthy lunch break, but he could at least see that the lager bottles were alcohol-free. They may have been pushing boundaries, but clearly not enough to risk their jobs.

'Well, now I'm here and meal break is over. So I'd like you all back at your desks in five minutes, please. I want a full run-down of everything the team is working on. And that includes your CIO's casework too, of course.'

Ted may not have had the same impressive stature as Big Jim. But the way he stood his ground, quietly waiting for signs of movement, left the three men in no doubt. Slowly, they stirred themselves and got ready to leave. Ted was not surprised that the older DC was the last to make any effort to get up and go. He could see that he was going to have to come down hard on him, and soon, if they weren't going to be wasting time with petty power struggles.

* * *

'As you can see, nurse, my wife's had a nasty accident. She managed to pull the car door shut on her leg. I don't think you realised how gusty the wind was, did you, darling? I thought I'd better bring her straight in because it looks quite bad.'

The nurse looked round the small cubicle, assessing the situation. For some reason, the man's opening remarks put her on alert. She hadn't put her nose outside for much of her shift but when she had done, for a quick breath of fresh air, she hadn't noticed it being windy at all. And her sharp eyes hadn't missed the look the young boy had given the man when he'd mentioned what had happened.

The woman was sitting passively on the bed, keeping her eyes cast down while the man was speaking. She didn't seem inclined to say anything herself.

Something about the family dynamics didn't feel quite right. But then, the nurse reminded herself, she might simply have been over-reacting after doing the safeguarding update training so recently.

'I think the first thing to do might be to take the boy somewhere he can have a drink of pop or something. Do you want to go with him, dad?'

'I'd rather stay with my wife,' he said, a fraction too quickly. 'He can stay too, can't he? He's a good boy. He'll be quiet and keep out of the way. Won't you, lad?'

'The thing is, it's a bit crowded in here. And it might be nicer for your wife to have some privacy while I examine her. I have to go and get the equipment I'm going to need, so I could take him and leave him quite safely with one of my colleagues.'

'He's not supposed to go off with strangers,' the man said, almost sharply.

She ignored him and smiled at the boy.

'I'm not a stranger though, am I? I'm the nurse who's going to be looking after your mum. I'm in my uniform and here, look, here's my name badge. My name is Jo. So would you like to come with me and I'll get you a drink?'

She pulled the curtain partly open for him to go out, but made no attempt to touch him, or take his hand. She sensed he would be resistant to any such gesture.

'I know mum's leg looks a bit nasty, but we can soon fix her up, so try not to worry.

'Is she a bit accident prone, your mum? Does she often get hurt like that?'

The expression of suspicion on the small face looking up at her spoke volumes. The boy said nothing. She could almost see the shutters coming down. She handed him over to a colleague without asking him anything more, found the trolley she needed and went back to the cubicle.

The woman was still sitting with her head lowered, but it was clear she'd been crying. The man stepped back swiftly as soon as the nurse reappeared to begin her examination.

'Can you manage to slip your trousers off all right? And perhaps pop your cardigan off for me. I'll quickly check your blood pressure, while you're here, as routine.'

She didn't need to take her BP really. She might be reading too much into nothing at all. But she did want to have a quick look for any signs of other injuries.

'Is the leg very painful? Could you manage to walk on it?'

The man made to answer, but she stopped him with a gesture.

'I'd really like your wife to tell me, please. It's helpful if she can rate the pain level for me herself.'

She wanted to hear the woman speak. It seemed clear she wasn't going to give her version of what had happened with the husband there. But Jo really wanted to hear her say something. Anything. So she could gauge whether or not she was overreacting.

'I'm so sorry to be a nuisance. I'm so stupid. I pulled the door to before I'd moved my leg. The wind just caught it somehow and banged it shut. My own silly fault.'

She managed to wriggle out of her trousers, the in-jured leg hampering her slightly, although there was movement there, so hopefully no fracture. The nurse helped her off with her cardigan, positioning herself so the man couldn't do so.

'That's a nasty looking scar. Are you OK with me tak-ing your BP on that arm? How did that happen?'

She was careful to ask in a matter of fact way, as she slipped the cuff on the woman's arm to take the reading.

The woman gave a nervous little laugh.

'Oh, that was so silly it's embarrassing. I was trying to sharpen a knife, on the sharpening steel. I've seen my husband do it before and I thought it would be easy. Not when you're clumsy, like me, it seems. The knife slipped and caught me. What a good job my husband had just come home from work and could help me to stop the bleeding and put a bandage on it.'

Jo was finishing up when another nurse from outside the cubicle said, 'Jo, have you got a minute, please?'

She excused herself and went to see what he wanted.

'There's been a bad accident on the motorway. We have a lot of incoming heading our way so any minor injuries will have to take a back seat for now.'

She would have liked more time to talk to the woman, preferably on her own. But she had to hustle the couple out with almost indecent haste now to make way for more serious patients coming in.

She made herself a mental note to find time to put something at the end of the treatment sheet. Something along the lines of, 'Query possible domestic violence incident??'

Chapter Five

Ted was on the phone to Hector once more as he walked briskly back to the station.

'Change of plan, 'eck,' he told him. 'It looks like it's going to take me a bit longer than I thought to knock this lot into some sort of shape. Like I said, Big Jim warned me they might want to push boundaries, but it seems they're taking the piss more than a bit.'

Hector chuckled.

'Ask them about cuffing, Ted.'

'Cuffing? Surely Jim wouldn't have missed them shelving cases they couldn't be bothered to do the donkey work for? I'm sure he'd have mentioned that to me.'

'Yes, but don't forget Jim's area was a lot bigger than yours. You're sharing part of his workload with another DCI. And because of the size of his empire, he chose to do most of his checking up by video link when he could. Otherwise he'd never have kept on top of it. Sometimes, there's a lot to be said for the old-fashioned ways, though. Modern technology can't always tell you what's really happening on the ground. As you're now finding out.

'I was having a brew with some of the blokes I know at this nick and they tell me they call the CID office "the black hole". Because things they send on to that lot have a habit of disappearing, never to be seen again.'

'Have Uniform said what the DS is like? Why he's not on top of this?'

'Good, knows his theory, but too soft, is the unanimous verdict. Classic case of why officers are usually moved to another team when they get promotion. Pete was allowed to stay on. Compassionate grounds. His mother is severely disabled and his dad can't always cope by himself. Pete's the only other relative. So he was given special dispensation to stay on here.

'Trouble is, he and Alan Burgess were always big mates before, and Ramsay hasn't learned how to leave that behind, now he's in charge. Burgess is older. He helped Pete out when he was wet behind the ears, so it's led to problems. Burgess is also a gobby sod, by all accounts. Does the bare minimum and Pete lets him get away with it because he's not got the balls to jump all over him like he should now he's a rank higher.'

Ted sighed. It was a situation he really didn't need, with such an increased workload. He knew it could happen. His own team member, Rob O'Connell, had been allowed to stay on when he got his promotion to DS, because of his wife's work in Stockport as an RSPCA inspector. He was coping well with outranking his long-term friends and knew where to draw the line. They respected him for it, so it worked. It seemed Ted would have to waste precious time giving DS Ramsay some guidelines on doing the same. Unless he could look at moving Burgess somewhere, perhaps swapping him for another officer, until the DS got a grip.

Ted was nearly at the station now. He paused before going in. Getting the inside story from Uniform via Hector would give him a useful head start on how to begin to tackle the situation. He'd walked back briskly but he was not best pleased that there was no sign of the others following him yet. They were clearly not in a hurry to be back within the five minutes he had given them.

'And what about the third musketeer on the team?'

Hector made bleating noises down the phone, then said, 'Milo Sharp? A total sheep. That's his nickname, too. Sharp the Sheep. He'll always do whatever the strongest collie dog tells him to do. And at the moment that's Burgess and not Ramsay. Good luck sorting that little lot out, Ted. Let me know when you're done. I'm happy enough chatting to Uniform while I wait. You never know, I might dig up some more useful info for you.'

The Civilian Investigator, Lee Wu, was still working away at her computer.

'Have you actually taken a meal break yet, Lee?' Ted asked her, then went on hastily, 'Is it all right to call you Lee?'

He had a sudden anxious moment, a vague memory about Oriental names sometimes being given with the surname first.

She looked at him again. The same mildly curious expression, as if he were some strange alien species she'd never formerly encountered.

'No, not yet. And yes, Lee is fine. Thank you for asking. I thought someone ought to be in the office in case of any calls.'

It was a statement of fact, more than a dig, Ted thought. She was right, of course. His own team members were careful to work their breaks so that there was always someone in the office unless it was unavoidable.

'The others are on their way back now, hopefully, so please feel free to go and have something to eat. I can answer any calls until they arrive.'

He was looking round the office space for somewhere to talk to team members one to one. Open plan was becoming popular, with officers on different shifts often hot-desking rather than having designated desk space. Ted rather like the old-fashioned ways. He certainly appreciated having his own broom cupboard sized space partitioned off for the rare occasions when he needed to read the Riot Act to any of his officers.

'Is there a room anywhere? If I want to talk to people one at a time?' he asked Lee, who was standing up and putting her things together in readiness to go out.

'There's one next door,' she told him. 'It's a small kitchen-ette place where we can brew up or make toasties and such like. If you need the loos, they're directly opposite. I'll see you shortly, then, if you're sure it's okay to leave you to it.'

'Not too shortly,' Ted told her. 'Take a nice leisurely break. An hour should do it, especially if you haven't yet had a meal break.'

The door opened as she was about to leave the office. Ted noticed she had to stand aside as the three officers trooped in. He didn't like that. He'd been brought up the old-fashioned way by his father. He was prepared to accept that it might be her own preference, although he doubted it.

'Right, DS Ramsay, I gather there's a rest room next door, so shall you and me adjourn there for now, for a little discussion?'

This time Ramsay made sure he opened the door and stood aside for Ted to go through first. Ted spoke quietly and politely enough but Ramsay sensed he was in trouble. He made another to pre-empt things and excuse his actions.

'Sorry again, guv. I wasn't really sure what time you were coming here so I thought me and the lads could have a catch-up over a pint. We were talking shop, though. And not drinking alcohol on duty, of course.'

'I don't expect officers to be talking about work in a pub where they could be overheard by anyone. I also expect to find some sort of activity log, so I know where people are when I call in.'

Ted was leaning against a work surface in the small space, his arms folded. He left Ramsay standing like a spare part, al-though the DS had the grace to look contrite.

'Sorry, guv, understood.'

'So what are you and the team currently working on? Who's on what? It has to be said that your clear-up rate to date is not very impressive, in the absence of your DI.'

Ramsay looked uncomfortable now. It had clearly been

simpler to spin Jim Baker a line via video link than to stand in the confined space of the kitchenette looking into the unwavering hazel stare of this DCI from Stockport. He wasn't sure quite what he'd been expecting. It certainly wasn't the intensity of his gaze and the set of his jaw.

'Well, sir,' Ramsay thought he'd better make a bit more of an effort. 'Me and the lads have got this alleged assault and robbery. A young lad. The report came in from Uniform. Apparently he was jumped by two blokes who've knocked him about and stolen his wallet and his phone. The thing is, there's no witnesses, so it's just his word, and the descriptions he's given. We're thinking it's not likely to go very far with only that to go on.'

'There are no witnesses?' Ted asked levelly. 'Or you haven't found any yet? What about CCTV? What does that show?'

He could see from the DS's guilty expression that they'd clearly made little effort to find any. He hoped they were simply lazy and incompetent rather than bent. Massaging the figures and marking crimes as No Further Action to lessen their workload was something he could probably sort out with a few chosen words. He didn't like to think it might go any further than laxity, because there was nothing Ted disliked more than a dishonest copper who might be taking backhanders to cover up crimes.

Ramsay was starting to sweat, visibly, finding himself on the spot.

'We were going to get started on that this afternoon, sir. It's one of the things we were talking about just now.'

He must have realised how lame his excuse sounded.

'When did this incident happen?' Ted asked him, trying to keep the rising irritation he was feeling out of his voice.

'At the weekend, sir. Saturday night, to be precise.'

'The weekend?' Even Ted's normally quiet voice rose at that. 'It's Thursday today. What have you been doing, for goodness sake?'

He didn't wait for an answer. He had a feeling there wasn't one.

'And what about the victim? How serious was the assault?'

Ramsay looked relieved at a question he could, at least, answer.

'Not too bad, sir. The hospital only kept him in a couple of nights and now he's back home. One of us is going to see him this afternoon for a full statement. To see if he's remembered anything more since he spoke to Uniform when the incident was reported.'

Ted took a moment to look up at the ceiling and count silently to ten. Now he couldn't decide whether Ramsay was stupid, inept or dodgy. Or possibly all three. He was starting to wonder how he'd got his promotion in the first place.

'Two nights in hospital is significant, DS Ramsay. These days more than ever, patients don't get kept in for no good reason. So to sum up, you've had this case on your books for five days now without making any kind of progress at all. Would you agree with my summary?'

There wasn't a lot Ramsay could say to that. He gave a brief nod of acknowledgement.

'Not a good start, really, is it?' Ted asked him, now he had his voice under control again. 'Not to the case, nor to our first meeting. There are other places I need to be now, so here's what's going to happen. Before you leave here today, you're going to send me a detailed report on everything you have on this case to date, and who is investigating what aspect of it.

'I suggest you make good use of your CIO. She made a good impression on me. You seem to forget that the team is not just "you and the lads". You and the other two get out there and do some proper policing. Track down any CCTV close to the scene. There'll be some somewhere, even if it's from private premises. Get Lee onto checking that while you and the others go out and find some witnesses.

'It would seem to me, at first sight, that you haven't tried hard enough from the beginning to find anything to make a case out of this. I'd like to see a lot more of an effort made before you start deciding it's not got legs.

'I'll be back to check on you soon. And unannounced. Count on that.'

When Ted went back to the car where Hector was waiting for him, he got into the front seat.

'Before you say anything, I want the ins and outs of everything Uniform told you about that useless shower who have underwhelmed me with their progress, or lack of it, to date.'

'Right you are, Ted. So where to next?'

'I really wish I could say take me to the nearest pub, after that experience. But I'll settle for Longsight nick. My old stamping ground from my time in Uniform. I hope the CID lot have changed since my days there. We didn't exactly hit it off.

'But meanwhile tell me anything else you found out about the three not so wise monkeys.'

* * *

He stopped to buy things several times on the way back home from the hospital. He didn't say anything by way of explanation. Each time, he came out of the shop carrying a small, white, paper bag with a green cross on it, which he dropped into the foot well by the woman's feet.

The boy took the opportunity of one of his absences to ask his mother, 'Why did you say that about the wind to that nurse, mum? It wasn't windy. There was no wind when we were walking away from school. Why did you say something that wasn't true?'

She gave one of her short, nervous laughs.

'You wouldn't have noticed because you'd already got in the back seat and shut the door. It was one of those funny little gusts that suddenly blows up from nowhere.

And at the very minute I was pulling the door to. I probably did that a bit too hard, I think. You know how clumsy your silly mum can be.'

Then she went on, trying to sound casual, 'What did the lady say to you when she took you somewhere to sit down? Did she ask you anything?'

The boy frowned at her question. It wasn't right to tell lies. He knew that. He'd been told that often enough, at home and at school. But mum had just told him a whopper. There'd been no gust of wind. He wasn't stupid, and he wasn't a little child. He knew when it was windy or not. And there'd been no wind to slam the door shut on her leg. He didn't know why she'd lied, but she had done. It was true that she often got hurt. Perhaps for some reason she didn't want the nurse to know that. But if she'd lied to him, then he could reply with a lie of his own.

'She asked me what sort of drink I wanted and if I needed anything to eat with it. I said a fizzy orange, please, and nothing to eat, thank you.'

Despite the pain and the anxious anticipation tying knots in her stomach, she had to smile her pride at him. He was always such a good boy and so polite. They both instinctively stopped talking when the man came back, clutching another bag with a green cross on it, which joined the first one on the floor.

There were three such bags lying there by the time they got back to the house.

'Look, here's the key, lad. You go on ahead and open up while I help poor mum out of the car. Can you amuse yourself on your Playstation for a while? I'll have to sort out a bit of supper for us all, because clearly mum is going to need to lie down and rest, and that might take me a bit of time. Off you go, and don't worry about your mum. I'll take good care of her. I've bought her something to help with the pain, so that's a start.'

He was the picture of concerned compassion as he went round to the passenger door to help her out. The next door neighbour on one side was in her front garden, doing something to the plants in the border.

He gave her a beaming smile and a friendly wave.

'I've just had to take the wife to Casualty. She managed to trap her leg in the car door, poor thing.'

He was almost tender as he helped her to her feet, giving her his arm for support.

'Oh, you poor dear!' the neighbour exclaimed. 'That sounds so painful. Do give me a knock or a shout if there's anything at all I can do to help you when your hubby's at work.'

He saw her carefully to the front door before the mask slipped and he was sneering at her once more.

'Get upstairs to bed, you stupid bitch. I'll see to you in a minute, once I've got your bag out of the boot.'

It was as much the fear of what was to come as the pain of her leg throbbing under the bandage which made tears start to her eyes again. She bit down hard on her lip to stop any sound escaping. Nothing which would unsettle and upset the boy any more than he already was. She'd seen the suspicion in his eyes. Had hated lying to him. Hated even more the certainty that he had been lying in return when he talked about what the nurse had said to him.

Did that mean she was on record somewhere as being at risk of domestic abuse? And was that going to make her situation better? Or worse?

She wasn't quite sure what was going to happen next. Go to bed, he'd told her. But surely he wasn't thinking of...?

Surely not.

Even he wouldn't do something as sadistic as that.

Would he?

She slipped off her cardigan. The trousers were going to need washing anyway, because of the blood on them. She changed them for something with a looser fit, so they wouldn't press on the painful area. She sat on the bed and carefully lifted her legs to stretch them out, pulling a cover over them.

Then she waited. Starting to shake with the delayed shock, the pain, and the fear of what was to follow.

She heard his heavy tread on the stairs not long after. Then heard him open the door of the boy's room and go in there. The sound of drawers opening and closing.

The anticipation of waiting was as bad as anything he might have come up with to inflict on her.

When he came into the room and she saw the knife in his hand, she had to make a conscious effort to clench her pelvic floor muscles to stop the threatened flood of urine. It was the biggest, sharpest and most lethal of the butcher's knives from the block in the kitchen.

His other hand gripped the three green cross bags, and the handles of the new holdall she'd bought when she was planning her escape. He put all the bags on the end of the bed near her feet. Put the knife down while he carefully, neatly, he took out all of her clothes and put them away, each in the right drawer or on the correct shelf.

Then he picked the knife up once more and brought it down savagely, onto the holdall, slashing and tearing at the material until it was in pieces.

Almost conversationally, he told her, 'You won't be needing that any more. Don't even think about trying that trick again, and certainly not taking the boy with you. His place is with me.'

She was shaking so violently now that he must have been aware of it; seen the way the cover was moving with every convulsive twitch of her muscles. She couldn't tear her eyes away from the methodical way he was ripping the bag to shreds.

When he'd finished, knife still in hand, he gathered up the three paper bags, moved closer to her, and emptied them out into her lap. Six packets of paracetamol.

Still without raising his voice, he said, 'I've told you before, bitch. When you decide to leave me, the boy stays with me. This is the way you do it.'

He jabbed the knife towards the small boxes, lying on top of her trembling legs.

Then he brought the blade up suddenly until it was touching the underside of her chin, the point digging in but not yet piercing the skin.

'That. Or this.'

Chapter Six

'Right, pay attention everyone. You should all have a copy of the Operation Order for tomorrow.'

Kevin Turner was briefing his Uniform officers on Friday morning in preparation for the weekend, when they were expecting things to get lively in the town.

'You will have noticed that us mere mortals have been joined by four extra bodies from up there in the hallowed grounds of CID. For those who don't know them, our other reinforcements from elsewhere, for instance, we have DS Rob O'Connell, and DCs Virgil Tibbs, Jezza Vine and Steve Ellis. Don't let the sharp suits put you off. Come tomorrow, they'll be digging their uniforms out of their lockers, blowing off moths and cobwebs, and coming to join us for the fun.'

His tone had been light-hearted up to now, but he became more serious as he went on.

'You all know that when the barking mad idea of allowing rallies for two such diametrically opposed groups of individuals to take place on the same day in the same area was first raised, there were strenuous objections. Not just from the police, but from the other emergency services, too. Not to mention various shopkeepers worried about getting their windows kicked in.

'But the powers that be in their wisdom, or lack of it, decided it smacked too much of a police state to ban either or both. So it's up to us to deal with the consequences. And not to put too fine a point on it, it's not likely to be a teddy bears' picnic.

'DCI Darling has kindly lent us his four finest. Even more appreciated as we know they're stretched to the limit themselves at the moment, with a suspected murder and a nasty scam on their books.

'The observant amongst you will also have spotted our colleagues from the Mounted unit here. I'd like to thank them for coming to this briefing. That means we've also got a mounted presence for additional crowd control. So Ronan,' he looked directly at a tall and lanky younger officer sitting in the front row, where he could stretch out his long legs, 'try not to get your big feet trodden on by a police horse, okay?'

There was some laughter, as the constable self-consciously bent his legs to draw his large feet back underneath him, where they were less noticeable.

Then Kevin switched abruptly back to formal mode once more. There was a visible change in the atmosphere. Officers instinctively sitting up straighter at the change in him.

'Our presence at the fun and games is for one purpose only. We are there to calm and contain. We are there to stop the two factions knocking lumps out of one another. We are not – repeat, not – there to fan the flames until it becomes a full scale riot. And don't forget, if we all survive tomorrow, there's a strong possibility that we'll have to do the same thing all over again on Sunday, too. If they're all enjoying themselves, and Stockport's hospitality, not all of them will leave tomorrow night.

'There is to be no question of any behaviour at all which could get us press or social media headlines about police brutality. Remember, it's not only the press and media we have to look out for these days. It's people with their mobile phones out, doing everything they can to make us look bad, at every opportunity.

'I'm in charge of this whole operation and believe me, if anything bad appears on social media about any of you, and if your body cam recording doesn't clear you of any wrongdoing beyond any doubt, you'll have me to answer to. So make sure you all read the Operation Order and are very clear about your deployment tomorrow. Understood?'

Heads nodded. There were a few mutters of, 'guv' or 'sir'. They all knew how easily phone footage could be manipulated to make their actions look worse than they were, which is why they were glad of the body cameras front line officers now wore as standard, to show what actually happened when it got contentious.

Kevin Turner was looking round at the assembled officers. He had no doubts at all about putting Virgil, Rob and Jezza in the front line. Young Steve Ellis was a different matter altogether. He looked as if he wouldn't say boo to a goose at the best of times. Which was why he'd paired him off with Rob O'Connell for the operation. Rob should be able to keep half an eye on him, at least. Today Steve looked even paler than usual, and as if a good night's sleep wouldn't go amiss.

Kevin decided to have a word with Jo Rodriguez at some point, to see if there was anything going on with Steve which he needed to know about. Now Ted was high-flying in his new role, Kev wouldn't get to see as much of him as he had previously. If the weekend was even half as lively as he feared it might be, he couldn't afford to be carrying anyone. So if there was anything of concern, he'd sooner drop Steve before things began than deal with the repercussions if he didn't.

DS Ramsay's report had reached Ted by end of play Thursday as requested, but only just. It was light on detail, so it hadn't taken him long to read through. He wished he could spare someone senior, like Jo Rodriguez, to go over there for a few days to shake the lot of them up, but his team had enough on their own books to keep them all busy.

Reading it, then replying in strong terms to leave Ramsay in no doubt that he was not happy, had made Ted slightly later home than he'd anticipated. Trev had the meal ready and it was his turn to be in Riot Act reading mode from the moment Ted walked into the kitchen.

'You have remembered that you can't be so much as one minute late tomorrow, haven't you? Not one second. I am so looking forward to this handfasting lark of Bizzie's. I may never speak to you again if you don't get me there for the start of the fun.'

Trev had been wardrobe consultant for the occasion to forensic pathologist Bizzie Nelson, as the two of them had become somewhat unlikely but very good friends.

Ted was busy greeting cats while Trev dished up their food.

'And more importantly, you have remembered that we are going there on Saturday as well? And possibly even on Sunday, depending on how long the festivities keep going?' Trev asked.

'It seems a strange sort of a ceremony to me, running over the entire weekend.'

'It's a new one on me, too, but it sounds an absolute hoot, so I'm determined we should be there for as much of it as we can. Now, what was that word I told you to memorise and apply, now you're the Big Boss?'

Ted smiled patiently at him as he sat down and Trev put their plates on the table.

'Delegate.'

'Exactly! Remember how many times you had to cover for Big Jim when he was DCI and you were his DI. So now it's your turn to take advantage of your new position and delegate to Jo. You know he's more than capable.'

'Jim was always on the end of the phone if I needed him, though ...'

'Don't you even think of it, Ted. I mean it. If necessary I'll hide the battery out of yours so you can't be summoned. Delegate. Leave it to Jo. Anyone would think you didn't trust him.'

Ted gave Jo the edited highlights of his conversation when they caught up with one another after briefing on Friday morning.

'I'm glad Trev has faith in me, at least,' Jo told him with a smile.

'I do too, Jo, honestly. It's only the control freak in me who finds it hard to let go. There's a lot going on this weekend and we're stretched thin.'

'And the most important thing for you this weekend is to be at this handfasting ceremony. I'm intrigued by it all. I never imagined the Professor to be some sort of closet hippy, I have to confess.

'And speaking of the Prof, with her going off on her honeymoon, it will be someone we don't know as well for the PM on our potential murder victim, so let's hope they can give us as many answers as she would do. Do you want me to send Mike to that?'

'It's his case, so I think he should go, don't you? He doesn't have to look at anything, and tell him to put some Vick's under his nose if he's worried about the smell. What else on that case?'

'I've been trying to find out from Children's Services about getting someone to talk to the son. I know he's very young, but he could still possibly give us some valuable insight into what was going on in that household. It would need someone with the right training, of course. They'll have their own people with him, no doubt, but we need one of our team to talk to him. I was going to send Maurice, as long as the lad wasn't likely to be afraid of men. He must have seen some terrible goings on, I imagine. If we could just get him to meet Daddy Hen it would probably be all right.'

DC Maurice Brown, in famous Daddy Hen mode, had been worth his weight in gold on more than a few occasions, dealing with traumatised young victims of crime in particular.

'The best thing would be to get Maurice to go and talk to Children's Services himself, then let them decide if he'd be all right talking to the boy, with them chaperoning. If not, we'll need to find a female officer with Victim Support training.

'What about the victim's medical records? Have you managed to get hold of those yet?'

He knew he wouldn't have to chase his own team up like he was doing with those from Ashton. He simply liked to keep himself up to date with everything which was happening.

'We're following up that up at the moment. She was apparently on pills for depression or something like that. There were also some incidents which could have been accidental, self-inflicted or things done to her by the live-in partner. Hence the need to interview as many people as possible who knew either of them.'

'But nothing flagged up anywhere about possible domestic abuse?'

Jo shook his head.

'If she'd been seen by anyone who had any suspicions of something going on at home, it never got noted in writing, for whatever reason. More's the pity, if it's been going on on a regular basis for some time. There's a chance her life could have been saved, if it had been picked up and acted on.'

'You're sure we're all right, dressed like this?' Ted asked anxiously.

There were so many cars parked near to Bizzie Nelson's large house in Davenport that they'd had to park some distance away and walk down.

'We're not going to be the only ones not in black tie, or anything like that?'

Trev laughed at the question.

'Ted, no one wears black tie to a hippy handfasting. Trust me. We're both going to be fine. And just wait until you see Bizzie. I can guarantee you won't recognise her after my stylist sessions.'

They were lucky with the weather. Bizzie's plan had been

to have as much of the celebration taking place in the large back garden as was possible. The house was big, but it would still have been a squash to get everyone inside. Ted was surprised by how many people were there. He'd always thought of Bizzie as someone quite solitary, too wrapped up in her work to have time for socialising. Perhaps most were guests of her partner, Douglas Campbell.

As they'd been instructed, Ted and Trev headed down the side of the house to the garden, where people were congregating. There were flowers everywhere, strewn from trees, filling vases on the long tables laid with drinks, glasses and nibbles.

Bizzie saw them first, before they spotted her, waved enthusiastically, and came striding over. Ted was stunned. Trev hadn't been exaggerating. The pathologist was wearing a long, embroidered ivory kaftan which transformed her. Her short, wiry grey hair was softly curled and sporting random rosebuds. She also had on some light and discreet make-up, the first time Ted had ever seen her wear any. She was positively beaming with evident delight at the sight of them.

At her side trotted a young Staffy dog, all lolling tongue and lingering puppy fat, also wearing a garland of white flowers. Trev greeted Bizzie with one of his famous engulfing hugs and to Ted's surprise, she leaned towards him for a chaste touching of cheeks.

The dog had a cursory sniff at Ted's leg before mounting it and starting to hump away enthusiastically.

'Spilsbury, you disgusting hound! Stop that at once,' Bizzie admonished him. 'I'm so pleased to see you both. I do hope you'll be able to participate for much of the weekend.'

Trev fished into Ted's jacket pocket and pulled out his work phone.

'Look, Exhibit A. One work phone. Firmly switched off for the occasion. And Ted, tell Bizzie the word I've been teaching you.'

Ted grinned sheepishly.

'Delegate. I've left Jo in charge, with strict instructions not to contact me unless extremely urgent.'

'Wonderful! Come and get some drinks.'

She turned and swept away, Trev following her.

Ted stood rooted to the spot. Trev noticed and turned back to him.

'Are you coming?'

'I can't. The dog's sitting on my foot. And it's pissed in my shoe.'

* * *

She could see straight away from his high colour that he'd been drinking. He must have driven home like that. She could also tell at a glance that he would be well above the limit if he was tested. He was arrogant enough to think he'd get away with it if stopped.

It seemed to have put him in good spirits, literally, at least for the time being. Unusually, he moved to plant a beery kiss on her cheek as he walked into the kitchen. She tried not to recoil in horror from his touch. She didn't want to do anything to anger him. She knew the good mood wouldn't last long, but she was anxious not to precipitate its end too soon.

'What's to eat? I could eat a scabby donkey.'

'Smoked haddock,' she told him anxiously.

He usually liked that, but she could never tell. She was always so careful to remove every single bone or piece of skin before she served it to him.

'With a poached egg on top?'

'Of course, if you'd like one. I can easily do that for you.'

She was silently praying as she spoke that she would manage to get it exactly right. He was always so fussy about how he would eat his poached eggs. Which was why she avoided making one, unless he insisted.

'Where's the boy? Has he done his homework?'

The good mood seemed on the brink of evaporating already. It made her nervous. She fumbled and so nearly dropped the eggs as she took them out of the fridge.

'He's watching one of his programmes. I think he's done his homework.'

'Think? You haven't checked it?'

There was a warning edge now. He was looking for things to find fault with. She didn't want to give him any ammunition so she said meekly, 'I was going to do it as soon as I'd made your tea. Shall I put your egg on now?'

The mask was slipping rapidly. The look he gave her was one of angry contempt.

'Of course not, you stupid bitch.'

As ever, he didn't raise his voice. He might simply be talking about the weather. Except the scorn in his tone was like a physical blow.

'I'm going to check up on the lad's homework, since you couldn't be bothered to do it. If you put my egg on now it will be like a golf ball by the time I've done that.'

He went through into the sitting room. She heard him turn off the television and start speaking, still in that same quiet voice.

'Have you done your homework yet, lad? You know the rules. You should have finished that, properly, before you even think of watching television. Your education is far more important than some stupid rubbish on the telly. Get your books out and show me what you've done.'

She paused for a moment, her head cocked to hear what was going on. She wasn't brave enough to stand up to him when he started on her. But if he so much as sounded like he was about to raise a hand to the boy, she would be in there like a shot, determined to do whatever she could to protect her son.

'Well, I can see that you've tried. That's something, at least.'

He was speaking patiently, now. Reasonably. For the moment, at least. She'd go and put the water on to boil for his egg, so she could have his meal ready as soon as he'd finished checking the homework.

'But you could have done so much better than this. It just isn't detailed enough. And look, here, you've made mistakes with your spelling. Basic mistakes. You can do a lot better than that. I'm disappointed with this. If you're serious about going for the career you want to, you've got to do better than this. Remember, lad, the devil is in the detail.

'Now, I want you to sit back down at the table and have another go at it, while I go and eat my tea. You can do better. I know you can. And you're going to need to, to make anything of yourself. Do it again, while I eat. Then I'll come and have another look.'

Her hand was reaching for the egg box when he came back into the kitchen. He crossed the small room with angry strides, one hand reaching out to grab her wrist, hard, to stop the movement.

'He's writing rubbish. An infant could do better than that garbage,' he hissed into her ear. 'It's an embarrassment. You might be a half-wit, but I expect better of him.'

He was still gripping her arm with one hand. With the other, he turned off the gas and lifted up the saucepan in which the water was starting to bubble up to boiling point. He held her hand over the sink as he slowly and methodically emptied the pan of water over it.

Tears started from her eyes as she bit down so hard on her lip to stop the scream escaping that her teeth drew blood.

'Now give me my tea. And make sure the egg is cooked just the way I like it, if you know what's good for you.'

Chapter Seven

'Ted Darling! That better not be an in use work mobile I see in your hands.'

Ted gave a guilty start as Trev stumbled into the kitchen, yawning widely, wearing a hastily pulled on pair of boxers, back to front. He hadn't expected to see him surface for a while yet.

It had been some ungodly time in the wee small hours when they'd returned from Bizzie's house. Despite his earlier reservations, Ted had found the whole thing more fun than he'd imagined he would. Douglas had been resplendent in his kilt, in the green and blue Campbell tartan. Several of his friends were also sporting their clan colours.

One of Ted's abiding memories would long remain the sight of his slightly inebriated and more than a little bit stoned partner attempting to master the intricacies of dancing Strip the Willow without falling over.

Ted was there as a guest of a valued friend, not as a police officer, so he'd turned a blind eye to the group of people who would occasionally assemble under the apple trees at the far end of the garden to partake of something which was clearly not tobacco. He couldn't really do otherwise when, to his astonishment, he witnessed Bizzie join them on one occasion. He was seeing a totally different side to the pathologist.

Ted was happy enough in his usual pastime of people watching. To his surprise, he had a devoted companion. Despite Ted's long fear and mistrust of dogs, the young pup,

Spilsbury, appeared to have adopted him. Ted knew the dog was named after the founder of modern forensics, Sir Bernard Spilsbury, someone whose work Bizzie admired.

Something which had surprised him even more was that he had, by trial and error, found a way to control the young miscreant. The dog was mostly white with a large brindle patch over one eye. It gave him a roguish look, which certainly suited his nature.

'Leave,' Ted tried, experimentally, when in the absence of his mistress, Spilsbury once again mounted his leg. 'Get off. Sit.'

It was only when he prefaced the command with an attempt at Bizzie's stern tone saying, 'Spilsbury!' that the dog obeyed. It first sat on its haunches, grinning up adoringly at him. Then it slowly collapsed onto its side, offering up its underbelly for stroking. Very cautiously, Ted bent down to give it a fleeting rub, which sent it into excited wiggling contortions. From that moment on, it became his inseparable shadow for the whole weekend.

'I was just looking to see if there were any messages from work that I needed to deal with before we go back to Bizzie's for the next round,' Ted began, but Trev cut him short.

'Ted, I'm always telling you, you are a totally rubbish liar,' Trev said, going to put the kettle on. 'I could hear you talking from upstairs. And unless we've suddenly acquired a cat called Jo that I don't know about, you were talking shop with your DI.

'Delegate, Ted. Delegate. How often have you been told that? And not only by me. Let the poor man get on with his job and show you what he can do without you.'

It was hotting up at Rob O'Connell's end of town. He was heading up a serial of twelve officers. He'd made a couple of requests for Mounted support but been told that the horses were currently deployed at another scene of disorder. The mounted officers had been obliged to draw their batons, something they seldom did, to get the unruly throng of pushing, shoving protesters, to move back as ordered, in an attempt to keep the two factions apart and avoid a flashpoint.

Rob was right up in the front line, flanked by Virgil and Jezza on one side, Steve on the other. Virgil was doing his usual job of looking solid and menacing. Many of the protesters were giving him a wide berth because of it. But Steve was visibly shrinking in the face of the open aggression he was facing. At one point he started to take a step back until Rob grabbed him and bodily hauled him forward to keep the line unbroken.

At the very least, if he couldn't get much in the way of back-up, Rob was going to need a replacement for Steve. The mob had already seen him as the weakest link and were doing their best to exploit the knowledge.

One man was shoving his considerable beer gut right at Steve like a battering ram, jeering into his face, trying to wind him up.

'Come on then, sonny. Think you're a hard man, do you? Let's see what you've got, then.'

Steve was doing his best to stand firm in the face of it. Rob could sense the effort it was costing him. For a brief, optimistic moment, he thought the line was going to hold. Then Steve whirled abruptly, doubled over, and threw up, spattering the footwear of anyone nearby with vomit.

At least it made Beer-gut hesitate, long enough for Rob and the other officers to close up the gap once more and start to push back against the crowd.

It took a long time for things to calm down to the point where most of the officers could stand down and head back to the station for a debrief with Kevin Turner. There was no sign of Steve anywhere as Rob and the other officers made their way back.

'Anyone know what happened to Steve?' Virgil asked, as

they were putting caps, vests and equipment back in their lockers.

None of them bothered to change into their own clothes. As soon as they did, they would no doubt be called back out. It was just tempting fate.

'I don't know whether he was ill or something else,' Rob told them. 'I don't want to judge him, but it didn't look good from where I was standing. It look like he lost it. I'm not going to bring it up in public at the debrief unless I have to. But I'm going to have to tell Jo and he's going to have to talk to Kevin Turner. And to the boss, at some point.'

'Where is Steve, anyway?' Jezza asked, a note of concern in her voice. 'Shouldn't we at least find him to check if he is actually ill or not, and make sure he's okay?'

She was fishing for her mobile, finding his number and dialling. After the briefest of pauses she looked at the other two and made a face.

'Straight to voicemail,' she said, then, 'Steve? It's Jezza. Where are you, mate? Let me know if you're okay, at least.'

Jo Rodriguez turned up for the debrief, which was led by Kevin Turner. Standing in for Ted as he was, Jo knew the boss would expect him to have a handle on anything and everything the team had been up to over the weekend, while he'd been off enjoying himself. It was one of the things he'd phoned up about that morning, full of apologies for checking up on him.

Rob stayed quiet about what had happened with Steve. He knew he was going to be asked about it at some point, but he was hoping it would not get mentioned in public. Not until he'd at least had chance to find out if Steve was okay, and to ask him for his own version of what had happened.

One or two of the others who'd been nearby and seen what had gone on looked at Rob expectantly, but then appeared to accept he'd decided not to discuss it in an open debrief. It was clear someone had already put the word in to Kevin Turner though, because when they'd finished, he invited Jo and Rob to follow him to his office and told them both to sit down.

'So what happened today, with Steve, Rob? Not the edited highlights, either. I need to know what really happened. Did he bottle it?' Kevin Turner asked him outright.

'Honest answer? I don't know,' Rob told him. 'He wasn't right from the start, but he could have been coming down with something, I suppose. He was physically sick, after all.'

'Where is he now?' Jo wanted to know.

'Another thing I don't know. Jezza tried to phone him, but it went to voicemail. She left him a message, but I don't know if she's had a reply yet.'

Kevin looked from one to another.

'Well, sick or lost it, I can't take the risk of having him back in the thick of it, if we do have to do this all over again tomorrow. I'm hoping we don't, but if we do, is there anyone you can find to replace him with, Jo?'

'If we have to, I will, of course. Even if it means me pitching in. But like you said, let's hope it doesn't come to that, eh?'

Jezza was the one who got the text from Steve, but not until later that evening. She'd arrived home and headed straight for the shower. Luckily for her, her boyfriend, Nathan, who now lived in, had a meal waiting in the oven and was busily helping her brother Tommy with his endless quiz question compilation.

Jezza had initially felt wary of letting Nat into her life. She'd been fending for herself and taking care of Tommy for a long time and it felt intrusive at first. Watching the two of them together when she got in, she felt a warm rush of affection for both of them, in different ways. She paused to plant a kiss on Nat's cheek but made no attempt at physical contact with Tommy. Some days it was allowed. Others it led to meltdown, and there was no visible trigger warning, or none that she had yet learned to determine, of which it would be.

'Do you mind if I have a shower before we do anything else? All this front-line police malarkey is harder than it looks.

I'd forgotten what it can get like on the sharp end.'

Nat gave her a suggestive smile.

'I do like the look of a woman in uniform, though.'

She smiled as she headed for the en suite bathroom opening off from her bedroom in the flat her parents had bought for her. Her phoned pinged with an incoming text as she was peeling off her uniform top and putting it in the laundry basket. The trousers would have to do another day.

'Sorry about earlier. Some sort of gastric flu. Staying with Océane tonight but I doubt I'll be in work tomorrow. Please can you let everyone know. Thanks. Steve x'.

She wasn't sure she entirely believed the story. She tried to call him, but once again it went straight to voicemail. She didn't bother to leave a message this time. Steve knew he could talk to her if he needed to. He'd probably be best off staying with Océane. Bill Baxter, with his long years of service in the force and his bravery medal, might be the last person Steve would want to talk to or confide in after a day like today.

* * *

She was, as ever, on the alert for signs of danger from the moment she heard his key in the front door. She'd never managed to learn to read his mood properly. It must be her fault. She couldn't tell when he'd had a stressful day at work, so she did and said stupid things which acted like a trigger to his pent-up frustrations.

There was a soft clink as he put the keys down on the little table in the hallway. That was encouraging. At least he hadn't flung them down with a clatter.

'Hi, honey, I'm home,' he called out.

His voice was light, jokey.

Another good sign.

'I'm in the kitchen,' she replied, trying to keep any in-tonation out of her voice. To make it bland and neutral, so he couldn't read anything into it which would give him cause to react.

He strode in to find her and, to her surprise, moved closer and planted a kiss on her cheek which felt almost affectionate. There was a hint of whisky on his breath but not much. He'd probably stopped for a swift one with colleagues before he came home. It seemed to have put him in a good mood, for once. She'd have to do everything she could not to break it and spoil the moment.

He leaned back against the kitchen units, muscular arms folded across a big chest, as he watched her fiddling about with a pan on the hob.

'What are we eating? I'm starving.'

'It's chicken curry. I'm making it just the way you like it.'

He sneered at that. Put on a whining falsetto voice as he mimicked her words. '*I'm making it just the way you like it.* I doubt that. You never do anything just the way I like it. Why do you think I have to shop around for what I like?'

She kept her eyes on the pan's contents. Watching the wooden spoon stirring as if fascinated by its every movement.

'And speaking of what I like, we're going out for a meal on Saturday night. Some of the blokes I work with, and our other halves. A curry night. A proper curry. Not that bland swill you're mixing up there.

'I want you to look good. Sexy. I want to be getting a stiffy just from looking at you. Not see you in some sort of shapeless sack thing like you always wear.'

He reached in his back pocket for his wallet. Took out a few banknotes. Grabbed a handful of the top she was wearing and stuffed his hand down the front of it, jamming the notes into her bra, then pinching her nipple. So hard it made her eyes water.

The gesture was so full of disdain she wondered if that was how he paid some of the women he went with. When he couldn't get what he wanted for free, as he was always boasting he could easily do.

For a moment, he seemed to calm down again. She didn't dare get her hopes up. She simply carried on stirring the meal.

Then she said cautiously, 'I'll need to get a babysitter for him. If we're going out on Saturday. I hope I can get one easily at quite short notice.'

He made a noise of annoyance.

'Always so bloody negative. Always looking for any excuse to stop us going out and having some fun. Like a proper couple.'

She waited for the explosion. It didn't come. He seemed, for once, to be making an effort to control himself.

'What about the boy today? Has he done his homework, and has he made a proper job of it, for once?'

'Yes, he did it as soon as he got home from school. I've checked it all to make sure it's right, then I said he could watch some telly.'

Once again his face twisted into a scornful grimace.

'You checked it? What bloody use is that? We both know you can barely write a shopping list and get it right. I'd better go and check it myself. Don't burn that slop while I'm doing that.'

She turned the heat down low. Put a lid on the pan. Whatever she did with it clearly wasn't going to meet with his approval. The earlier good mood was now well and truly gone. Yet again she'd done the wrong thing. She needed to try much harder.

She fished the money out of her bra and went to put it in her purse. She'd start by making an effort to dress up nicely for him on Saturday. She didn't like the clothes he thought were sexy. Hated to dress in a way which drew attention to herself. But if she made an effort to dress to please him, perhaps things might start to improve between them.

'Now then, boy, let's have a look at this homework, shall we? Your mum says she's checked it, but we both know she's not looking for the same standards I am. She doesn't know what you need for your career. But I do. I want you to do well, lad. To make me proud.'

Chapter Eight

Ted was in early on Monday morning. He wanted to catch up on everything which had been happening over the weekend. Trev had been strictly monitoring his access to his work phone, so he felt a bit out of the loop. He didn't like the feeling.

He'd expected to be the first person in and to profit from a bit of quiet time at his desk. Instead he found Steve already installed in front of his computer. He looked dreadful. He never really had the look of a healthy, outdoor type, but he was now paler than Ted had ever seen him. He also looked as if he had dropped some weight, and he didn't have any to lose.

He lifted his head at Ted's entry, his expression more anxious than usual around his senior officer.

'Morning, sir.'

'Morning, Steve. Are you all right to be in work? You don't look on top form, I have to say.'

'That's what I wanted to tell you, sir. I came in early, hoping to catch you. I had to take the weekend off. I had some sort of gastric bug or maybe food poisoning. I started being sick at the demo and I've spent most of the weekend throwing up ...'

'It's fine, Steve, you can spare me the details. You've got an excellent record, so a couple of days off sick isn't an issue. As long as you're sure you're fit to be back at work.'

'Yes, sir, there's nothing left to come up.'

Ted headed for his own office to tackle whatever had landed on his desk in his absence. He rather wished Steve hadn't shared so much information with him. He wondered fleetingly if he had been doing what suspects so often did in interview. Supplying too many details in an attempt to make something sound credible. But then he pushed the thought aside. He'd no reason to suspect Steve would be anything other than truthful, or would pull a sickie when he knew how stretched they all were. To be on the safe side, he'd need to have a quiet word with Jo and Rob to get the full picture. If Steve needed their help and support, they would all rally round him. But first they'd need to know what was going on.

He'd made a small dent in the catching up when his mobile rang. He recognised the number but even if he hadn't, he would have known immediately the voice which greeted him with, 'Eddie, dahhhling, how are you?'

Gina Shaw. An undercover Drugs officer he'd worked with on a previous case. One which was still frustratingly unfinished. Her speaking to him like that meant she was either somewhere she needed to stay in character for her PR cover, or she was enjoying teasing him. When he hesitated slightly and she laughed, he knew it was the latter.

'Hello, Gina, what can I do for you?'

He tried not to get too optimistic, but if she was calling him out of the blue, there was a slim chance she might have some good news for him about the still-open case. It would make his day to hear there was a chance of getting some justice, finally.

'It's more what I and my colleagues might be able to do for you. I don't want to get your hopes up too high, because it may yet not come off, but I've been covertly and carefully watching your delightful young drug dealer, Data, for some time now. It's just about possible that we may shortly be in a position to arrest him for possession with intent to supply. I thought that might perhaps be of interest to you?'

'It certainly is. Especially if I can be there to see the little bugger get his collar felt. We want him for quite a few other things too. Most importantly, we want him to lead us to our famous blind dwarf drugs baron, if we can.'

'I thought you might. I'd already raised the possibility with my powers that be and got a very guarded agreement. Apparently I'm meant to remind you that you would be there to observe only and not to do any special agent stuff abseiling down buildings, if that means anything to you?'

Ted laughed at her words. They'd clearly come from someone who knew about his previous role as a Specialist Firearms Officer, when operations like that had been routine work for him.

'Right, I'd better love you and leave you, Eddie,' she stuck ironically to the name she'd given him for their cover when they'd first met. 'I promise to keep you posted, and look forward to meeting you again soon, hopefully in positive circumstances.'

Jo Rodriguez came to find Ted before the rest of the team arrived, as they'd arranged. He paused to ask Steve how he was feeling and if he was really fit to be back at work. Steve looked uncomfortable and replied with a, 'Yes, sir, thank you,' which surprised Jo. No one on the team ever called him anything but Jo. Not even Steve, in normal circumstances.

Jo's tap on the door of Ted's office was cursory, to say the least. Merely a formality. As he went in and took a seat in response to Ted's nod, he observed, 'Well, you look pleased with yourself, Ted. Was the hippy-fest as good as that?'

'I actually enjoyed myself a lot more than I thought I would. It was like nothing I've ever attended before, but it was great fun. The happy couple have gone off on their honeymoon up to the Highlands and Islands now. Or whatever the equivalent is called in hippy-speak. So let's hope the Professor's replacement for the next two weeks is as easy to get along with, and as efficient as she always is.

'What's really put a smile on my face this morning is that Drugs have their eyes on our old friend Data once more, and are hoping to mount an op to pull him in. I've already declared an interest for us and pointed out that we're keen to use him as a possible way to get to the man behind the whole drugs operation. The famous Big Man. Not to mention the rest of it.'

'Now that would be a very welcome tick on the books all round. Especially if he can lead us to the mysterious Big Man, whoever he is.'

'I want to try to be involved in briefings on this from the beginning, if I can. I need to make sure everyone concerned knows exactly what we're up against. Not just from him but from his Special Forces henchmen. It would be a serious mistake to underestimate any of them.'

'As long as you're not spreading yourself too thin,' Jo told him. 'You can't be everywhere at once. That's what I'm supposed to be here for. To spread the load a bit.'

'I know and I appreciate it, Jo. I'm leaving you in charge again later on. I'm going back over to Ashton to see if they've achieved anything yet. I've a mind to ship DC Burgess back here, so you can ride shotgun over him a bit. Have a think about who we could send in exchange. It needs to be someone who can guide DS Ramsay without undermining him. Or maybe I should shift Burgess across to Trafford for Sarah Jenkins to sort out. Then once things ease up a bit here, we could replace him by sending Graham Winters to Ashton. He'd be an asset.'

Ted had briefly told Jo about his visit to other stations when they were discussing best use of available officers.

'So tell me, how it's been. And what about Steve? He looks shocking this morning. Have you managed to find out anything more about what's bothering him? He told me gastric flu or food poisoning, but he really isn't himself, is he? If we can get to the bottom of it, we might be able to help him, but he doesn't open up easily.'

'Steve was the first thing on my agenda to talk to you about. It started on Saturday, apparently, as soon as things got lively with the crowd control. He was at the front with Rob and the others when it all started to kick off. Rob said he looked ready to turn tail even before he was sick. Clearly once he started throwing up he had to leave. The thing is, we don't know if it was genuine illness or if he really did bottle it.'

'Who's going to talk to him about it? It's time we tried to get to the bottom of whatever is going on with him. He's clearly not right. We need to make it clear he's not in any sort of trouble, but we can only help him if we know what the problem is.'

'I was going to leave it to Rob to talk to him, initially. He was in charge on Saturday, after all. Steve was answerable to him. I thought it might seem as it we were undermining Rob's authority if either of us waded in initially. If necessary, we could refer it on to Kevin. It was his op, he was in overall charge, and he can do tactful. Perhaps you should make time to have a quiet, unofficial word with Kev about it? On the off-chance that someone else there had a clue about it all.'

'That sounds like a plan. Shall we go and catch up? Sounds like the rest of them coming in now.'

'Before we start, Ted, I keep meaning to say, and forgetting. I have the perfect video footage to blackmail you with whenever I need to, which I'll hold over your head for ever more,' Kevin Turner warned Ted as he went into his office and sat down later on.

'What, Moondancegate? That's has been all over social media and goodness knows where else. There's no blackmail mileage left in that at all.'

Kevin looked sly and tapped the side of his nose.

'Not Moondance, no. Something much, much better to threaten you with.'

'Give me a clue, then.'

Kev gave a sadistic chuckle.

'You're the clever detective. It's up to you to work it out. But it gives me total power over you for as long as I want. All I'm saying for now is, nice legs.'

Ted stared at him in dawning horror. He thought he'd got away with having had to do a hasty striptease in the station car park to get out of a suit which stank like the crime scene he'd just left. He should have known that nothing like that went unnoticed at the nick.

He made a clumsy and obvious change of subject.

'Anyway, I gather there was a bit of a problem with Steve on Saturday. It may have been genuine illness, of course. But until I find out more about what's wrong with him at the moment, if you need us for any more fun and games, I'll either substitute him with someone else or make sure he's done some update training before we put him in a similar situation again.'

He went hurriedly through everything else he needed to discuss with Kev, then beat a retreat as hastily as he could, Kev's threat about the video, and his laughter, ringing in his ears.

He decided to go to Ashton earlier than he'd planned. He'd prefer to be somewhere else if CCTV footage of him in his kecks really was circulating in the station. The mere idea was making him paranoid. Were the two PCs who stood aside to let him go through a doorway first really grinning at him with knowing expressions, or simply smiling politely at him?

He hadn't booked Hector for this journey. It wasn't justifiable use of his time to keep him hanging around when Ted didn't know how long he was going to be. He would take his service vehicle. He was turning up unannounced, as he said he would. The optimistic side of him was hoping to see an improvement in the team over there, and there was certainly room for it. The realistic side warned him it was probably too soon for results.

Only DS Ramsay and Lee Wu were in the office when Ted walked in. He could see that Lee was trawling through CCTV footage. Ramsay was doing paperwork. The look the sergeant gave Ted when he saw him raised his hopes once more. He would really like to see a result from this team.

'Hello, sir. You've come at exactly the right moment. Alan, DC Burgess, has just gone out with Uniform assisting to bring in one of our suspects. You were absolutely right. Once we started going out and about checking for private CCTV footage, we found some. And it shows a regular of ours. Nasty piece, with previous for robbery and assault. So hopefully we might be getting somewhere at last.'

'Good, I'm pleased to hear it. Are you planning on interviewing him yourself?'

'I thought I would do, guv. I've dealt with him before. I've sorted out a warrant to search his place for any of the stolen property.'

'Excellent. I'd like to stay and watch over the monitor, if that won't cramp your style.'

'Fine by me. Oh, and I should say, the credit for this goes to Lee. She was the one who spotted him on the footage.'

Ted smiled at that. He was pleased with the progress, but even more pleased that the DS gave credit where it was due instead of grabbing the glory for himself. Perhaps there was hope for him.

* * *

The chicken was in the oven, on a low light. It should be fine for when he got home. Nice and tender. Just the way he liked it. The boy had eaten earlier. She'd have something with her husband when he got home. If all was going well. Perhaps, for once, they could sit together at the table and enjoy their food. Like normal couples did. It would be a long time since that had happened.

As ever, she listened out for warning sounds as he came through the door at the end of his shift. A way to gauge his mood. Sometimes, if he was feeling calm, he gave a little two-tone whistle to announce his arrival. He did that this evening, as she heard him put the car keys down quietly.

'We're in the living room,' she called out. 'I'm helping him with his homework.'

She realised she'd made a mistake, saying that, as soon as she heard his snort of derision. She was so stupid. Always saying the wrong thing. She wished fervently that she could bite back the words. But it was too late. She'd said them, and he'd heard her.

'Good god, woman,' he said as he strode in.

His tone was mocking but he didn't have the dangerous edge to his voice.

Not yet.

'Don't you think he has enough difficulties getting it right, without you adding to them? Come on, then, lad, show me what you've been doing with all this wonderful help from your mother. Between us, you and I might be able to sort it out into something that's worthy of you handing in.'

Mother and son were sitting at the table together. The resemblance between them was striking. There was nothing of the father in his appearance, although there was no doubt the boy was his. There's no way the woman would have dared to cheat on him.

The boy was as skinny as she was, with that same permanently anxious look. As if he was sure everything he did was wrong and he was about to be punished for it. Yet always striving so hard to get it right. Seeking his father's approval.

He was holding up his exercise book now, his hand visibly shaking. Two faces looked up at the man, both with the same look of desperately wanting everything to be right.

'Oh dear,' the man said, shaking his head. 'Oh dear, oh dear. This is no good at all, lad. What have I told you about relying on your mother for help? This is a pile of crap, to put it mildly. You can't hand this in. You'll only embarrass yourself if you do. Let's you and me sit down together and see if we can't make a better job of it.'

He put the book down on the table and moved round to where the woman was sitting. For such a bulky man, he could move with surprising speed. He gripped her by the back of the neck and hauled her bodily from the chair, shoving her aside so roughly that she lost her balance and fell over with a small cry of pain.

The boy was on his feet in an instant, his chair tipping over backwards with the speed of his movement. He flew at the man, pulling powerlessly at him, trying to get to his mother, as his father stood over the fallen woman,

'Leave her alone! Stop bullying her! Mum! Mum!'

The man turned slowly towards the boy as the mother struggled to get up off the floor to protect him.

'Well, what have we got here? The cub trying to fight the alpha male to save his mother's worthless hide?'

He didn't bother to raise his voice. His tone was measured, reasonable. He simply picked the boy up, gripping both upper arms and holding him effortlessly aloft.

'You'll thank me for being strict with you now, my lad, when you land the job you want and you do well at it. And I know you will. As long as you listen to me about what standards are acceptable and not to her,' he jerked his head to where the woman was now pulling herself up off the floor, trying to get hold of his arm to stop him hurting her son.

He set the boy carefully back down on his feet and told him, 'Sit back at the table, lad, and let's go through this again. The two of us. Until it's worthy of being handed in.'

His casual back-handed slap to the woman's face as she managed to get up off the floor had little more force than he might have used to swat a fly. It still knocked her back off her feet and made her gasp.

'You. Go and see to my tea. And make sure it's edible, for once. Goodness knows how long I'll be, sorting out this rubbish. But I'll see to you later.'

Chapter Nine

It was a smugly self-satisfied DC Alan Burgess who strode into the office having arrived back from bringing in the suspect. He was clearly so pleased with himself that he failed to notice the DCI sitting, head down, going through the case file, at a desk in the corner. It was finally coming together, although there was still a lot of work to be done on it before it was fit to send to CPS.

'Got the bastard downstairs, Pete, so I'm ready when you are. Stick the kettle on, Chop Suey, love, I could murder a brew before we get stuck in.'

It was only when Ted lifted his head and spoke quietly that Burgess seemed to notice him.

'If you're brewing up, DC Burgess, mine's a tea, white, two sugars, please.'

Burgess recovered his stride quickly enough. It was obvious that it was a rare thing indeed for him to be office tea boy. He knew roughly what his male colleagues drank but he clearly had no idea about Lee Wu and had to ask her. It emphasised that this was the first time he had ever made a drink for her.

When Burgess left the office to go to the kitchen with their orders, Ted soundlessly got up to follow him. He was in his famous stealth mode, which his own team knew so well.

Burgess was opening and closing cupboards to find things. The unfamiliarity of it all was noticeable. Ted was so tempted to shut the door of the kitchenette behind him with a high-flying karate kick – the action his team called his kick-trick –

but he held himself in check. He decided it didn't quite go with the image of Head of Serious Crime. In addition, he could hardly have the talk about equality he intended to have with Burgess if he left himself open to allegations of bullying and intimidation.

'How long have you been with the Force, DC Burgess?'

'Twenty-five years and counting, guv.'

'Long enough then to know that it's not the nineteen-seventies any more and that any form of racism, sexism or any other type of discrimination is not tolerated.'

'Chop Suey?' Burgess asked, his expression all outraged innocence, getting tea, coffee and sugar out of a cupboard now he'd found the right one, as he waited for the kettle to boil. 'That's just a bit of a joke. A nickname, like. Lee doesn't mind.'

'She doesn't mind? Or she's perhaps raised an objection and been told she doesn't understand your idea of humour?'

Ted could see from Burgess's reaction that his comment had hit home. He didn't want to be wasting time dealing with issues like this. Ones which DS Ramsay should have been all over. But he wanted to mark Burgess's card for him, well and truly.

'DC Burgess, I don't expect to be spending time on my visits here with this sort of outdated and unacceptable behaviour. I shouldn't need to. I'm here for Serious Crime. So I expect it to stop. Right now. Lee is a valued member of the team. You treat her as you would any of the others, please.'

The please surprised Burgess, judging by his expression.

'Fair enough, guv,' he replied, plonking all the mugs onto a small tray and adding coffee or teabags and sugar as request. 'As soon as we've had the brew, I'll go and help Pete with the suspect interview.'

'There's no need. I'll be watching over the monitor, in contact with the DS. The most profitable use of your time right now would be to write up your notes of the arrest in detail, and to see if you can find the other suspect by some means. Who's overseeing the search of the first one's premises?'

'I left that to the Woodentops to sort out,' Burgess told him dismissively, sloshing the freshly-boiled water into the mugs, fishing out the teabags and tossing them into the sink together with the used teaspoon.

'Whereas I prefer always to have a CID presence during the search on a case like this. Then we have a first-hand account of exactly how it was conducted and what was found where. I generally find it works better that way. And once again, talking about respect and equality as befits the Force in the twenty-first century, you will refer to Uniform officers as precisely that and nothing else. Especially in my presence.

'So clean up in here, don't leave it to someone else to do, finish your drink quickly, then get back to the house search for a progress report and remain there until it's been done to your satisfaction.'

Ted could imagine the gestures Burgess was making behind his back as he turned and left the room. It bothered him not the slightest. He wanted to make something of an efficiently functioning unit of this team, then he could get on with the more important aspects of his new role.

It was later in the day before Ted was happy to leave the Ashton team to it. The search had revealed some of the missing property, although their suspect was still denying everything and refusing to name the second man involved. They at least had enough to charge him with, then release him on bail with strict reporting conditions.

Ramsay's interview of him had been competent though not outstanding. Ted had made a few suggestions through the earpiece he was wearing, but it was a good enough result, although there was still the second suspect to find and bring in.

It was pouring down by the time Ted left to drive back to Stockport. Typically, he'd left his raincoat in the car so he got a soaking on the sprint to where he'd parked it. He took his jacket off and draped it on the passenger seat to be drying out a bit on the drive back, then put his coat handy for when he arrived. It made him think once more about the footage Kevin was threatening him with. He'd better make time to take him for a drink at least once in the week as a down payment on the blackmail he was threatening.

Trev phoned as he was driving.

'Not wishing to force you to incriminate yourself, but can you give me a rough idea of when to expect you home? Your answer will determine which of two options I cook for supper. I know you can't always be sure, so I'll settle for knowing which day.'

Ted chuckled.

'I've improved recently, though, surely? And my answer is whichever will gain me a sticky sweet pudding.'

'Play your cards right and you might get more than one treat.'

'I'm on the way back from Ashton now. I need a catch-up, a brief one, with Jo and the team, then I'm all yours. I'll give you a bell when I'm leaving, but it shouldn't be too late. Hopefully.'

A different attitude greeted Ted when he walked into the main office at his own station. All the team members were at their desks, finishing jobs and sorting paperwork before they went home for the evening. Quietly harmonious, with an air of purpose. Steve was busily working on his computer. He looked marginally better, at least. The deathly pallor had given way to a bit more colour, though not much. Ted didn't want to make a point of singling him out. He'd find out later how he was.

'We'll have a quick round-up of developments, boss, now you're back, before we knock off. Don't get too excited. There's nothing definitive yet. But there's some progress to report, at least. The PM on our suspicious death is tomorrow.

Mike's covering. The Professor's replacement is a Dr Sinclair. I don't think we know him yet.'

'It's not going to be the easiest case to meet him over, either, I imagine,' Ted said. 'Mike, I know you'll do your best to get the information we need, but I'm wondering if there is actually any way to tell if marks from hands gripping can be shown to be from pushing someone or pulling them in an attempt to stop them from jumping.'

'There would be in crime fiction,' Jezza put in with a grin. Ted ignored her and carried on.

'You've probably already thought of this, but have we asked at the school the boy goes to? In case they've noticed anything about him recently. Although if they had, it might have been passed on to Children's Services already. And where are we up to with them?'

'I'm going to the school tomorrow, boss, to see if there's anything at all they can tell us,' Jezza told him. 'Then I'm going with Maurice to see Children's Services, about us talking to the boy. They're being reasonably cooperative, but clearly they have to protect his interests. I thought it might help if I went. I know I've not done the Victim Support Training, but if I tell them about living with Tommy, I thought that might get us somewhere.'

'Somehow we need to speak to that little lad. I know it will all be very traumatic for him. He's lost his mam. There's a chance the man he's been living with is as innocent as he says he is and the boy's being kept from someone he would feel safe with. But we can't take risks with him. We need to try to find out what's been happening in that household.

'At some point I'll talk to you about one of the ideas I put in my report to the ACC. Another way of looking out for warning signs. But not now. You've all got homes to go to. Anything else to report?'

'Two more Black Mould Scam victims on our patch, boss,' Rob O'Connell told him. 'Not such good descriptions from them as from Mrs Hamer. Claire and I have been working through what we have for similarities and differences. We're pretty convinced we're dealing with the same people in both our areas. The good news is that we've thrown up some possible matches.

'I thought we'd start by taking a few photos to show Mrs Hamer. Claire can come with me, in case Mrs H starts giving me those teacher looks again. Then, depending who, if anyone, she picks out, we can try the photos out on the other victims. We might possibly be getting somewhere.'

'Excellent, well done everyone. Now, just before you all rush off. Some of you may know Mrs Skinner, who's cleaned our offices for us since long before any of us were here, and generally kept us in order.'

He wasn't about to admit to the team the number of times he'd kicked a wastepaper basket to a state beyond redemption in frustration when things weren't going well. Nor the number of apologetic notes he'd had to leave for Mrs Skinner, who always discreetly sorted out a replacement for him. Not to mention the reproachful messages she left for him in return.

'Long past retirement age, but they've always let her carry on. She's a police widow. A valued officer from this station, killed in the line of duty, and everyone knows the extra cash has been a big help to her. But now, as is always happening these days, the cleaning firm who employed her has been taken over by a bigger one. Impersonal. All they've done is look at her age and decide based on that she can go. Goodness knows what she'll do with herself without her work.

'Anyway, I thought it might be nice to get her something. A small gift to show our appreciation. A card at least. So let me know if any of you want to chip in, or sign it or something. Purely voluntary, of course.'

Ted went for a quick flick through his emails and any notes on his desk before he left. He had his phone in his hand and was telling Trev, 'I'm on my way now. Just putting my coat on,' when there was a light tap on his door and Jezza came in.

'Sorry, boss, have you got a minute?'

'Cancel that,' Ted told Trev, motioning to Jezza to take a seat. 'I will be putting my coat on very shortly. Hopefully.'

'I didn't mean to delay you but I thought you might like to know what I've managed to prise out of Steve. Although it's probably easier to get info out of an MI5 agent. I dragged him out for a sandwich and a coffee at lunchtime and asked him outright what was bothering him.'

'I hope he realises there's no question of him being in any trouble. His sickness record is excellent. Two days off being ill is nothing to get worried about. And if it was all a bit much for him with the demo, he only has to say and there is help available.'

'Simpler than that, boss. Affairs of the heart. Océane is going to the States for six months, the jammy thing. She's very highly regarded in her field, you know. So much so that she's off to share skills with the FBI. And Steve is going to be totally lost without her. Knowing someone like her thinks he's okay means the world to him. You know how low his self-esteem is.'

'I do, but I don't know why. To my shame I know very little about him. I don't think he has family, does he?'

'There's a father, or perhaps a stepfather, I'm not sure, somewhere, but he has no contact with him and won't talk about him. I know his mother died suddenly, not long after he joined up, but I don't know any more than that.'

'You know a lot more than I do. I don't even know where he's from.'

'Hampshire, I think. He's always very vague about himself. But you know I studied language and speech patterns as part of drama training, so that's where I'd put him as coming from. Oh, and I've heard him say grockles on occasion.'

'I'm not even sure what they are. It sounds a bit suspect.'

Jezza gave an exaggerated eye roll at that.

'Tourists, boss. The invading hordes, who appear as soon as the sun comes out. Like the ones who descend on the New Forest every year and manage to run over some of the ponies and donkeys. Anyway, you're clearly in a hurry to get off, so I won't delay you.'

'By the way, before you go, Jezza, I'm hoping you can help me with part of the present for Mrs Skinner. I want to get her a really nice, very solid wastepaper basket.'

Jezza gave him one of her looks.

'Wow, boss. Just what any woman has always dreamed of.'

He smiled at her tone.

'It's a bit of an in joke between us. She's had to replace mine a few times, for reasons I'm not prepared to go into for fear of incriminating myself. So I thought a nice stylish one, a designer one, if they do such things. Maybe wooden, perhaps? And then put some presents in it. I've no idea what. Bath stuff? Hand cream? Trev will have some ideas, no doubt.'

Jezza had her phone out and was scrolling through some searches.

'Er, boss, you do realise a wastepaper bin like you're describing is going to cost you a good three figures?'

She held the phone out to him to show him the screen. He looked at it in astonishment.

'I'd no idea it would be that much. But I think she'd appreciate the humour. Could you send me the link, please? Then I'd better get going or I'm going to be in trouble.'

* * *

She was in the kitchen, making his breakfast. She and the boy had already had their tea, and he was in the living room, doing his homework. She'd decided it was best if she didn't try to help him. She only made things worse and angered his father.

She preferred it when he was on nights. His mood

was generally better when he first woke up. Which meant that at flashpoint moments, like checking homework, he wasn't usually on such a short fuse. His work took a toll on him, of course. She understood that. He had a lot of responsibility. And accountability.

She was always so stupid. She'd never learned to judge the sort of pressure he was under when he got home. Always saying the wrong thing. Or not serving his tea just how he liked it. It was no wonder he got angry with her.

The signs were good so far. She'd heard him humming away to himself as he took his shower and had his shave. She knew he'd slept well. She'd looked in on him a couple of times to make sure.

The boy knew to creep round like a little mouse when he came home from school and his father was still sleeping. He'd barely made a sound. Now he was at the table in the living room, head down over his books. Trying so hard, as he always did.

She paused occasionally to put her head around the doorway. Simply for the pleasure of looking at him. Not to disturb him. He was oblivious to her in any case, studying as hard as he was. The feeling of pride, looking at his frown of concentration, almost took her breath away.

Then she heard the top stair creak as the man started down. He was in his sock feet, his work boots downstairs, ready polished. For a big man, he'd learned the art of moving quietly, but that step always made a noise. He kept saying he'd fix it one day.

He went into the living room first. She immediately stiffened with tension. She paused in her breakfast preparations. Every fibre on the alert for any sounds which would take her rushing in to try to protect her son. Even though she knew it was a total waste of time and would only enrage the man further.

'Now then, lad, how have you got on with your home-work?'

His tone sounded jovial enough.

'Much better without your daft mother thinking she's helping and making it worse, I bet.'

It was quiet for a moment. She interpreted the silence as the boy passing over his book, filled with trepidation, no doubt, then the father starting to look through it.

She hovered.

Waiting for the explosion.

Praying it didn't come.

'Well, this is a bit better, at least. Good boy for trying. There are still some careless spelling mistakes, though. Where's that desk dictionary I got you? It's no use relying on computers to correct your spelling for you like lazy people do. You need to take control yourself. Make sure you check how to spell new words. And it's very important your written work is beyond reproach. It will need to be to a high standard in your chosen career.

'You're never going to excel at sports or anything physical, a little lad like you, so you have to exploit your intellect. Get these mistakes corrected. And by that I mean do it again, don't just scribble on it. Leave it out and I'll check it again when I get back from my shift.'

She heard him coming towards the kitchen, even though he still made little noise. She hurriedly turned back to her cooking, desperate to get everything perfect.

So far his mood was better than she'd dared hope.

She mustn't do anything to spoil it.

'And how is the love of my life? I hope you have my breakfast ready, woman,' he said but he sounded jokey, almost affectionate.

For once she didn't cringe as he came up behind her. He even planted a soft kiss on the side of her neck.

She was trying to be so careful with the hot fat. Not

wanting anything he was doing to distract her to the point of splashing or spilling any of it onto herself. Or onto him.

Now he was running his hands, slowly, sensually, down her back. He cupped one to each of her buttocks, kneading so gently. It was almost seductive.

She tilted her head, eyes half closing, leaning back against him. Feeling rare arousal despite herself.

Then the pressure of his hands increased. Pinching, hurting. She tried to struggle, to say something. One of her hands was still gripping the pan. The oil was getting too hot now. Starting to spit angrily everywhere. She tried to use the other hand to switch off the gas under it but his weight against her prevented the movement.

Desperately, she dragged the pan off the heat, her clumsy action sloshing hot fat all over the naked flame which instantly flared up.

He grabbed her by the upper arms, flinging her bodily out of the way as the smoke detector started its shrill, frenetic beeping.

The boy came running into the room, calling for his mother as the father was soaking a towel under a running tap, dropping it over the flames. Extinguishing them quickly and efficiently.

'Don't worry, it's only your clumsy mother, trying to burn the place down. Again. What a good job I'd not left for work yet. And now I won't have time to eat here. I'll have to grab myself something on the way in. You take care of yourself while I'm out, lad, in case she does something else just as stupid.'

Chapter Ten

'Is there any way you'll be able to tell us, doctor, from the marks on the body, whether the lady was thrown or pushed over the handrail? Or whether the signs are more compatible with someone perhaps grabbing hold of her and trying to prevent her from jumping?'

Dr Sinclair, the stand-in pathologist in Professor Nelson's absence, gave DS Mike Hallam a rather old-fashioned look over the top of his glasses. He was a small man, slimly built, neat and meticulous in both his appearance and in everything he did and said. He countered with a question of his own.

'Do you watch a lot of crime fiction on television, sergeant?'

'No, sir, I don't. It's all too far-fetched for me. Not good for my blood pressure.'

'Doctor is fine, there's absolutely no need to call me sir. And I'm assuming you don't like it because of how it misrepresents the role of the police in sudden death investigations?'

When Mike confirmed his assumption , the pathologist went on, 'I probably wouldn't be exaggerating if I said that the function and powers of pathologists are possibly even more ridiculously portrayed than those of you and your colleagues.

'We may be asked to view a body in situ. Usually for an early opinion on whether a crime is involved or not. We certainly don't go chasing round the country carrying out any investigations ourselves. Nor does the Coroner. We leave that to the police, who are the experts in it.

'As I'm sure you already know, it's my job to tell the Coroner, and the police, based on forensic evidence, how this poor lady died. The Coroner will then decide whether or not an inquest is required to determine whether the death was natural, accidental, suicide or murder. Or a variation of any of those. Unless, of course, your investigations enable you to charge someone in connection with the death early on in your inquiries.'

Mike was biting his tongue. He knew all of that already. And Sinclair must realise that any DS would know. He could have asked the Professor the same question and received a much more helpful and detailed response. One which didn't sound like teaching a grandmother to suck eggs.

Sinclair seemed to sense his frustration as he continued, 'I know you need to know as much detail as possible, to determine whether this is a murder case or not. So I'm happy to share my preliminary findings with you, although my written report will, of course, be more detailed. With the caveat that things might change on more in depth analysis which will follow today's procedure.

'So, from preliminary superficial examination, the victim shows a number of old injuries which could be compatible with a history of abuse. Possibly. Note my emphasis on the word "could". Also, initial visual examination would seem to suggest that death was due to a broken neck.

'Now, in the most unscientific of ways possible, we could play about with this being a piece of crime fiction and do some speculating, if you would find that at all useful. But please don't hold me to any of this. You could say I'm simply humouring you.'

'Thank you, doctor, I really appreciate any pointers at all.'

'The first thing which would spring to my mind, if I were to write this as a crime fiction piece, is based on my own experience of other such deaths. And that is that although people have been known to kill one another by throwing the victim down the stairs, it's quite hard to prove pre-meditation for such a case. So it is usually extremely difficult to prove any form of intention to kill.'

'How far did our unfortunate lady fall?'

'Down two flights. But not carpeted. Those concrete steps in communal blocks of flats.'

'So presumably not a big, impressive, wide stairwell, as you might see in, for instance, an old-fashioned smart hotel, such as might feature in an Agatha Christie?'

Mike had to smile at that. He was starting to warm to Dr Sinclair after all.

'Nothing remotely like that.'

'So therein, you see, lies your problem. Unless your perpetrator obligingly confesses, or left a note somewhere saying he fully intended to kill this person – his wife, perhaps?'

'Live-in partner. They weren't married.'

'What used to be called a common law wife, then. My point being that the very architecture of the scene is going to make it almost impossible to show pre-meditation to kill. Your suspect might, under questioning, admit to having pushed her against the bannisters in the heat of some domestic dispute. He might even, under the right conditions, concede that he lifted her up and helped her on her way. But could he have foreseen that his actions would lead to her death rather than mere injury, albeit potentially serious? With a narrow stairwell, could he have predicted that she would fall further than the two flights? And would he have the necessary knowledge as to how far she would need to fall to suffer fatal injuries? Those would be the burning questions for the Coroner's Court, and for any trial in Crown Court.

'I will, of course, be testing for any type of drug in the system, which might suggest she was unconscious when she went over the bannisters. Possibly to make her easier to manhandle. That might indicate pre-meditation, although not necessarily.'

'The trouble with that is that a lot of neighbours heard shouting, from both of them, before they went out to find out what was going on, and found her apparently dead on the stairs. Which suggests that she was awake when she fell. Or was pushed. Unfortunately nobody came out until it all went quiet.'

'By which time the poor woman would almost certainly have been already dead, based on my initial observations. It's too early to say for sure but I would expect death to have been more or less instantaneous, judging by my first superficial examination of the cervical vertebrae.

'Again, letting my surprisingly vivid imagination run away with me, I could foresee a scene in which some enterprising defence lawyer has a dummy made to the exact height and weight of the victim. They might then experiment with repeatedly throwing it over the bannister, to see what was the maximum distance it could reasonably be expected to travel. I could see that looking rather dramatic on the small screen. Although it's totally fanciful, of course.'

'And for the moment, our suspect is sticking to his story that she was trying to jump and he was simply attempting to stop her from doing so, hence my earlier questions.'

'Are these flats all on one floor inside? Not split level?'

Mike frowned.

'As far as I know they all are. I've not heard of flats being on more than one level. Is it significant?'

'I lived in one in London for a time. They're quite widespread, in the north, too. They're sometimes called maisonettes, I believe.'

'Oh, maisonettes, yes, I've heard that term. I think there are some of those in Stockport. I somehow didn't associate it with what I would call flats. But no, not in this case. I've been to the crime scene and there weren't any stairs inside that one. It's all on one level.'

'I see. And yes, in my little game of playing a TV pathologist who would do half of the police's work for them, if not more, I would venture to suggest to you that it could be significant. You see, if it was one of those apartments with stairs inside, the defence would pounce on that in respect of motive. They might well pose the question as to why, if the man had decided to throw the unfortunate woman down the stairs with malice aforethought, did he not simply do it in their own home, then claim it was an accident? Why go out into a communal area and risk being seen by someone? But the layout in this case rules all of that out.

'I take it you have no eye witnesses?'

Mike shook his head.

'Lots of neighbours giving statements to say blazing rows were a regular feature in the flat. But no one yet prepared to claim to have seen the fatal incident itself. We still have some more door-to-door still to carry out. We haven't managed to speak to everyone, so there's the outside chance of a witness somewhere.'

'And I see from the cadaver that this lady has had a C-section at some point. So is there a child involved in this unfortunate incident? And did they witness the fatality?'

'There's a little boy of nine. Very traumatised, as you might imagine. Two of my colleagues are going to talk to Children's Services today about the possibility of speaking to him. Even if and when it might be possible, it's going to need to be a long and slow process, with all the safeguards in place.'

'It's never easy for any child involved in something like this. There's an unfortunate and totally irrational stigma to being a child in a family where one parent has killed the other, even if it's a step-parent. I will do my very best to give you all the answers I can. I know Professor Nelson's shoes are big ones to fill, but I'll certainly try my best for you.

'And I have to say I've rather enjoyed the unusual experience of giving my imagination free rein, rather than relying on scientific facts. Perhaps a new career as a writer of crime fiction awaits me in my twilight years, when I finally hang up my scalpel.'

Ted was talking to Sarah Jenkins at Trafford via video link. Hector was right. There simply weren't enough hours in the day for him to go out and about on his new enlarged patch, as well as keeping an eye on things with his own team, as he liked to do.

'So far we've talked to the nan and to the daughter, now she's back on leave. She and the boy are staying with their nan for now, but we've not talked to him yet. We're liaising with Social Services about the best way to handle it.'

'Whose parent is the grandmother?' Ted asked her.

'She's the mother of the victim. And to say she had little time for the son-in-law is putting it mildly. Both she and the granddaughter had been continuously trying to persuade the woman to leave him and take the boy with her. The trouble is, as is so very often the case with domestic violence, she'd been conditioned to believe that some of it must be her fault. She wasn't quiet enough when he was working nights and sleeping in the daytime. She didn't make his meals the way he liked them. We've all heard the sort of thing before.'

'What about his story of her associating with drug dealers?'

'Her mother says that was an absolute load of rubbish. Her daughter had no friends. She shut herself away from everyone because the other half got insanely jealous if she showed interest in anyone. She would certainly never have dared to have someone round to the house, and definitely not a man.

'The PM's tomorrow, so that should hopefully show us if there was any evidence of her taking drugs at all. The daughter also says that's pure nonsense. Her mother didn't take anything. She barely drank, either. Just one glass of wine on the rare occasions he took her out anywhere, to show her off to his friends.'

'Will the daughter testify against the father? It's largely

circumstantial anyway, but it might help to build a case to show intent to kill.'

'Ah, now, there we do have the one glimmer of hope on the horizon. She's not his daughter. The boy's his, but she's from an earlier marriage. Very sad story. Her father died very young from a rare disease, shortly after she was born. The mother brought her up on her own for a few years, but then she met this charmer and fell for him, for heaven knows what reason. Her own mother warned her off him. I imagine she was probably very lonely and clutching at straws, perhaps.'

'Keep me posted on what happens at the PM, please. These cases are some of the hardest to get a murder conviction on, so all we can do is build the best case we can. We'll have to let CPS decide what charge we can go with.

'We have something similar on our own patch at the moment. No grandparents around for the little lad in this case, as far as we know, so we're not sure at the moment what will happen to him, whether or not we get a conviction for anything against the father.

'Oh, by the way, I don't want to add to your workload but I wondered if I could send you a DC for a few days. Put him on legwork, statement taking, that sort of thing.'

'It sounds, in theory, as if that should be lightening our load. Reading between the lines, I imagine he's not yet all that much of an asset to a team, is he?'

Ted smiled at her.

'He might be all right with proper firm direction. Where he is at the moment, the DS is too much of a mate and he tends to take advantage. It's only fair to warn you that he probably has a very old-fashioned attitude towards women, and not in a good way. Could you at least try him out for a day or two? If he's too much of a pain, let me know and I'll swap him for someone easier. We're making good progress on our scam case, so we're getting a bit less stretched, at least for now.'

'I'd be delighted to try him out. I do love a challenge.

What's his name?'

'DC Burgess. Alan. Twenty-five years served and behaves as if he joined in the early seventies.'

She was still laughing as they ended the call.

* * *

She woke to a rising feeling of panic.

Air.

She needed air.

Her lungs were craving it, her brain sending her urgent signals to breathe. Take a deep breath.

She opened her eyes, though at first she saw nothing but flashing lights. She tried to take in some of the air she so desperately needed. Her legs were starting to pedal frantically as adrenaline flooded her body, provoking the flight reflex.

There was a heavy weight across her chest. A choking feeling in her throat. Pressure at the side of her neck starving her brain of vital oxygen.

When she finally managed to focus, she saw his face, inches away from hers. A sadistic smile twisting his lips as he watched her struggles.

She managed to move her lips in an almost silent plea.

'Please. Please.'

He relaxed the pressure slightly. Immediately she gulped air, making her start to cough and gag. Blood vessels in her neck and throat seemed to be pulsing much more strongly than usual. She was convinced she could feel the much-needed oxygenated blood once more bringing urgent relief to her brain.

'I love it when you beg for it.'

His tone was conversational. Nothing more. It could have been a simple greeting.

Her focus was coming back. She could see that he was naked. It scared her as much as anything to think that he could have been in the room for some time without her even being aware of his presence.

It must have been the pills. She usually slept so badly, living in ever-present fear. The constant fatigue was stopping her from functioning at any useful level. She'd been to the chemist's. Bought herself the strongest over-the-counter remedy they could sell her. She'd gone somewhere she wasn't known. Spun them a tale about noisy neighbours with a fondness for parties and music at high volume. She could tell that the person serving her didn't believe a word of it. Could see, too, that they weren't all that interested. Clearly she wasn't going to do herself any serious harm even if she swallowed the whole packet at once. She would have been tempted to try that. But there was her son to think of. She could never do anything which would hurt him. Never.

She'd remembered not to take her mobile phone with her when she went out to buy the pills. She didn't want to have one. She had nobody to call, except him, and she would never have voluntarily phoned him. She suspected there was some way he knew of which would tell him where the phone was, wherever she took it. So he would know where she was at all times. She didn't understand enough about such things to tell if that was even possible. But he did. If there was such a way to do it, he would know. He loved to tell the boy about anything technical like that which he knew about. Showing off his superior knowledge. The boy always listened in rapt fascination. Eager to know all about it, his thirst for knowledge overcoming the ever-present fear brought on by the man's company.

To be on the safe side, on the rare occasions she dared to go anywhere she didn't want him to know about, she always left the phone behind in the house. If he ever found that out, she could always say she'd simply forgotten to pick it up and take it with her. He was always saying how stupid she was. He would easily believe that she had forgotten.

The instructions on the packet of pills had said to take one to two tablets, half an hour before going to bed. She had been so desperate for sleep that she'd taken three. Clearly a serious mistake. At the very least, she could have been sitting up in bed when she'd heard him come in. Anything to stop the desperate feeling of being helpless on her back with his strength and weight pinning her there. At his mercy.

Her eyes went automatically to the door. Her ears straining for any sound that the boy was awake and risked coming in to find her.

The man saw her action and sneered.

'I've locked the door. Of course. A man wants some privacy when he comes home to his loving wife. After a totally shit shift. With everyone acting like fucking muppets and not enough work getting done. Especially when he finds her gagging for it. Begging him for it. That's the cherry on the cake. So go on, then. Beg me again. You may get lucky.'

The latent menace behind his words scared her so much her mouth went instantly dry. She couldn't form any words.

'I can't hear you, bitch. Beg me again.'

Her lips were desperately trying to make the shape of the words, even if no sound came out. One of his powerful hands shot out and gripped her throat once more. She tried not to choke. Willed her mouth to form the words he wanted her to say. Even if they weren't audible.

'Please. Please.'

Chapter Eleven

Mike outlined what he'd learned at the post-mortem when the full team got together at the end of the day. Ted had already told Jo he intended to get away at a decent time, as soon as he was up to date. He hadn't told him the reason.

'Lots of caution and caveats, but basically Dr Sinclair was able to tell me that our victim died from a broken neck, and that death would have been pretty much instantaneous.

'He noted a lot of old injuries on the body, too. Bruising, cuts of various ages, some burns which, again with lots of reserve, he said could all indicate possible domestic abuse. Or, as he was at pains to point out, she could simply have been clumsy or unlucky.

'No track-marks or any other outward signs of any substance use or abuse, but we'll need to wait for the results of the various blood and other tests for a more detailed picture. So in short, as it stands, we're not really much further forward, other than it appearing obvious that it was the fall down the stairs which caused her death rather than anything which may have happened to her before that.'

'Where are we up to with witness statements?'

'I'm collating those, boss,' Jo told him. 'So far we've found no one with a good word to say about our prime suspect. If he has any friends, we've not yet encountered them.'

'The management all speak well of him at work, though,' Maurice put in. 'Good at his job, runs a very tight ship and has exacting standards. Just what they need.'

'Which is why I couldn't find anyone who worked with or under him with anything positive to say about him,' DC Nick Cross reported. He'd been with Maurice to the engineering plant where their suspect worked. 'I'm not sure I could repeat some of the more colourful language in what I was told, although you could all have a pretty good guess. The general picture was a hard man who was there to do his job rather than win friends.'

'A bully, would you say, from what you were told?' Ted queried.

'Definitely. That and a thoroughly nasty individual. I was careful not to lead any witnesses, and only the top management appear to have been informed of the reason for his absence. It's a smallish place so inevitably it's got round that his wife has died and quite a few of the blokes I spoke to asked me straight out if he'd had anything to do with it. He didn't talk to any of them much, except to kick backsides if production rates started to slide. But I got the impression of quite a piece of work with a bit of a dark side to him.'

'But no report of any physical violence in the workplace? And he has no record of any?'

'No record for anything,' DC Cross told him. 'No one said anything outright, but there were a few hints. I got the impression that if he ever did thump someone they would have known better than to say anything about it to anyone, if they wanted to keep their job.'

'What about family? Jo, have we traced any relatives of either the victim or the suspect?'

'Not for him, yet, no. Our victim has a sister somewhere, apparently, but not locally. We're still trying to trace her. It doesn't seem as if they were in close contact at all. From what the neighbours have been saying, our victim lived a solitary life, apart from the boy. No visitors, and she didn't seem to go out much at all.'

'Where are we up to with the boy? Maurice, Jezza, how did

your meeting go?'

'Maurice and I appear to have passed Stage One with flying colours, boss,' Jezza told him. 'There'll need to be a full interview strategy meeting next, to make sure the boy is safeguarded as a witness, and we'll be at that, tomorrow. They want us to give them a day or two before we start talking to him. They need to find someone he trusts who can also attend to make sure he feels safe and comfortable at all times. At the moment, he's finding it a bit hard to form a relationship with anyone, but they do understand we're a bit on the clock and we need to crack on as soon as we can.'

'And the Black Mould Scam? Rob?'

'Coming along nicely, boss,' Rob O'Connell told him. 'Mrs Hamer is sharp. She picked out two people who are already known to us and have form. Very little hesitation. The other two victims on our patch were a bit more hesitant, but they both went for the same ones after studying them all for a bit. One of the victims of Claire's cases ID'd one of them straight away, but dithered a bit over the second. We've been round to both suspect addresses we have so far but found no one at home yet. We'll try again tomorrow and keep on trying.'

'I'm sorting warrants to search both premises for possible stolen goods, boss,' Jo put in. 'Steve's been looking at similar cases further afield in case there might be a connection. Steve?'

The movement was slight but Ted noticed it. Once again Steve had appeared to be miles away until he heard the DI address him.

'Sir, yes, I've compiled a list of anything with the same MO, and cross-referenced any descriptions against the ones we currently have. Some of the descriptions are a bit vague. The older victims admit to having poor eyesight, which makes them easy targets as they might not spot things like dodgy ID.'

He stopped and looked round anxiously.

'I don't mean that in an ageist way, or anything.'

'It's fine, Steve. Factual. That's what makes these such

cynical crimes. Soft targets. That's why it would be nice to get it nipped in the bud, and soon.'

Trev saw Ted glance towards the door of the gym yet again and spoke quietly to him so no one else could hear him.

'If he said he's coming, he'll be here, Ted. Let's get started.'

The two of them were doing a series of stretching exercises, with the children who came to learn self-defence from them once a week.

Ted was visibly on edge. Much to his surprise, the ACC had phoned him, having read the report he'd put in about domestic violence, and asked if he could come along to the club to hear more about one of the ideas Ted had proposed. He'd apologised for the short notice but said he needed to be in the area earlier on in the day, so he could easily call in.

Ted always felt out of his comfort zone when different aspects of his life overlapped for any reason. He tried never to take work back to the house. And he was never comfortable about allowing work colleagues into any part of his private life. But this was important. Too much so to let his personal feelings get in the way.

The session was getting into full swing when the door opened and the ACC crept in, mouthing a 'Sorry' in Ted's direction. He spotted the protocol, the line of outdoor shoes neatly lined up by the entrance, so slipped out of his own, then went to sit on the low bench against the wall of the gym, where one or two parents were watching their children.

He'd obviously come straight from a work engagement as he was still in uniform. His appearance caught the attention of some of the youngsters, especially young Flip, who idolised Ted so much he was determined to join the police himself. Ted called a brief halt to explain.

'As you can see, we have a visitor, and he's a police officer. He's one of my bosses, in fact. He's come along this evening because I've told him about the code word system Trev and I have taught you. Arranging a word or phrase that you tell us and only us, which means that if ever you say it here, we know straight away that you need help with something you can't talk about with others around.

'But first, let's go over the basics. If you're frightened or you think you're in danger, what can you do?'

One or two hands shot up, but most of the children spoke up without hesitation, calling out, 'Phone Childline!'

'Good. Excellent. Now, if you can't do that for any reason, who should you talk to?'

'A teacher!'

'A policeman!'

Several voices at once were anxious to supply the right answer. Flip took it a stage further.

'A police officer,' he corrected, 'cos it could be a woman. An' if they've not got uniform on, like him over there has, you ask to see some ID to make sure it really is a police officer.'

'That's exactly right. Always make sure you know exactly who you're talking to. And remember, some people might tell you they're something like a police officer and it may not be true. So always check. And if you're in any doubt ...'

'Run away!'

The chorus of voices this time was unanimous.

'So now, Flip, without using your own code, can you give us an example of the sort of thing someone might use to signal to someone who knows the code that they're in trouble or danger of some sort and that they need to talk, urgently and in private?'

Flip beamed his pride at being singled out. Without hesitating, he said, 'Me dog's having puppies.'

'And Trev and I would know that isn't true because we know you don't have a dog. Good one. Now, who can tell me what you must never do with your code?'

Another chorus of young voices joined in at that point.

'Cry wolf!'

Trev replied to them this time.

'Exactly so. Never use your code if you don't really need to. You keep your special word or phrase for genuine emergencies only and you never, ever misuse it, even if you think it would be funny. Well done, all of you.

'Right, let's get you all moving again now so you don't stiffen up. Pair off and we'll go over that last move we showed you once again. Someone you don't know grabs you from behind unexpectedly, so let's see how you react.'

Ted was surprised to see that the ACC stayed to watch the session to the end. He'd fully expected him to slip away quietly once he'd seen the relevant part, but he seemed to be happily enthralled, watching the youngsters go through their training session. His presence made Ted hesitate about finishing up with his usual demonstration with Trev, but there was no way the youngsters were going to let him off the hook, no matter who was watching. They wanted it as fast and furious as it usually was and he didn't like to disappoint them.

Once they'd finished with the usual formal bows, Ted grabbed his towel to wipe his face then slung it round his neck as he walked across to talk to the ACC.

'That was very impressive, Ted. You have those youngsters eating out of your hand. And your code word scheme seems like an excellent idea. When we can both find a bit of time, let's get together and talk more about how we could roll the idea out to schools and youth organisations, as you suggested, for those who don't already have such a safeguard in place.

'Oh, and having seen your demonstration with your Trev at the end, I'd better think very carefully in future before I decide to jerk your chain for anything.'

* * *

110

She sat next to her son at the dining table as he did his homework. She resisted the temptation to reach out a hand to brush his fringe out of his eyes. It would only irritate him and break his concentration. He was trying so hard to get everything right. He'd found his dictionary and kept checking carefully the spelling of every unfamiliar word. Making sure his writing was neat and easy to read, and stayed on the line.

Occasionally he would pause to look at his mother, sometimes with a small smile. It made her heart melt.

She had the time to sit and enjoy being with him, for once. His father was on a day shift so he'd be home soon. The meal was under control. At least she hoped it was. The pie was in the oven, so it should be cooked through, with a nice crispy crust, by the time they were ready to sit down and eat. The potatoes were simmering on a low light. There were just the vegetables to put on as soon as he got home.

For once she'd decided to try having them all sitting down to a meal at the same time. He might like that. Like a proper family. She'd laid the table for them all in the kitchen so the boy didn't need to put all his books away while they ate, in case he hadn't quite finished his homework to the correct standard.

She hadn't bothered to try to help him with it. She only ever made things worse. The same way she did with everything she touched. She always tried her best, but her best was never good enough, she knew that. The boy had inherited his slight build and timid ways from her, but his brains were far better than hers, even at such a young age. She would never dare to say it but he was already showing signs of an intellect far above that of his father.

He was bright enough. Good at his job. He'd done well to get where he was. But it was clear his son was going to far outstrip him, as he got older. He was not yet at secondary school and she was already dreaming of university for him. Of going to watch him at his graduation. Would he have to wear one of those black gowns? She wasn't at all sure. No one from her family had ever been to university. But she knew her wonderful boy could get there.

She jumped to her feet as she heard the key in the front door. She'd been so lost in her thoughts and dreams that she hadn't heard him put the car away in the garage. Perhaps he was planning to go out again later so had left it outside.

She hurried into the kitchen to put the vegetables on. The timing might be all wrong now. What if the pie was starting to burn before they were cooked? She was so stupid. Of course the boy hadn't inherited any brains from her. She clearly had none if she couldn't even cook an evening meal properly.

'The food won't be long, love,' she told him as soon as he came through the door. She tried not to sound defensive, aware that she was, as usual, making excuses before they were even called for. Attempting to deflect blame before it landed. 'I was just giving the lad time to finish off his homework properly.'

He went through the motions of planting a kiss on her cheek, calling out as he did so, 'I'll be through in a minute, lad, to check up on your work. Make sure it's properly up to standard.'

'I haven't looked at it yet,' she told him. 'He's been getting on with it so nicely. I know I'm not up to helping him, especially now he's getting older. So I left it for you to look.'

He snorted at that.

'He's as skinny as you are but he certainly gets his brains from me.'

She spoke again. Hesitantly. So far he was calm,

though as contemptuous of her as ever. She hardly dared voice her dream in case it provoked an explosion.

'Will he get to university, do you think? I keep thinking how wonderful it would be if he did and if we got to go to see him graduate.'

'You think he'd want you there?' he sneered. 'Look at yourself. You'd be an embarrassment to him.' He mocked her voice as he said, '*I've helped him with his homework*. Yes, and we all know what happens to the standard of his work when you do. Of course he wouldn't want you there. He's got his brains from me so if he gets to Uni and if he graduates, it's me he'll want there on his big day. Not you.'

She bent her head over the pan so he couldn't see the tears spring to her eyes at his wounding words.

There was a sudden noise as the boy erupted into the kitchen and flew at his father, small fists trying to pummel at him as he screamed, 'Stop it! Stop staying things like that to my mum. I will always want her there, if ever I do well at anything. She's my mum and I love her.'

The man sighed. He simply used his strong arms to hold the boy away from him as he told him patiently, 'You're just a little lad at the moment so of course you love your mum. That's natural. But as you get a bit older, you'll start to see what an embarrassment it would be to have your new friends at Uni see what a stupid mother you have.

'That's always assuming she doesn't manage to do something really dangerous and kill one or other of you. Because believe me, lad, she's more than capable of do-ing that.

'Now I'm off to the pub. Whatever she's cooked will be shit, as usual, and it would stick in my throat.'

He looked directly at the boy as he let go of him, his expression not unkind.

'Believe me, boy, one of these days you'll wish you'd listened to me. Wish you'd seen what your precious mother really is and what she's capable of. I only hope it won't be too late, when that happens, to save yourself.'

Chapter Twelve

'That went really well, didn't it? The kids were fantastic,' Trev said, as they got into the car to drive home. 'I thought Flip was going to wet himself with excitement when he saw the ACC in uniform turning up. It was kind of you to give him the chance to shine.'

'Well, if he's serious in his plans to join the Force, there's no harm in bringing him to the attention of a senior officer. Although Russell Evans will probably have retired long before Flip is old enough to join.'

'Will he make it into the force, do you think? You're always saying they're looking for degrees or the equivalent these days. Is Flip up to that?'

'I honestly don't know. It's not all graduates, though. There are other routes to join. And if sheer determination is anything to go by, Flip will make it. I hope he does. I'll certainly give him a reference any time he needs one.'

'You have remembered it's the weekend after this one that I'm going down to London for this "how to be a better prosecution witness" thing, and to meet up with Eirian, haven't you? So what are the chances of you taking one full day off this weekend, so we can spend some uninterrupted quality time together?'

Trev laid a suggestive hand on Ted's leg as he posed the question, and cautioned him, 'Think very carefully before you answer, Ted, for fear of incriminating yourself.'

'Has your sister got permission for the weekend, or is she

going to be nicking off, yet again?'

Trev threw his head back and laughed.

'Yes, Mr Policeman, it's all above board. An official exeat, and I've phoned the school myself to check.'

The traffic lights were on red so Ted turned to look at him for a moment before they changed and he needed to drive on.

'And are you still all right with this? Seeing old faces, dredging up memories? I'm sorry I can't come with you, but phone me whenever you need to.'

'It will be very strange staying in the London flat again. Goodness knows how long it is since I was last there. I have very mixed memories of that place. But, yes, it'll be fine, I'm sure. Eirian will cheer me up, if needed.

'So what about a day this weekend? Blow away a few cobwebs. Anywhere you fancy. Kinder, if you like.'

Ted put the car in gear as the lights changed, then pulled away smoothly.

'Sunday,' he said confidently. 'I'll book it as a definite day off. Do not disturb, and all that.'

Trev's chuckle was slightly rueful.

'That's enough to put the kiss of death on our plans. But I'll hold you to it. Sunday it is. No excuses.'

Most of the team members were out as Mike started the day by feeding back what he had so far from the post-mortem. Maurice and Jezza had gone to their pre-interview meeting about the boy, their potential witness. Rob and Claire were out in search of their scammers, taking Steve and Virgil with them, so they could hit both properties at the same time. They hoped to get lucky with at least one of them that way. Graham Winters had been sent up to Ashton to replace Alan Burgess. He'd be a useful addition, quietly keeping things on track. Nick Cross and Andy Green were both still on statement taking from the flats where the Stockport victim had died. For once they were finding no shortage of people with plenty to say on the subject of what they had heard going on in the flat. Steve Ellis was at his desk, collating anything involving both cases. Ted noticed he at least appeared to be more focused on his work.

Mike was interrupted by his mobile phone ringing. He checked the screen, then said, 'It's the pathologist, so we might hopefully have an update.'

He headed to the office he shared with Jo to hear what Dr Sinclair had to say to him.

'DS Hallam? Mike, is it, did I see from your photo ID? Robert Sinclair here, the pathologist. I promised to keep you up to date with anything I discovered after you left. I hasten to point out that this is not very scientific, not at all, but it may possibly be of some help.'

'Thank you, doctor. Anything you can give me would be useful, especially as I'm due to interview our suspect in a little over an hour's time.'

'Please call me Robert. I feel I should thank you because you've managed to unleash a fanciful side within me which I had no idea existed. I didn't want to say anything while you were there so as not to raise false hopes, and I noticed that you studiously avoided looking too closely at the victim.'

Mike gave a guilty laugh at that.

'I'm not known for having a strong stomach, I have to confess.'

'I did notice some bruising to the victim's throat. Faint, but perceptible. Under magnification, it showed up more distinctly as a human handprint, in effect. The thumb mark was to the right side of the throat, the fingers to the other side. I've taken extensive measurements, should the need arise to attempt to identify the owner of the hand in question.

'The first thing you will no doubt have picked up on is that the indications are that, as the print was made from the front, confirmed by where the palm print is, this was done by a right hand, which may be helpful to you.

'Now, this is where it starts to get right outside what I usually do. My only excuse is as I said, I suddenly started seeing it from a crime fiction perspective, and wondered what I could come up with were I to be writing it as such.

'Strangely, the current Mrs Sinclair couldn't be persuaded to allow me to grip her round the throat in simulation. Luckily, I have a teenage son who, as he is already convinced his Aged Parent is beyond redemption, didn't seem to think it all that bizarre a request. So we did some role play.

'Two things struck us as very odd, in our re-enactment. They might very well jump out at you too, with your superior experience of such things.'

'Well, the first thing which strikes me is that if I was trying to stop someone intent on jumping to their death, I think I'd be more likely to grab an arm or a leg, or both, rather than a throat hold. That doesn't sit right, somehow.'

'Exactly so!' The pathologist sounded pleased with his deduction. 'Not really a natural reaction at all. I hasten to add that I wasn't really trying to throw my son and heir over the bannisters. His mother was not at all keen on that either, strangely. But we did simulate it, as far as we could, he being a reasonably similar height to our victim, though heavier. And no matter how many different ways we tried it, my natural instinct was always to take hold of him by the upper arms. I did check, too. If I was in a position to grab him by the throat, I was most definitely in a position to take hold of his arms.'

'And the second thing?' Mike asked him.

'Well, on this one, you have the advantage over me of having visited the scene, so you will be the best judge of this. It occurred to me that, this being in a communal block of flats, the stair rail would have to be at a reasonable height. Otherwise there would be the risk of people routinely falling over it, especially if they were coming home slightly the worse for wear.

'So taking the height of the average domestic bannister, it's not a terribly easy manoeuvre to hitch oneself up onto it backwards, as it were. And it doesn't seem to me to be entirely logical. Although I appreciate that people desperate enough to want to kill themselves are not always thinking rationally. But, and you'd have to test this theory out with our famous dummy, without a gaping void of a big, wide stairwell, I would say there was a possibility that by going over backwards, like a diver from a boat, the person might do a sort of somersault in the air and land on their feet. That would probably result in some nasty lower limb fractures, but would it be guaranteed to kill?

'I know none of this is exactly scientific, but I thought it might at least give you some ideas when you speak to your suspect.'

Mike was making movements with his right hand in the air as the doctor was speaking, trying to picture the scene. In particular, he was looking for ways to pre-empt anything the suspect might come up with as an excuse for the marks.

'At a pinch, you might grab someone by the scruff of the neck as they were trying to jump, with their back to you, as well as an arm or something. But then, if our suspect is right-handed, which I need to check, the thumb mark is on the wrong side of the neck, surely?'

'Exactly so! I've carefully noted all the details of each and every mark on the body and they don't appear to me to be consistent with grabbing hold of someone to pull them back from the brink. Quite the reverse, in fact.'

'It's all incredibly helpful, Robert. Thanks very much. He's coming in with his solicitor this morning, so I doubt I'll get more than a succession of "no comments" from him. But it at least gives me some idea of what questions to pose.'

'I'm sending all of this over right now in writing as I know you'll need to make disclosure of my initial findings. There were rather a lot of injuries of various ages on the poor lady's body. I've highlighted the more recent ones in my report. And don't worry, none of my wild theories appear in it. Those are between us two, and for you to do with as you wish.

'Would you mind keeping me posted on this case, Mike? It's becoming really intriguing to me and I'd love to know the outcome.'

'Before I forget, Jo, I've promised to take Trev out somewhere on Sunday, so I'll need you to cover for me. He's away the following weekend, so I can return the favour then.'

'Ted, at the risk of repeating myself, it's what I'm here for. You must have done your fair share of covering for senior officers in your time.

'So tell me how things are going in your new extended kingdom. It sounds as if the clowns at Ashton have been taking advantage of Judy Collier's absence to play silly beggars.'

'They certainly got a surprise when I turned up unannounced and told them their fortune. Do you know Judy, then?'

'Not well, but I've heard she's a cracking good DI. There's no way she'd stand for any sloppy work on her team. But I hear too that she was pretty badly injured in that car accident, so she's likely to be in traction for quite a while.'

'The Trafford lot are sound as a pound. Sarah Jenkins is very impressive. Her DI shouldn't be concerned at all at having to be off sick.'

Mike came back in to join them at that point, to give them the rough outline of what the pathologist had told him. He'd printed out the written report in duplicate so he could give a copy to the suspect's solicitor at the start of the interview. A quick glance had reassured him it was a much edited version of what Sinclair had said to him over the phone.

'It's still going to be difficult for him to explain why he chose to grab her by the throat in an effort to prevent her attempting suicide. Certainly not hard enough to have left marks.'

'We'll need to get the victim's clothing thoroughly examined too,' Ted reminded him. 'If he had been grabbing hold of her to stop her from jumping, we might expect to see some tearing, perhaps.'

'Mike, you'll need to check if he's right or left handed, of course,' Jo put in. 'But I for one am struggling to see how it would be a reflex action to grab her throat to stop her from going over. If she was trying to go over backwards, which of itself sounds a bit strange, wouldn't you naturally tend to grab her by the legs? Or an arm and a leg, at least.'

'You're going to have to handle this very delicately, Mike' Ted told him. 'Is there time before the suspect gets in for you and me to go through the report quickly together and see how to handle it? Clearly we need to make disclosure, but if we're not very careful, we might inadvertently overplay our hand and give the defence a get out of jail card, if we finally have enough to charge him with.

'Who's his solicitor?'

'I'm not sure yet. He's only seen the duty solicitor so far, not got one of his own. And I'd really welcome it, boss. If you had any time to watch how the interview progresses and give me the odd steer, I certainly wouldn't object to that either.'

* * *

'We'll need to be thinking about the right secondary school for him very soon. He's growing up so fast. Should we start going to have a look at some?'

She asked the question as carefully as she could. Not looking at him as he stood leaning against the kitchen units, muscular arms folded across his big chest.

He was calm, for now. He must have had a decent shift where things hadn't gone too badly.

Nevertheless, it was clearly the wrong thing to say. She should have been more careful. Thought harder about how to phrase her question.

He gave a snort of contempt as he said, 'You're not going near any school we might think of sending him to.

You'd ruin his chances. They'd be worried he might turn out to be a half-wit like his precious mother.'

She put her head down so he couldn't see the tears which sprang so readily to her eyes at his words. She stayed quiet for a moment. But this was important. It was her son's future and she wanted it to be right for him.

'I would like to see the schools, though. I wouldn't show you up, I promise. I wouldn't say anything. I'd just like to be there.'

His voice was louder this time as he scoffed, 'For god's sake, woman, if you sit there in total silence they'll think you're even more of an idiot than you are.'

There was a noise from the living room and the boy appeared through the connecting doorway. His face was dark with anger and his voice was loud as he said, 'Stop bullying my mum! It's not up to you. She's got the right to have her say, too.'

The woman stopped what she was doing and moved instinctively to stand between her son and his father. She could feel the tension building in both of them.

The father's voice was equally loud when he replied. Angry.

'Don't you speak to me like that, my boy,' he bellowed. 'Not unless you want to feel the back of my hand. I'm your father. It's me who says what happens in this family.'

She could feel her son trembling with pent-up anger, as well as fear at the consequences of his behaviour. She reached behind herself to catch hold of him and keep him there. Sheltered from harm, with herself as a human shield.

The boy was still shouting at the top of his voice.

'Leave my mum alone, you big fat bully. I hate you! I hate you!'

The man's voice was an enraged roar now.

'You'll apologise right now, boy, if you know what's good for you. I know what's best for you with the career you want. What does she know, eh? She can't even cook a meal without ruining it. Can't even look after herself properly, the clumsy bitch, never mind deciding what's best for you.'

He was leaning past the woman, trying to grab a fistful of the boy to drag him out from behind her. The boy in his turn was screaming every swear word he knew, while trying to bite the large hand which was groping for him.

The woman would remain passive in the face of an attack on herself. Her instinct made her stand up and fight back to protect her son. The minute she brought her hands up to claw at him, the man lifted a hand to fetch her a backhanded slap across the face which sent her sprawling onto the floor, her head banging against a cupboard door, blood starting to spurt from her nose and cut lip.

The boy was beside himself now. He launched himself at his father in a ferocious but pointless fury. Rather than enrage him, his attack seemed to make the man calm down. He simply took hold of the front of the boy's shirt and held him effortlessly at arm's length. His voice was lower, more in control.

'Well, you've got some bottle, I'll give you that. I wouldn't have thought you had it in you. But you need to learn to choose your battles carefully. You'll never be big enough or man enough to take me on. Never. There's too much of your mother in you. And that,' he gave a contemptuous nod to the woman on the floor, still seeing stars too much to think of trying to get up, 'that's just not worth fighting for.

'I'm going back out now, to the pub, where I can at least get something decent to eat for a change. When I get back, I want to see your homework done to the best standard you've ever produced. And I want an apology from you, for your behaviour. If not, you're going to find out how much trouble you're in.'

With that, he turned on his heel and stalked out, pulling the front door to behind him with much more force than he usually did.

The boy grabbed a clean towel, ran it under the cold tap, and crouched down next to his mother, dabbing as gently as he could at the source of the bleeding, wincing with her as he saw the pain it caused her.

'It's all right, mum, it's all right. I'm here. I'll look after you. I'll always look after you. Don't cry. Please don't cry. As soon as I'm big enough, I'll get a job and we can move away from him. I'll keep you safe. Come on, mum. Let's sing our song. That always makes things better. You said so.'

The tears which spilled down her cheeks were of love, of pain and of a terrible sense of shame that he was the one trying his best to take care of her.

Simply opening her mouth made her split lip scream with pain, but she forced the best smile she could manage as she started to sing.

'When you wish upon a star ...'

Chapter Thirteen

Mike Hallam started the recording by identifying those present as he sat down opposite the suspect and his solicitor. He slid a copy of the pathologist's initial report across the table.

'I've just this minute had the preliminary report from the post-mortem, so you'll no doubt want an early break to discuss the details with your client,' he told the solicitor. 'For now, if neither of you has any objection, I can give you the basic outline.'

The solicitor inclined a cautious head in agreement but added a caveat, 'Be prepared for me to stop you if I feel I need time alone with my client before we proceed any further.'

'Of course, thank you, Ms Castle.'

He looked straight at the suspect as he started his questioning.

'These are merely the initial findings, of course, so there will be more to come, by way of blood analysis, for instance.'

'She were on pills, the wife. For her nerves. Mood swings, and the like. If you find owt like that.'

'The wife?' Mike queried. 'I think you told the first officers attending that you weren't married.'

'Not official. But we lived together for years. I thought of her as the wife.'

'And what about the boy? Are you his biological father?'

'I'm the only dad he's ever known. But no, I didn't father him, I've just been like a father to him for ages. And a good 'un, too. When can I see him? He must be going frantic without either his mam or his dad.'

'He's being well looked after, I can assure you. And you must understand that we need to establish who has legal custody of him. As his home is currently a crime scene ...'

'Scene of a suspected crime, officer,' Ms Castle corrected him at once.

'Excuse me, a potential scene of crime. But that means the boy can't go back there for the moment, any more than you can. So would you have anywhere safe for him to stay if you had custody?'

'I'd sort summat. I'm dossing with a friend for now, so he couldn't come there, but I would find somewhere. The lad needs to be with his dad. Especially now.'

'There are no grandparents, as I understand it?'

He shook his head.

'The wife lost hers years ago. Mine are both in homes now. Dementia. Both of them. It's a bastard of a thing. Especially as they weren't old when they started with it.'

'Sorry to hear that. As you probably realise, as you're not a direct relative, and there's no one else we can trace, the custody issue will need to be decided by Social Services.

'But now that I have the initial post-mortem results, I'd like to ask you a few more questions. No doubt your solicitor has advised you that you're not obliged to answer them, but obviously it would help us if you would.'

He saw the solicitor open her mouth to speak and cut in smoothly, 'So to make sure you understand your rights, I will caution you again, for the recording, as I did when we spoke initially.

'You do not have to say anything, but it may harm your defence if you do not mention, when questioned, something which you later rely on in court. Anything you do say may be given in evidence.

'Now, would you mind telling me once more exactly what happened on the night your partner died. In your own words. I know we've spoken about it before, but it's possible that in the intervening time you may have thought of additional details.'

'The wife had serious issues. We argued a lot, I'm not denying that. I was worried about her with the lad sometimes. That she might do something stupid with him around.'

'But not worried enough to contact Children's Services, for example?'

Again the man shook his head, more emphatically, this time, at that question.

'I never thought she'd harm him. Not deliberately. She worshipped him. And he doted on her. But she was very accident prone. Always managing to hurt herself somehow or another. We had rows about it. They got a bit heated sometimes when she got hysterical, so now and then I had to try to shout over her to make her listen to reason.'

'Can you tell me exactly how she fell?'

'Jumped,' the solicitor put in. 'I understand my client has already told you that his partner ran out of the flat then jumped over the handrail, despite his best efforts to stop her. Are you now saying this incident is more than the tragic suicide which it appears to be? And if so, do you intend to charge my client with something?'

'We're a long way from any conclusions yet. The PM report I've handed you shows that the deceased died from a broken neck, which appears to have occurred as the result of the fall. I'm simply trying to establish all the details I can about how she came to fall.'

The solicitor indicated to her client to go ahead.

'We'd had another big row. I was trying to tell her she might need to go into hospital or somewhere. Just for a bit, like. Until she got herself back on an even keel. But she took it that I were trying to split her and the boy up. To take him off her. But I would never do that. I only wanted her to get some proper care. So she'd be able to look after herself, and the lad, better than she was managing to do. That's all I wanted.

'She went hysterical. Screaming that she couldn't take it any more. I tried to stop her but she ran past me, out the front door and onto the landing.'

'And what did you understand her to mean by that? She couldn't take what any more, do you think?'

'Being like she was, I thought she meant. It were bloody hard for me to live with, when she got like that, but it must have been hell on wheels for her, I reckon.

'I thought she were just going to run off down the stairs or summat. I don't know where she would have gone, but that's what I figured. Then I saw she was making for the bannisters. She started trying to climb on them so I ran up to her and tried to grab her.'

'Can you remember which part of her you grabbed?' Mike asked him.

'No, I bloody can't,' he snapped, sounding angry for a moment. 'I was concentrating on trying to do something – anything – to stop her from hurting herself.'

'Are you right or left-handed?'

The solicitor held up her hand to her client at that point to indicate to him not to answer.

'I really must stop you at this point, officer. I'm not prepared to allow my client to answer such a question until I've had time to read the PM report, which I presume is going to shed some light on its relevance.'

Ted's quiet voice in Mike's ear told him, 'Offer her a break, to take instruction. Refreshments, the works. Full on good cop mode.'

'I was about to suggest that, Ms Castle,' Mike replied. 'I'm quite happy for you to take a break now to talk to your client. Please take as long as you like. I could also arrange some refreshments for you, if you would like that?'

'Some water would be a good idea,' she told him, without bothering to consult her client. He looked as if water was the last thing on his mind, but he said nothing as Mike left them to it.

The drinks sorted, he went to find Ted.

'What do you think to him, boss?'

'He was quick to get angry when you pressed him. That would seem to fit with what we've been told about him at work. Possibly a low flashpoint. I may have been reading too much into his expression, but I also thought he didn't look at all pleased when his solicitor asked for just water without even consulting him. It might indicate that he's not a man used to women making decisions for him. I'll certainly be interested to hear what the boy has to say about him, if we manage to get that far with him.

'I'll go and call DS Jenkins at Trafford, and DS Ramsay at Ashton, now, to see how things are going with them. Let me know when they're ready to restart. I know his solicitor, Ms Castle, of old, so I thought I might come and sit in with you, if you don't mind.'

Mike gave a chuckle. 'Be my guest, boss. It sounds as if it might be a good spectator sport.'

'Thanks for sending us Alan Burgess, Ted,' Sarah Jenkins told him, to his surprise, as they spoke.
'After a bit of basic house-training, he's turning out not too bad at all. He had his little "*Alpha male, twenty-five years on the job*" moment when he first arrived. Once he found out it impressed nobody, especially me, he shut up a bit and got down to some work.

'I put him on checking CCTV and he spotted our murder suspect walking towards the pub he claimed to have been in at that precise time, confirmed by all his mates. There's no way he could have walked from where the camera shows him, with the timeline, to the pub. Even if he had somehow got there – maybe someone stopped and gave him a lift – it would still put him there much later than he said.

'And remember our Neighbourhood Watch type next door neighbour who found the body and notified the emergency services? He's a gem of a witness. He wears a step counter, with a clock and everything. He's been advised to take plenty of walking exercise for his health conditions, and he's got into the habit of checking it all the time. When he went in and found the woman dead, he looked at the time on the kitchen clock in the house, then checked it with his step counter. He said she clearly hadn't been long dead when he found her, and that was confirmed by the paramedics who attended. So we have quite a big discrepancy in the husband's version of events, compared to the footage.

'We're going to speak to our suspect again later today, when he comes in to report, before he goes off on his night shift. I'm going to interview him myself and he's got a lot of explaining to do, in view of what we've found. I'll contact him to come with his solicitor, for further questioning.

'Meanwhile the rest of the team, including Alan now, are going out to talk to all the supposed alibis again and to remind them of the penalties for perjury, if they stick to their stories as far as trial. I reckon there'll be a domino effect if even one of them starts to change their version.'

'It sounds like you've made excellent progress. Any news about the boy? And the post-mortem?'

'I've spoken to the lad myself, very briefly, with the agreement of Children's Services, who had someone present, as well as his nan. Quiet little lad. Not much to say for himself. But he did say his dad got angry and shouted a lot and it made his mum cry. I'm going to sort out a strategy meeting to see if he could be a witness, and whether or not it would be in his best interests to do so.'

'We're at a similar stage with our own suspected domestic violence death. There's just the young boy in ours, no other siblings. No eye witnesses to the actual death, as far as we know. But the boy was in the flat so he might be able to tell us what was going on before the incident.'

'Our PM's tomorrow morning, so I'll keep you posted with what it can tell us. I'll let you know the preliminary findings, at least. It's all a bit circumstantial at the moment. Even if he lied about the timings, for whatever reason, we might still struggle to place him at the scene at exactly the right time, or to prove intent to kill.'

Ted's next call to DS Ramsay at Ashton was equally as encouraging.

'Graham Winters has been a big help, sir, thank you. I had my eye a bit off the ball, and it showed. I think we're back on track now.'

'I'm pleased to hear it. How did the interview go with your suspect?'

'Denied everything from the start. Then we showed him the CCTV footage which puts him in an area he'd previously said he didn't know, had never been to. Then he suddenly remembered he might possibly have been somewhere in that area but definitely not for the purposes of robbing or assaulting anyone. And he, of course, had no explanation at all as to why some of the property our victim reported as stolen could possibly have ended up in his flat, where it was recovered when it was searched.'

'What's your next move?' Ted asked him.

'I want to see if our victim can pick him out from photos first, then if he does, we'll take it from there.'

'Good. Keep me informed, please. It looks as if you might get a good result on this one. How is DI Collier doing?'

'She phones me most days. Still in a lot of pain, but mostly climbing the walls at the inactivity. Sir,' he went on hesitantly, 'will you be mentioning to her about me and the others being in the pub? Only we really were on the alcohol-free.'

'We're not at school, DS Ramsay,' Ted told him. 'If I have a problem with you or any of your team, I'll deal with it. I wouldn't dream of bothering your DI, especially while she's off sick. Just make sure you build a good solid case against your suspect so you can give her some good news. That should cheer her up a bit.'

* * *

'You've managed to get through an entire day without hurting yourself, then? Wonders will never cease.'

Compared to some of the greetings she was used to from him, it wasn't too bad. Hopefully he'd had a reasonably good day at work. He made a token show of pecking her on the cheek. A gesture devoid of any warmth, with more of a sense of duty than anything. If he even noticed the efforts she had made with her hair, or the delicate touch of perfume about her, he made no comment.

She was trying to gauge his mood. There was something she wanted to talk to him about. She'd been trying to pluck up the courage all day. For several days, in fact. She was afraid of his reaction, as always, but it was important. Everything to do with her son's future was important to her. If she could only manage to start the conversation without provoking him.

She'd been practising what to say, over and over. She'd even stood in front of the bathroom mirror to try it out loud. She'd been horrified by the mousey, anxious face looking back at her from the glass. No wonder he found her so unattractive.

And then there was her voice. He was always telling her how whiny she sounded and he was right. She was ashamed when she listened to herself.

'Pathetic,' she told the image in front of herself. 'That's what you are. Pathetic.'

She mocked herself as she stood there, using the snivelling voice he put on when he made fun of her.

'*Please. Please. Please don't hurt me.* Listen to your-self, for goodness sake. No wonder it annoys him. Just talk in a normal voice. Ask him what it is you want from him without all the cringing. Grovelling like that is enough to make anyone angry. Especially someone with a lot of responsibility, and when he's had a hard shift. You're an utter disgrace. You'd make a saint lose his temper with you. Do it again.'

She picked up a brush and ran it through the dry, brit-tle hair which hung round her face. Hideous. That's what she was. Enough to turn anyone off. Why had she let herself get into such a state? How long had she been looking like that? It was a wonder he bothered coming home to her at all. Perhaps if she made more of an effort, things might slowly start to get back to how they had once been between them. When they'd first got together.

She straightened up. Gathered her hair up in one hand and held it up, instead of letting it hang round her face like a protective curtain to hide behind.

'I wanted to ask you something ...' she tried experi-mentally, trying to make her voice firmer.

'I would really like to go with you when ...'

No, that sounded too much like asking for permission. Perhaps if she could be a bit more assertive. Try to hide the fear which always bubbled just below the surface.

'I want to come with you when ...'

'I want to come with you when you go to the school to talk about his future,' she said now, to his face. 'They al-ready know me there, so I'm not going to spoil his chances there because he'll be leaving soon.'

She'd had a shower earlier using the gel her son had bought her for Christmas. She'd shampooed her hair and used enough conditioner so that for once it felt softer than an old pan scrub, which was its usual texture. Then she'd pulled it up at the back, securing it with a claw clip.

She'd made an effort with what she wore, too. Not exactly dressed up, but still a bit better than the usual shapeless layers of baggy trousers and dowdy cardigans she wrapped round herself in a protective layer.

As soon as he turned his head to study her, as if fully noticing her for the first time, she felt her courage start to fail.

'Well, what have we got here? Mutton dressed as lamb? What have you got yourself all tarted up for? Gagging for it, are you?'

She willed herself not to react. To stick to what she'd practised in front of the mirror. Assertive. That's what you were supposed to be, faced with a bully. And that's what he was. A bully.

'No, I just want to go with you to the school tomorrow. To the parents' evening. He's my son, too. I have rights.'

Too late, she realised she'd gone too far. That's not what she'd planned to say. Looking at the way his eyes darkened and narrowed, it was completely the wrong thing to have said. But there was no taking it back now. She'd said it.

'And I have rights too, you bitch,' he spat, half under his breath. 'Rights I'm about to exercise. Brace yourself.'

He grabbed her by the arm. Called out to the boy, 'Get on with your homework, lad, I'll be in to check up on you in a minute. Your mother and I need to talk about something for a bit. We shouldn't be too long.'

Then he dragged her to the stairs, bypassing the living room where the boy was working, hauling her up them and into their bedroom. He shut the door firmly and turned the key.

She bit her lips so hard she tasted blood but she couldn't stop the cries of pain which escaped her.

Please don't let the boy hear this.

Please.

Chapter Fourteen

Mike Hallam gave a time check as he restarted the recording, once the solicitor had finished her consultation.

'Interview resumed. For the recording, also now present is Detective Chief Inspector Darling.'

'Ms Castle,' Ted said to the solicitor, as he took his seat opposite her.

'Chief Inspector,' she acknowledged.

If she was surprised by his promotion, she was too professional to show it. It had been some time since they had last met. Back when Ted was a newly appointed Detective Sergeant, on his first murder case. He'd been a large factor in getting a conviction against her client on that occasion. Doggedly ploughing on with the interview in the face of her constant attempts to stop him.

'I hope you have now had chance to go through the report, both of you,' Mike Hallam continued. 'If so, you will have seen that the pathologist has noted that the deceased had signs of a handprint to her throat, apparently made by a right hand.

'So I'd like to repeat my earlier question,' Mike looked directly at the suspect as he said it, 'and ask again if you are right or left-handed?'

The man looked to his solicitor to check. When she gave a slight nod, he replied, 'Right-handed.'

'And could that handprint have been yours?'

Once again he looked for confirmation before he continued.

'It could have been,' he said grudgingly. 'When the wife flipped, she really totally lost it. She'd attack me sometimes. Never the lad. Like I said, she worshipped him. But she'd go for me in a big way. Vicious, like. I sometimes had to fight her off any way I could. I might have grabbed her neck, trying to stop her going out of the flat when I could see she were in no fit state to be going anywhere.'

Ted spoke again at that point. His tone was always calm, reasonable. Nothing to arouse the suspicions of whoever he was interviewing.

'The handprint suggests a hand round the throat, though. Not the neck. Applied with some degree of pressure in order to have left marks. From the front, based on the person being right-handed, which you have already indicated that you are. That would seem to be a rather extreme form of restraint.'

He was looking directly at the man as he spoke. Sizing him up. Noting in particular the thick neck, broad chest, powerful arms.

'You're quite a lot bigger than your late partner, going on the details from the post-mortem report. Stronger too, I would imagine. Would it not have been possible to restrain her simply by holding her arms, for instance? Rather than grabbing her throat, which she might have perceived as a threat to herself and struggled hard against?'

Again, Ted detected a spark of anger in the man's eyes, directed at him. Another indication that he might be someone with a low flashpoint.

'You don't know what she could be like when she went mental. She'd attack me. I had to try to hold her off any way I could so she couldn't do me no harm. Without hurting her, if I could, of course.'

'I see,' Ted told him levelly. 'So you're saying that your partner was sometimes violent towards you? And that you were acting in self defence, using minimum force?'

He looked from the man to his solicitor as he posed the

questions. She was visibly bristling as she snapped, 'You're attempting to put words into my client's mouth, Chief Inspector.'

'Not intentionally, Ms Castle, I assure you. I'm simply trying to establish whether your client is putting forward a defence to any charge we may bring against him that he was seeking to protect himself from assault by his partner.'

Ted was deliberately sticking to the term partner. He would normally have used wife, since the man had already stated a preference for it. He was looking to see what reaction pushing the man's buttons might have on his seemingly short temper.

'Wife. I've already said. She were the wife to me.'

His tone, in reply, confirmed what Ted was looking for.

'Wife. Excuse me. So you're saying your wife could show violent behaviour towards you? Was this a regular thing?'

The solicitor moved as if to intervene but Ted cut across her, polite as ever.

'Ms Castle, please excuse me, but if your client is putting this explanation forward as part of his defence, should it become necessary, you must understand that we need to explore this avenue now.

'For example, you are quite welcome, of course, to produce your own medical report, but we would also reserve the right to get our own examination carried out. To look for signs of injuries on your client. And that would need to be done soon. Preferably today.

'Time is clearly of the essence here, because if your client was attacked by his wife on the day in question, there may still be some marks on him which could help to corroborate his version of events. The longer we leave it, the more likely it is that any such marks would disappear.'

The man started to speak, blustering. Ted turned to him to reply.

'You must see how important this is, though, in terms of any future defence? If this incident was provoked by violent assault on you by your wife, then we need to get you examined by the police doctor, and to get photographs of any marks, defensive or otherwise, we might find on your body.'

There was an awkward pause as the man turned to look at his solicitor for guidance once again. Ted spotted the look and responded to it.

'Perhaps you'd like another short break with your client, Ms Castle, to take further instruction?'

Mike Hallam paused the recording once more, then followed Ted out of the room, heading for the stairs and the CID offices.

'Sorry if I was muscling in there, Mike. I wanted to see how he might react to being needled.'

'No worries, boss. That was masterful. He does seem to be on a bit of a short fuse, doesn't he?' He was following Ted who was heading for his office, in need of a brew.

'Tea? Coffee?' Ted offered, putting his kettle on.

Mike opted for tea. Ted busied himself with mugs and the makings, keeping his back turned towards the DS, while he posed his next question. He didn't want him to feel awkward.

'Are you all right with this one, Mike?'

'The battered husband defence, you mean?'

Ted was one of the few people who knew that Mike had been through abuse at the hands of his wife while she was suffering from mental illness. All now sorted, with treatment, but he didn't want to risk him being affected by the current case.

He put the drinks on the desk and sat down opposite him.

'It's fine, thanks for asking. Joan is absolutely back to normal these days, as long as she takes her tablets. For what it's worth, speaking from personal experience, no matter how bad things got with her, I could never have laid a finger on her. Not even to defend myself.'

'And speaking as someone who teaches self-defence, I'm struggling to see how someone of his size and build couldn't quite easily hold her at arm's length without having to grab her by the throat. No matter how violent she might have become. He has the reach, and clearly the strength, to have done that.'

'It will be interesting to see if there are any defensive wounds on him at all.'

'My feeling is he won't consent to being examined, because he knows full well there aren't any. So by mentioning the "something which he later relies on in court", but refusing corroborating evidence for it, he might have effectively shot himself in the foot as regards to using that as his defence.

'When we go back, I'm going to leave you to it once more, Mike, and I'll watch from the monitors. If he won't allow himself to be examined, you're going to need to press him as to why he used that particular method to restrain her. Not to mention how she managed to free herself from his grip round her throat. That's much harder to do, without training, than people realise.

'At some point can you get back to the pathologist and press him for a precise location of where pressure was applied. Again, speaking from personal experience of various martial arts techniques including choke-holds, I know that it doesn't require much pressure, nor a lot of time, to render someone unconscious that way.'

'So what's the history between you and Ms Castle?'

'She was defending on my first ever murder case, as a DS. I was working with your predecessor, Jack Gregson. Nasty case. Her client raped and murdered his young step-daughter.'

'And who won that time?'

Ted grinned at him.

'Not Ms Castle. Her client was convicted and sentenced to life, with a recommended minimum of twenty-five years.'

'After discussion, my client has decided he does not wish to be examined by a doctor,' Ms Castle began once Mike had re-entered the room and resumed the interview. 'This is not in any way to be taken as a retraction of what he has said previously.

He simply feels that, given the time lapse, there would be nothing of significance to see on his body as a result of his wife's attacks on him. He stands by his previous statement, that he took hold of his wife by the neck in order to restrain her and to try to stop her inflicting any serious injuries on him.'

'In which case, I must ask your client how, if he was holding his wife by the throat, presumably still inside the flat, she was somehow able to escape from that hold and run outside onto the landing.'

'She were scratching me and kicking at me and trying to bite me.'

'Despite being held by the throat? Firmly enough to have left marks?'

Again there was the spark of anger in the man's eyes as he snapped back, 'I were trying to protect myself, and to stop her doing herself any harm. It's what anyone would do.'

'Had she spoken about harming herself? Perhaps about taking her own life? We have, of course, requested her full medical history. Might she have spoken to her GP about wanting to end her life?'

There was no mistaking his reaction to that news. The knuckles on his right hand whitened as he clenched the fingers.

'She ... she wouldn't say much to anyone. Only to me. She didn't like going to the doctor.'

'You said she was taking medication, though? For her mood swings, I think you said. So she must have seen the doctor at some point to be given those, surely?'

He looked uncomfortable now. Mike noticed and pressed on.

'We are talking about prescription medication here, I take it? When you said she was on tablets?'

He looked to his solicitor for advice on that question. None was forthcoming. Ms Castle clearly realised that, as he had mentioned the pills in the first place, he could hardly refuse to talk about them now.

'Well, no. Like I said, she didn't like going to the doctor, so I got her summat online.'

'And can you remember what it was called?

'Not really. It seemed to be okay, though, I checked it.'

'Yet so far our search of your property hasn't revealed any such medication. Can you explain that for me?'

Ms Castle was quick in her reactions. But not quick enough. Her client blurted out the answer she didn't want him to give, before she had time to stop him contradicting what he had said earlier.

'She'd run out.'

Mike left a prolonged pause. Long enough for the man to realise what he'd just said.

'Wind it up there, Mike,' Ted was telling him through the earpiece. 'Bail him this time, pre-charge.'

'I think we'll call it a day there. I understand that you have to get to work. I must tell you now that this time you will be remanded on bail pending possible charges. Your solicitor will explain to you exactly what that means. I should also say that the terms of the warrant to search your home includes all property there, so with any luck, we'll be able to find out, from your computer, exactly what the medication was which you ordered online for your wife.'

* * *

She was curled up underneath the bedclothes. Had been there since he'd finished with her and gone back downstairs to check on the boy's homework, then gone out for the evening, to the school.

She'd used the top sheet to keep dabbing at her split lip until it had stopped bleeding. It was now throbbing steadily, shooting up to sharp stabbing pitch any time she moved her mouth at all.

She would have loved a glass of water. Cold relief for

her parched throat and sore mouth. At the moment it was more than she could contemplate to move her battered body.

She stayed where she was. Arms wrapped round her legs. Trying to hold her world together as it seemed in danger of falling apart around her.

He was much later getting back than she thought he would be. He must have gone for a drink after going to the school. It might perhaps have made him more mellow, but nothing was ever guaranteed.

Part of her was willing him to come back. Another part dreading what might happen when he did. But she wanted to know about her son. How he was doing. What his prospects were. Where he might be best to go next for his secondary schooling, to put him well on his chosen career path.

She'd heard the boy come upstairs. Pause outside her door, then give it a hesitant tap. His voice was full of concern as he asked quietly, 'Are you all right, mum?'

She pulled the covers back from her head so she didn't sound muffled when she replied. Her barely-healed lip split open again the moment she tried to speak. It gave a metallic taste of blood in her mouth.

'Sorry, darling, dad should have told you before he went out. Mum's got one of her stupid bad heads, so I just need to lie down quietly for a bit. Are you all right? Can you manage? It's time you were going off to bed now, anyway.'

'Do you want me to bring you something? Shall I make you a cup of tea?'

It took so little to move her to tears. The kindness in his worried voice did so straight away. She dabbed her eyes now with the sheet. Worked hard to swallow the lump in her throat.

'That's so kind, love, but you know how sickly these

headaches make me feel. I couldn't manage anything. But thank you, that's so nice of you. You go off to bed now, like a good boy. Your dad will be cross if he comes home and catches you up past your bedtime.'

'He's always cross about something. He's a bully, mum. Why do you stay with him? Why can't we go and live somewhere else?'

Tears again. Why did she cry so readily? Why couldn't she find the courage from somewhere to do something? Her son was right. As young as he was, he was right. She should do something. To protect him, if not herself.

Yet he always seemed to know. If she so much as thought about leaving him. He always knew.

'Go to bed now, son. Everything will be better in the morning. I'll be better. I'll make you a nice breakfast. You'll see. It will all be better. Night-night, darling. Sleep tight.'

'Night, mum. Mind the bedbugs don't bite.'

She listened to the sounds of him getting himself ready for bed. Heard him brush his teeth, without needing to be reminded. He was such a good boy.

Then he went into his room and she heard him put a CD into the player they'd bought him. She couldn't stop the tears when she heard the track he'd chosen.

'When you wish upon a star.'

She must have fallen asleep, listening to the soothing, familiar song. She woke with a start when the man came into the room, peeled off his clothes and slid under the covers next to her. It was later than she'd expected him to get home. She tried to stem the violent trembling his closeness provoked. To lie still and quiet, feigning sleep.

He gave a snort of contempt.

'Don't worry, you stupid bitch. Who was it who said

why go out for hamburger when you have steak at home? Well, I've been out for steak, after the parents' evening. Nice, juicy, tender rump steak, so I'm not interested in a bit of scrag end. You're safe enough for now. It's like fucking a frozen dead pig in an abattoir, anyway.'

The flood of relief she felt at his words was tempered by a desperate need to know how the evening had gone. What the future had in store for her son.

As if reading her thoughts, he said, 'And luckily it seems the boy has definitely inherited his brains from me and he's not doing too badly. But if he really wants to get on in the career he's chosen, he's going to have to up his game. Quite considerably. He'll be facing stiff competition.

'So every evening, it will need to be head down over his homework for as long as it takes to have it absolutely word perfect. Or he'll have me to answer to.'

Chapter Fifteen

'How's it going, Ted? What cases have you got on? For god's sake talk to me about something which doesn't have to do with bloody stately homes and which monarch might have spent the night in which four-poster bed.'

It was the voice of Ted's old boss, former Detective Superintendent Jim Baker, on the phone, and he sounded desperate. Ted couldn't resist the chance to wind up the man who was also a good friend outside work.

'You must realise, Mr Baker, that I can't possibly discuss confidential police matters with a mere civilian.'

'Piss off, Ted,' Big Jim growled. 'Look, don't get me wrong, being married to Bella and having time to spend with her is really good ...'

'You can spare me the details.'

'You're supposed to be my friend. You know, supportive.'

Ted was trying not to laugh at his tone.

'I'm trying, Jim, honestly. But seriously, you're retired. None of this concerns you any more. Not unless you get called in to consult on a case, and at the moment, we don't have anything big enough to warrant that, as far as I know.'

'At least tell me what you've got on, in case there's anything I can wangle my way into running, with a word in the right ear. Seriously, consider it a public service. I'd no idea how tiring and frustrating this retirement lark is or I'd never have considered it.'

'Look, I haven't time to chat now, but what about later, if

you can get away? It's Trev's karate night. I've already said I doubt I'll be able to join him, so he's going for a meal with his mates afterwards. That means I have an excuse for staying out late.

'I'm taking Kev for a pint when he knocks off because he's trying to blackmail me, so why not come over and join us? Kev won't stay long, I don't suppose, so if Dave will let us have the back room we could have a hotpot or something in there and I'll tell you what we're working on. I daren't do it in the bar, having had to kick the backsides of the Ashton lot because I found them in the pub having a long lunch and claiming to be talking shop when I called on them, without telling them what time I was going.'

'They weren't!' Big Jim exclaimed. 'How were they getting away with that with Judy Collier? She's a stickler for the rules.'

'You've not heard, then? She was in a bad car crash and is still in traction. So DS Ramsay is in charge in her absence.'

Jim made a scornful noise.

'So don't tell me, Burgess has his hand up the back of his jacket, working his mouth and making his own words come out of it. Right, I'll definitely be over later. Apart from anything, I want to hear what Kevin's found about you that he could blackmail you with. I never found anything in all the time we worked together, you jammy bastard.'

Ted left it to Mike to coordinate an update with the full team present at the end of the day. He perched in the background, as he often did, ready to add anything if necessary.

'The suspect has been sent on his way, not very happily, on pre-charge bail. What we need now is to look at where we're at collectively in respect of what we can possibly charge him with, to have any remote chance of getting it to stick. He's gone from denying everything and swearing blind she jumped intentionally to admitting he may have grabbed her but in self-defence because she could be violent towards him.'

Jo Rodriguez was coordinating all the evidence. He spoke up.

'The picture I'm getting of him, from what I've read so far, is of a bully in the workplace. Management by fear. But he works exclusively with men, as I understand it. So we need to know what he's like with women other than his partner. If he's been regularly knocking her about, it might indicate some deep-seated issue with women in general. Does he have any interaction with any other women, perhaps socially? What do they think of him?'

DCs Nick Cross and Andy Green had been interviewing the neighbours in the block of flats where the fatal incident had occurred. Cross spoke up for both of them.

'None of the blokes we've spoken to so far had a good word to say for him. Arrogant, overbearing, up himself, not interested in anyone else's opinion, was the general view. Not someone you'd want to tangle with. The women didn't like him either. Always polite, but patronising, one of them put it. Liked to mansplain things, put the little woman in her place, if any of them tried to have an opinion. We couldn't find anyone who chose to mix with either of them socially but they'd sometimes bump into one another in a pub, exchange a few words. That sort of thing. The little lad didn't mix with any of the other kids in the block, not that we could find out. Everyone said he was like a little mouse. He'd barely speak, except to return a greeting politely enough, if anyone passed him on the stairs on his way going to and from school.'

'But no one thought about raising concerns for his welfare anywhere?' Ted queried.

'I can probably answer that, boss,' Jezza told him. 'I spoke to his school. They also reported him as very quiet, no friends to speak of, kept to himself. But there were no real trigger warning signs. Nothing in his behaviour to signal he was experiencing abuse. He always looked well-fed, clean and well presented, no physical signs or marks to raise suspicions. He always did his homework well. A model pupil in many respects. Just a quiet one who didn't mix a lot.

'And Maurice and I have now had our first meeting with him. He is clearly traumatised by what happened and it was hard going. Even Daddy Hen couldn't immediately work his usual magic,' Jezza smiled fondly at Maurice as she spoke.

'He actually seemed to focus on me more than Maurice, but it's early days. It was a very brief visit, to test the water. He didn't ask about the man, at all. Nothing to indicate he considers him in any way a father figure. Certainly not asking if he could go back to him, which is probably revealing of itself.'

'And yet screaming rows were apparently a common feature in the home. So why did nobody report anything? Suspicions, at least?' Jo asked.

Steve spoke up, hesitant as ever with other officers he didn't know present. Although Mike was running things, with Jo inputting, it was to Ted that Steve's anxious gaze kept being drawn.

'Sir, perhaps the neighbours were simply afraid to get involved. If the man really does have a bad reputation as a violent bully, it would take a lot of courage, either to go up against him or to risk what his reaction would be if they reported him anonymously. Because he'd probably guess it was the neighbours and it might have got nasty with all of them.'

'That's a valid point, Steve,' Jo conceded. 'I always confess to not being the bravest of people. It's so sad, though, to think that a woman is dead when perhaps she could have been saved.

'How are you getting on with his computer? Is it giving up any secrets yet?'

'Oh yes, he's not got a clue about computer security at all, so it was easy. He thinks hitting delete means it's all gone for ever.' Steve's tone immediately gained confidence when he was back to talking about one of his specialist subjects. 'He's been buying drugs online, and doing his research to choose which ones to buy. He never clears his search history, either, so it's all there.

'He's gone for a veterinary drug which is banned from general sale in several countries, including here, because it's dangerous, easy to overdose on and the after effects can be very nasty. It's also proscribed everywhere for human use. It's not designed for it and is considered risky even in low doses.

'It's used to anaesthetise larger animals and farm animals, like horses and cattle, in particular. It knocks them right off their feet, literally, so it's the drug of choice in emergencies.

'One of the risks with it, with animals, is that as they're coming round they tend to get very panicky and can be violent. I believe, with horses, they deal with it by putting something over their head and eyes, like a coat, so they don't struggle quite so much. Which might, possibly, explain the victim's violent episodes, if they occurred as she was coming down off the drug.

'It's also addictive, and he would know that, from his research. So another part of the abuse was probably not to keep her topped up regularly, causing bad withdrawal symptoms.'

A long speech, for Steve, without hesitation. When he'd finished, he looked again to Ted first for any comment, a flush of colour rising up from his neck when Ted told him, 'Excellent, Steve, good work.'

'So when was he drugging her and for what reason?' Mike asked.

'I could take an educated guess at that one,' Jezza put in. 'I know some domestic violence victims stay with their abusive partner, for reasons of their own. But not all of them do. Some of them make a break for it. Some even get lucky and find a refuge which can take them. They may even manage to break free forever and go on to get their lives back on track.

'He must have been worried, every time he went out to work, that he would come back to find her gone, having taken the boy with her. Knocking her out whenever he left the house would ensure she would be in no fit state to do that.

'No wonder she went hysterical whenever she came down from the effects. That would be not only the drug itself, but you can imagine her frustration and sense of panic to realise he'd spoiled her escape plans yet again.'

'How was he getting the stuff into her, though?' Mike Hallam asked. 'Is it injected? Only Dr Sinclair didn't flag up any signs of needle marks and surely there would have been something to see. I can't imagine her sitting there calmly and letting him do it, so if she struggled, wouldn't that tend to leave bruises?'

'It is mostly injected into animals,' Steve told him, still speaking with confidence. 'He's been buying it in liquid form which can be given orally, so my guess is that he was simply slipping it in her food or drink and she wasn't noticing. Perhaps she simply thought that sleeping so deeply was her body's reaction to the tensions it was under. Trying to heal itself through sleep. Or perhaps he'd convinced her that she really was seriously mentally ill.'

Jezza nodded her agreement at that.

'That sounds plausible to me, Steve. And it must really have heightened the terror, her finding herself so often powerless to do anything and not truly knowing why.'

Claire Spicer, the civilian investigator who was principally involved in the scam and not directly working on the possible murder case, spoke up.

'I know that no one can know or judge what goes on in another household, but could she really not have been aware? Would she not have started to get suspicious? Perhaps even to the point of not eating or drinking anything when he was in the flat?'

Jezza visibly bristled in an instant at her words.

'No one outside a home or family can possibly know what goes on inside it.'

'No, sorry, I appreciate that,' Claire told her. 'It didn't come out right. I'm lucky enough for it never to have happened to me, or to anyone I know, so I'm having difficulty imagining how it would have been and how I would have reacted in the circumstances.'

'We really can't know what was going on,' Mike said. 'He might possibly have been encouraging, or even forcing her to drink. Perhaps telling her she was dehydrated and would feel much better if she drank more water, for instance.

'Steve, how long does the drug stay in the system? Will it show up post-mortem?'

For the first time Steve's confidence wavered.

'I've not got quite that far in my research yet, sarge. Not enough to give a definitive answer. It's next on my list. As soon as I have the info, I'll add it to what I have up to now and make sure it gets circulated.'

'So does this latest lead mean we're getting closer to show-ing intent to kill, boss?' Jo asked. 'I'm struggling at the mo-ment to find an innocent explanation for knocking your wife out regularly with an illegal cattle drug. I'm assuming this was a fairly regular thing?'

'Going by the amount he's been buying, then yes, defi-nitely a regular thing I would say,' Steve confirmed.

The team members were all quiet for a moment, thinking of the implications. Then Maurice muttered, 'The bastard,' ignor-ing Ted's look.

'I don't know that it advances us much on intent to kill,' Ted answered Jo's question. 'But it no doubt opens the way up to some significant charges, at least. Let's see what you've got by way of a case at the end of the day tomorrow and I'll talk to someone at CPS about what charges to throw at him. Even if they're only holding charges until we get a bit more.'

'Are you driving home, or can I ply you liberally with enough booze to get you to hand over the tapes?' Ted asked Kevin

Turner as they took a seat together in the bar of The Grapes with the first round of drinks, which Ted had paid for.

'Even if I go on a bender it still won't be enough to buy yourself out of trouble on this one. I can have fun with this for a long time yet. Anyway, it will have to be just the one for me this evening. I've promised to take Sheila out shopping when I get home so it wouldn't go down well to have me staggering up the drive stinking of booze and unfit to be driving. What about you? Time off for good behaviour tonight?'

'Trev's at karate this evening. And Big Jim's coming in to join me later for something to eat. It seems he's missing work already.'

Kevin gave an exaggerated sigh, smiling at his words.

'Bloody coppers, eh? We moan like buggery about the hours when we're working, then as soon as we stop, we want to go back to it.'

True to his word, Kevin only stayed for the one drink. He passed Big Jim coming in as he was leaving and stopped for a few words.

Ted and Jim got drinks and took them through to the small back room, as Dave had agreed, where they chatted while they waited for him to bring their food. They'd both decided on the special, the steak pie. Ted filled Jim in on the details of the various cases while they waited for the food to arrive.

'It's a bugger getting a successful murder conviction on these domestic violence cases, Ted. You know that as well as I do. Unless you have independent witnesses, it's often next to nigh on impossible to show intent.

'Sometimes the signs are there and people spot them. Any-one who would knock their wife about is a special sort of low-life, in my book, and there are often flashes of it in their atti-tude to other women. God knows, Margery gave me every pos-sible excuse to treat her badly, the way she was constantly car-rying on. Not even behind my back, sometimes, it got that bla-tant towards the end. But I swear I never once lifted a hand to her. Not once.'

'There have been cases though where something like this has come out and everyone says they would never have guessed, never suspected a thing. Do you believe that, or are some men much better at hiding that side of their nature than others?'

Jim took a thoughtful pull of his pint before he replied.

'Well, I suppose I'm living proof that you can know someone very well without really knowing anything about them. I thought I knew Mickey Wheeler inside out and that we were friends. You know that the shock of finding out about his gambling addiction, and him knowing all those years that my daughter was alive and well, damn near killed me. So I suppose it's possible.

'What do your blokes do? An engineer and a security guard? Be thankful you've not got a copper. If anyone would know how to cover their tracks over something like this, one of our own would.'

* * *

He strode into the kitchen without so much as a greeting and dropped the glossy brochures on the table.

'Those are the ones I've chosen for him, in order of preference. First choice at the top. You can look at them, but that's as close as you're getting. I'm not having you do anything at all to wreck that lad's chances. God knows, he's got an uphill battle to get where he wants to go with your weak and pathetic genes pulling him down all the time. The one thing he's got going for him is my influence and the brains I've given him. I just hope it's going to be enough.'

She paused in her preparation of the evening meal, wiped her hands on a towel and reached out a timid hand to pick up the top brochure.

'Could we perhaps all sit down together and look at them all, after we've eaten? Perhaps to see which one he likes the look of?'

She was trying to keep her voice neutral. Not to say anything which he might take as her daring to criticise him. She was simply anxious that such an important decision as her son's future schooling was not one he took alone without consulting her.

His face screwed into a sneer and he put on the whiny voice he always did when he was mimicking her and the way she spoke.

'*Which one he likes the look of?* What have looks got to do with anything, for god's sake, you half wit. He can't possibly know what's going to be the best choice for his future education, and you certainly don't. I've selected what's best for him. At least I've brought the bumf for you to look at. Think yourself lucky.'

He moved suddenly closer, with surprising speed, grabbed one of her arms so tight it made her wince and cringe.

'Don't bother serving up any of your usual pigswill for me tonight, either. I'm going back out. I only stopped by to bring you those, and to make sure the boy has his nose to the grindstone to get the grades he's going to need. I'm on a promise, so don't expect me back until late, if at all.

'And think on, you're as much use to the boy as a chocolate teapot, with where he wants to get to. Time for you to take a long, hard look at yourself and ask if you're anything more than a millstone round his neck as he starts to spread his wings and chase his dreams.'

Chapter Sixteen

'I've just this minute had the lab reports on substances found in our victim's blood,' Ted told the team as they got together at the end of the day for updates before the weekend. 'It makes very interesting reading. I've copied everyone in, but I can give you the broad outline now.

'First off, Steve, well done with the computer records. The lab were most impressed. It's not a drug they've come across before so they had to do a lot of research. Not licensed for use in Britain, as you said, not even for veterinary use. Certainly not for use on people. There were only faint traces remaining and as it wasn't something they would have routinely checked for, it could easily have been missed entirely if you'd not been through the computer and picked up on it.'

Steve put his head down, visibly flushing, but he looked pleased at the praise, despite his embarrassment.

'I've only had chance for a very brief call with CPS about this latest development, and we're going to need to put all of this new information to our suspect before we know where we can go from here. But this is clearly a significant development.'

'First thing he's going to claim, no doubt, is that his wife bought the stuff herself, using his card,' Jo put in.

'He can try that, although he is on record as saying he got it for her from the internet. He'll almost certainly want to go back on that once he hears this, by saying he found the drug for her to try, but she became dependent on it so kept ordering more, with his card.'

'We certainly haven't found any record of her having a credit card of her own,' Mike put in. 'Not wishing to make a judgement on that, but it could perhaps indicate more controlling by the partner. It's not uncommon in domestic abuse for one person to keep control of the purse strings.'

Mike was speaking from bitter experience. When his wife had been ill, he'd had no access to his own money much of the time.

'Sir, it won't be infallible, but credit card statements were found at the flat. I could try going through those and cross-checking them against his shifts at work, if we can request those. Like the DI said, no doubt he'll claim he left his credit card at home and his wife must have been using it.'

'Would anyone really leave their credit card at home these days?' Jezza asked. 'Occasionally, maybe, if you changed clothes or handbag, if you carry one, and you might forget to transfer it. But repeatedly? That doesn't sound likely. Does he have a car for work, or use public transport? If he has a car, he must need to put fuel in it sometimes, for one thing. So why would he go out without his card?'

'He does drive,' Mike replied. 'He's a car owner. The shifts he works don't always coincide with available public transport so he's an essential car user. And yes, I agree with Jezza. It would seem unusual to me for someone to go out without their credit card.'

'Maurice might, if we were all going to the pub and he didn't want to pay for a round,' Jezza couldn't resist teasing her friend.

'And given how unusual a drug this seems to be, I imagine, Steve, that our suspect must have spent quite a bit of time researching to find out about it?' Jo ignored her and carried on.

'A lot of research, yes, sir. This one wasn't the cheapest, either, not by a long way. He'd also been searching to find what the side effects and after effects of any of the heavy duty tranquillisers were. He did his homework thoroughly before starting to buy.'

'More evidence of pre-meditation there, boss?' Jo queried. 'Setting himself up with his defence in advance, with this story of her being violent and attacking him?'

'Let's not get ahead of ourselves,' Ted cautioned. 'Although I'm struggling to think of any plausible excuse he could offer for buying an illegal drug. There must be an offence there, for a start, for us to charge him with. It will do as a holding charge, if nothing else, while we investigate further.

'Right, enjoy your weekend, everyone, those who have some time off. Jo, can we have a quick get together? Mike and Rob too, please, about cover?'

The four of them adjourned to the office which Jo and Mike shared. There was more room there than in Ted's.

'I'm going to work on a bit this evening. It's Mrs Skinner's last day and I wanted to give her the present in person. She's looked after us well, for a long time.

'I'll be in at some point tomorrow, too. I have a lot of paperwork to sort before Monday and like I told you, Jo, I'm strictly off the radar on Sunday. So have you got enough cover for both days?'

'All sorted, boss,' Jo told him. 'I'm on call for the whole weekend. I'll come in at some point both days, but I'm at the end of the phone as needed. I need to drop various sons at different sporting fixtures, but I'm never more than a phone call away. Mike's in charge tomorrow, Rob on Sunday, so we've got it covered. And seriously, unless you have a pressing need, there's no reason to come in tomorrow.'

'Budget figures, wanted for Monday, if you're volunteering, Jo?'

Jo laughed and held up his two index fingers to form a cross, to ward off the mere suggestion.

'Whenever you mention such delights it reminds me why I'm quite happy to stay at the level I am and play Robin to your Batman.'

Ted was head down over his desk putting the finishing touches to his figures when his office door opened without a knock and Mrs Skinner walked in. She gave a start of surprise to find him still working at his desk.

'Oh, I'm sorry, Chief Inspector, I didn't realise you were still here. Do you want me to go and clean the other offices first, if you're busy?'

'No, come in, please, Mrs Skinner,' Ted said, getting to his feet as he spoke.

He never forgot his father's teaching about it being polite to do so, and doing it for both of them, as his dad could no longer get out of his wheelchair unaided.

'I was hoping to catch you. It's your last day, I hear? I'll be very sorry to see you go.'

'I didn't want to stop. I love my work. It's all I've got left now, really.'

To Ted's consternation, her voice broke and she started to cry. He moved round the desk and pulled the spare chair out for her.

'I'm sorry, I didn't mean to upset you. Please, sit down for a moment. Would you like a cup of tea? I was about to make myself one.'

It wasn't quite true. He'd been hanging on until she arrived but had then intended to leave. Trev had been to something with his English students but wouldn't be late home and Ted had promised to try to be there in time for them to eat together.

'I don't want to put you to any bother. And I'm not allowed to take a break when I'm working, Chief Inspector. I'll get into trouble.'

'It's your last day, Mrs Skinner. What can they do to you? And I think you deserve a break. Tea, or coffee? And please, call me Ted. You've known me long enough. Not to mention covering up my little outbursts of temper.'

'This will sound strange, but whenever I clean your office, I always look at those little sachets of green tea you have and wonder what they taste like. I've never bought a box, in case I didn't like them. But could I try a cup of that, please?'

'Of course you can. I put honey in mine. It's quite an acquired taste and I have a very sweet tooth.'

Once he'd put the kettle on to boil, Ted reached behind the desk and pulled out the present Jezza had sourced and wrapped for him then put it on the desk in front of the cleaner.

'I wanted you to know that we've all very much appreciated the hard work you've done for us over the years, Mrs Skinner. The team had a whip-round to show their appreciation, and I wanted, in particular, to give you something to remember me by.'

He had to help her with the wrappings as emotion got the better of her. Then she laughed in delight at the designer wastepaper basket, and gasped in pleasure at the toiletries Jezza had chosen.

'This is so very kind of you, Ted. I shall miss coming here. It's the last bit of contact I have with my Cyril, when he was in the force. Almost like family. I've no idea what I'll do with myself now.'

'Here's my card. If ever I can do anything for you, anything at all, please don't hesitate to get in touch, at any time.'

'Thank you. And I rather like this tea. I must get myself some.'

It was much later than Ted had intended when he finally got home. In the end he'd insisted on staying and driving Mrs Skinner back to her house to save her having to carry her gift home on the bus.

Trev was less than amused and had clearly decided to go ahead and eat without him, although he hadn't yet got as far as dessert. Ted was apologising from the moment he set foot over the threshold, hurrying into the kitchen, dodging cats, even Adam, who was the first to greet him, as ever.

'Sorry. I'm really sorry, but I do have a good excuse. Honestly. I had to help a damsel in distress and in tears.'

Trev thawed visibly at the tale Ted told him, then stood up to give him a hug.

'You are very kind, and very sweet and more than a little bit soppy. I love that you looked after Mrs Skinner, even if it did make you late. I especially love it when you grovel. But you are on a final warning for Sunday. I want my promised day with you all to myself, or the consequences will be dire.'

'Think carefully before answering that phone, Ted Darling. It could end in divorce.'

Trev was lying on his back on the coarse grass on top of Mam Tor, his head pillowed on one of Ted's legs. A skylark, was singing overhead, his fluting tune having been rudely interrupted by the sound of Ted's mobile phone ringing.

Ted pulled it out, carefully extricating himself from under Trev's head and looking at the screen.

'Sorry, it's Rob, so it must be urgent. He knows I'm not officially on call.

'Yes, Rob?'

'Boss, I'm really sorry, but I need to run something past you to make sure you're happy with my decision. I can't get hold of Jo, except briefly. He's had to take his youngest son, Mateo, to hospital with a broken leg from playing football. It's a bad break, too. It will need surgery to pin it. Jo wants to stay with him. He doesn't want to phone his wife because she's taken the three girls to Bolton to see the family and he's worried she'd drive back like a mad thing and put all their lives at risk.'

'It's fine, Rob. What's the problem? Bear in mind I'm an hour and a half away, at best. I'm up a mountain and the car is down near Castleton.'

'I'm sure we can manage, boss, I don't need you to come in. I was after someone senior to say if I'm making the right decision or not. That's all.

'I'm up at the Lanky Hill flats. There's a bit of a siege situation going on. A well-known drug user, who's totally off his face. He's got a woman and three small kiddies in the flat with him. None of us can make out what it is he wants, but he keeps turning the gas taps on and waving a lighter around. He goes hysterical at the sight of uniforms, but he's talking to me so I don't want to leave him. He knows me. I've nicked him a couple of times, but for some reason, he seems to trust me. I'd never forgive myself if I left then he blew the place up and there were fatalities.

'But meanwhile we've got a suspected murder-suicide situation on the other side of town, and according to the first responders, it's a bad one. A man's come home from work and found his son stabbed to death and his wife having tried to slit her wrist but still alive. No signs of anyone else present in the property, no signs of a break-in.

'He's gone to phone the emergency services, realised he's left his phone in the car, run outside and the front door's slammed behind him. By the time the first responders arrived and helped him to break in, they've found the woman dead with a fresh stab wound to the chest, which looks self-inflicted.

'I've sent Steve for now to start the ball rolling. A CSI team is on its way and the good news is that Doug is back at work and going to manage it himself. Obviously, if it starts to calm down here, and especially if we manage to get the man out of the flat and into safe custody, I'll go straight over there myself to oversee. But for the moment I don't want to leave, unless you tell me to, and the chances of finding a trained negotiator on a Sunday aren't good.'

'You've done absolutely the right thing, Rob. Let Steve know he can call me at any time if he has queries or doubts. He'll do a good job on assessing the scene. He was very thorough when he went to the Honest John scene on his own.'

Trev had stood up to start packing away the remains of the picnic. He motioned towards Ted.

'Go,' he said, picking up from the one-sided conversation that Ted was needed. 'Your head's there already. Go. At least we got to enjoy the picnic in the sunshine. You can drop me off at home on the way, then do some proper grovelling when you finally get home.'

Ted's mouth moved in silent thanks then he spoke again into the phone.

'Rob? Tell Steve I'm on my way. I have to drop Trev off first but I should be with him in under two hours, if you let me have the address.'

The metallic stench of blood hung heavy in the air of the well-appointed kitchen of a semi-detached house. Crime Scene Investigators had arrived and were setting up, Doug once more back in his role as Crime Scene Manager, after his sick leave.

Steve went over to talk to him first outside the property, anxious not to do the wrong thing on what was clearly going to be a big case. Doug tried to keep any note of doubt or criticism out of his voice as he asked, 'Is it just you for now, Steve?'

'The DCI's on his way but he's got to come from Castleton, so I'm starting things off. I have worked a murder scene before, though,' Steve told him, painfully aware of how defensive he sounded.

'Well, why don't you have a quick word with the first responders to begin with, while I assess the scene and get some stepping plates down, before we all go wading in there contaminating everything. We'll get all the initial photos done, too. I'll give you a shout when you can go in.'

Steve had exchanged a brief nod with one of the first officers from Uniform at the scene. He was currently sitting outside in the area car with the husband who was looking pale and shaken, wanting to get back into the house. The man was wearing the green uniform of the ambulance service.

The second officer was outside the house, monitoring who came and went. She'd nodded briefly in recognition at Steve when he'd arrived. He knew both officers had considerably more years of service under their belts than he did. It made him more acutely aware of his own inexperience, and more determined not to get anything wrong. He went back now to have a word with her. At least she seemed more approachable than her male colleague outside in the car.

'So, is it just you for now, Steve?' she asked him, echoing Doug's words.

He tried to detect anything behind her tone, but found it neutral enough. He knew her name was Valerie Gabriel but wasn't quite sure how to address her, so he began with 'Erm, the DCI's coming later, but he's out of town. I'm only here to start things off. Please can you tell me what you know so far?'

'Ron and I were despatched following a 999 call reporting the fatal stabbing of a boy of eleven and an apparent attempt by the mother to kill herself. We were out on what turned out to be yet another false alarm, so it was about twenty minutes before we arrived.

'We found the husband in a right old state, trying to kick the front door in and getting nowhere fast. He said he'd come home to find his son dead from a single stab wound to the chest, and his wife unconscious on the floor, having apparently tried to slit her wrist. You're the detective, Steve, you'll have noticed he's a paramedic, so we took his word for it that the boy was dead and the woman was unconscious when he got home. No need not to.

'He said he realised he'd left his mobile phone in the car, so he ran outside to get it, phoned 999, but when he tried to get back in to help the wife, the door had slammed shut and he couldn't find any way to get back inside. He'd left his keys inside the house. He's been all round the outside, kicking the front and back door, throwing anything he could find at the windows, but it's the usual story. Double glazing. Not easily broken.

'When we got here he was hurling himself at the front

door. With Ron adding a bit of weight and me doing my best, we managed to break it open and he ran in. We heard him give like a howl of pain and he shouted that his wife was dead. We'd followed him in, right on his heels, and we could see that he was right. She had a big kitchen knife sticking out of her chest, with one hand still by the handle part. I double-checked and she was dead. No pulse, no signs of life, although she hadn't gone cold by then.

'He completely lost it at that point. Screaming that he could tell she'd not long died and that if he could have got in earlier, she might still be alive. Blaming the door for slamming. Blaming himself for forgetting his phone, and then leaving his keys in the house. Blaming us for not getting here sooner. You probably know the sort of thing.

'Ron took him to the car to try to calm him down a bit, but we've not made any attempt to question him. We called it in straight away and waited for the cavalry to arrive.'

'Are none of the neighbours around, and did none of them have a spare key?'

'Nice sunny Sunday afternoon for a change, Steve. Most of them are out at the nearest park or maybe on a trip to the seaside. We did ask him about a spare key but he says not. He doesn't like the thought of anyone else being able to go into his house when he's not there.'

At that moment, one of the Crime Scene Investigators came to the door to tell them Doug had cleared them to go in for an initial look, as long as they walked where indicated.

'Would you like me to come with you?' PC Gabriel offered. 'I mean, I'm sure you know what you're doing, but sometimes two pairs of eyes are better than one.'

Steve thanked her and agreed to the suggestion, then stepped into the hallway, walking where indicated, and headed for the kitchen at the back of the house as indicated. They passed a living room on their right as they went, the door open to show a television, on quite loud, blaring out the usual Sunday afternoon bland moving wallpaper. A continuity voice was announcing the next programme, an old favourite feel-good film.

As soon as the unmistakable first notes of the most popular Disney film song of all time started to blare out, Steve stopped in his tracks, the colour visibly draining from his face above the mask he'd donned for entry.

'Turn it off!' he said sharply.

The PC and the CSI exchanged surprised looks. Not much showed above the masks, only their eyebrows shooting up towards the headwear they both had on.

'It's not respectful,' Steve said, more quietly. 'Turn it off, please.'

Chapter Seventeen

'An architect,' Trev said reflectively.

Ted was concentrating on his driving. He wanted to get to the scene of the incident as soon as he could, but in his own car, he wouldn't risk getting stopped for speeding. He made a querying noise.

'Hmm?'

'That's who I'm going to have an affair with, to amuse myself when you keep abandoning me. I can't imagine they keep getting called out on a booked day off.'

Ted changed down to do a sneaky overtaking manoeuvre where there was just about enough room for it to be safe, saying reasonably, 'They might, if one of their buildings collapsed.'

'A draughtsman, then. They're pretty desk-bound. I did go out with one once but he nearly bored me to death. And he kept his socks on in bed. Ugh!'

'I can only apologise. It was all booked, but fate got in the way.'

He had already explained all the circumstances, but Trev was enjoying playing the martyr.

'I know, and I shouldn't complain. Poor little Mateo. And poor Jo, he must be worried sick. I do love it when you grovel, though, so I'm not finished with you yet.

'But I know you want to get there as soon as you can, so drop me off near Dialstone Lane and I'll walk from there. It'll save you a few minutes, at least.'

'Are you sure? I really am sorry. I've no idea what time I'll be back tonight, either. Not until I get there and assess the situation. I'll try to make time to take you out for a meal in the week, before you go away next weekend.

'And please don't find an architect. Or anyone else, come to that.'

Trev laughed as Ted pulled up at the side of the road to let him get out and grab his rucksack from the boot.

'You're safe enough, for now. Goodness knows why I put up with you, but I do love you, Mr Policeman.'

Ted drove straight to the scene. Police tape had gone up round the perimeter of the property now and the inevitable curious onlookers, mobile phones snapping away at anything interesting, had descended. Two more officers from Uniform had been despatched to keep them back.

Ted signed himself in and stopped to pull on coveralls, gloves and shoe covers before going into the house in search of Steve. He found him in the kitchen, making meticulous notes in his pocket book and taking photos and videos on his mobile phone. He looked up in surprise to see the boss arrive. Ted was quick to reassure him.

'Me being here is no reflection at all on your ability, Steve. You know we'd usually put a DS or above on a potentially complex case like this, but there's no one except me currently available. And I'm here to advise if you need me to, not to cramp your style.'

The bodies of the boy and his mother were still in the room. Ted was busily assessing the scene, looking for the slightest detail which might be useful. The boy looked to have been tall for his age but slim. Not much bulk about him yet. His life cut short at that gangly stage. Ted doubted he would have had much strength to put up any sort of defence and the blow from the knife which appeared to be what had killed him. Especially if the fatal wound had been unexpected.

The woman was small, too. Thin rather than slim. A

pinched face, an anxious expression frozen on it in death. She must have been in unimaginable torment to take the life of her own son, if that was what had happened.

'The coroner's office has been informed, sir. There's no pathologist available to come out today, so we've been trying to photograph everything as it is,' Steve told Ted.

'Do you have any doubts on the murder-suicide theory?' Ted asked him. 'From what you've seen so far? To want a pathologist to view the scene?'

Steve looked uncomfortable. There were Crime Scene Investigators in the room, going about their work, and he seemed reluctant to speak in front of them.

'Could we speak outside, sir, please? Perhaps in the car?'

Ted indicated to him to lead the way. The DC headed for the car he'd come in. Once they were inside, he turned to Ted and began talking, awkward as ever.

'Something isn't quite right, sir. About the scene. It looks a bit staged to me.'

Ted was careful to keep his tone neutral as he said, 'Go on.'

He knew how much effort it cost Steve to speak up about anything. He'd also learned to trust his judgement. Steve was observant. He had shown that on the Honest John case. Ted wondered if he'd spotted the same thing which had jumped out at him immediately.

'A few things, really. But mostly that first knife wound to her wrist. I mean, you've just stabbed your son to death, for some reason. That's unusual in itself. Statistically rare, I think. So in the kind of extreme frame of mind you would need to be in to do that, it wouldn't be out of character to want to take your own life. So the logical thing would be simply to turn the knife on yourself and stick it through your chest, surely? After all, you've already witnessed at first hand how effective that is.'

He was looking anxiously at Ted as he spoke, his tone still

hesitant, unsure of himself. Ted simply waited for him to continue, not wanting to rush him.

'Instead, you lie down on the floor and take a superficial slash at your wrist, then somehow lose consciousness. Because the husband, who's a paramedic, said she was alive but unconscious when he got home, and that the boy was already dead.'

'What are you basing that assertion on? That she was lying down when the wound to her wrist was inflicted?'

'The blood pattern, sir. If she'd done it while she was standing up, there should have been some drips, at least, on the floor. Perhaps down the front of her clothes, too. There weren't. The only sign of blood was the trickle down the side of her arm and onto the floor, suggesting she was lying down when that wound was inflicted.'

'She fainted after stabbing the boy?' Ted suggested, playing devil's advocate. 'Came to, saw what she'd done so was filled with remorse, and decided to take her own life? But she lacked the courage or conviction to make a proper job of it and fainted again from her effort, perhaps?'

'The husband's a paramedic, though, sir. He said she was unconscious when he came home and found what had happened. Wouldn't he know the difference between a faint and being actually unconscious and unresponsive? And then there's the time lapse between the two injuries. Not to mention leaving the knife with her.'

'What's your point about that?' Ted asked him.

'Well, sir, I've done some first aid training, and isn't one of the things they drum into you the need to do a risk assessment? Making the scene safe and preventing further injury? Again, he's a paramedic. If he had to run outside for his phone, why didn't he first remove the knife? Take it with him, perhaps? In case his wife came round and decided to finish the job off?'

'Would he be thinking straight, though? He'd just found his son dead, after all. Seemingly murdered by his wife.'

'A trained, serving paramedic?' Steve said, in a scornful

tone which, from anyone else, would have been questionable. 'Wouldn't he go into autopilot mode initially? Maybe fall apart later on? But at that stage, from what he told the first responders, his wife was still alive. Even if he hated her for what she'd done, wouldn't he want her kept alive? So she could stand trial, at least?'

'So are you saying he killed her? How could he have done that, if he was outside with the police? It should be fairly simple, at the post-mortem, to tell roughly when the various wounds occurred, in relation to one another, I would imagine.'

Steve hesitated, clearly unsure of his ground now.

'If you have a theory, Steve, I hope you know I'll listen to it. I might not agree, but I will certainly listen and give it full consideration.'

'It sounds far-fetched.'

'The truth is often far-fetched. Try me.'

Steve paused. Took a deep breath, then plunged on.

'What if he drugged his wife? What if he killed the boy, for some reason, while she was unconscious, from the drug? Then he set it up to make it look like she'd done it, by cutting her wrist to look like a suicide attempt. He'd know how much of an injury he could inflict without risking killing her. A cut like that one, across the wrist, isn't often fatal. You need to do it the length of the arm, open up the blood vessels. And preferably do it in warm water so the bleeding carries on.

'That's why I wanted to get a pathologist here, to view the scene and take blood and other samples. If he did use a drug, it might be a short-acting one, like GHB.'

'We're still stuck with the problem of her seemingly having died while he was outside with two police officers as his witnesses. How does that work, then?'

Steve was quiet again, seemingly reluctant to go on.

'You clearly do have a theory, Steve. I'm willing to listen to it, at least,' Ted encouraged him.

When Steve began to speak again, his tone was bitter. He

wouldn't look at Ted. His eyes stayed glued to the dashboard of the car as he sat in the driver's seat.

'If you tell someone repeatedly that they're worthless, not fit to look after their own son, everyone would be better off without them, they can start to believe it. Especially if they have low self-esteem to start with.

'Supposing he did drug her. Something short-acting, because timing was critical to his plan. She comes round to find her son dead, her with a knife in her hand and one apparent attempt at killing herself. He might have spent years telling her she was unfit to be a mother and would do something like that one day, and then she wakes up to the reality that she has. Apparently. Then surely she would go ahead and kill herself? That's why we need blood tests. Before it's too late.'

Ted was quiet for a long moment, weighing up what Steve had said. It was possibly the most far-fetched theory he'd ever heard. But one or two of the things which Steve had flagged up had already jumped out at him at the scene.

'Even if you're right, Steve, I have no idea if we could make a murder case against him. Drugging her and tampering with the crime scene is something we might be able to prove, but I doubt we could pin the boy's death on him. If, and it's a very big if, he did kill the boy, he would almost certainly have cleaned his own prints from the knife and made sure his wife's were the last ones on it. At the moment, with no pathologist available, it looks like an impossibility to do all the necessary tests for drugs. Especially short-acting ones. It would need a miracle.

'You go back inside and carry on. Leave me the keys to lock the car. This looks like a nice enough neighbourhood, but I don't want to take any risks. I need to make a phone call. I'm going to see if there's any truth in the old saying, "The impossible we do today".'

Ted got his phone out as Steve walked back to the house. His call was answered on the second ring. Professor Elizabeth

'Bizzie' Nelson's voice, booming in his ear, didn't sound in the least bit annoyed at being disturbed at home on a Sunday afternoon when she was still officially on leave.

'Edwin! How lovely to hear from you. An unexpected pleasure.'

'Bizzie, I'm really sorry to bother you at home, and I know you're not officially back to work until tomorrow, but I really need some help. How was the ...' he hesitated a moment, still unsure whether a hippy-style handfasting was followed by a honeymoon, or if it was called something else. '... how was your trip to Scotland?'

'Glorious,' she enthused, 'but I'm sure that's not why you're ringing. What can I do for you?'

Ted set out succinctly what Steve had told him. He realised as he said it how improbable it sounded, but added, 'So if there is the remotest possibility that she was drugged, we're clearly going to need samples taken as soon as possible.'

'Goodness me! If you or I saw something like that on one of those ridiculous crime shows on television, I think we'd both be throwing things at the screen.

'How much store do you set by this young member of your team?'

'He has good intuition.'

His response clearly amused her, from the chuckle she gave.

'Not a very convincing argument to someone of science.'

'All right, this might carry a bit more weight. One or two of the things he'd spotted as being not quite right had already occurred to me as needing further examination and explanation.'

'Right, well, Douglas is blissfully domesticated, although not a very adventurous cook, which is one of the reasons I allowed him to move in. So as your scene of crime is not far away, I shall leave him to unpack and put the washing on, feed Spilsbury, and prepare our supper. I will be with you in approximately fifteen minutes.'

True to her word, Bizzie Nelson arrived within a quarter of an hour. Ted had been keeping an eye out for her and went out to meet her. She was driving a car he didn't recognise, probably that belonging to her new partner. Again he was unsure of the correct terminology following a handfasting. He needed to check such things with Trev.

The Professor stretched as she got out of the car.

'It's a long old drive down from the Highlands. But your case sounds intriguing and it's practically on my doorstep, so I couldn't resist.'

She was looking round as she stood there, at the house, now a crime scene, and at the neighbouring properties.

'A nice property. Not cheap, I imagine. A paramedic, you said? Not paid for by his wages, I'd guess. Private means? Or inherited, perhaps?'

Ted smiled. She was voicing one of the first things which had gone through his own mind when he'd arrived at the scene. He'd already made himself a note to get that checked out, in case it proved to be relevant.

'Is he still here, the husband and father?'

'In the area car with a PC, one of the first responders who was with him when they gained entry and found the wife and son, both dead. With no senior officer present, the decision couldn't be made as to whether to arrest him for something or let him go somewhere for now.'

Bizzie gave him one of her looks as she started donning her coveralls from the back of the car.

'As long as you realise that I'm not psychic, Edwin, and it's highly improbable that I can give you any concrete answers based on initial observations. But if there is anything I can tell you, I will certainly do so.'

Ted followed her into the house, directing her to where the bodies were, then introduced her and Steve to one another.

'I hope the Chief Inspector has explained to you, DC Ellis, that I am not a miracle worker. I've come to look at the scene because I live locally and was available. But it's unlikely I will have a sudden lightbulb moment, such as might be seen on the telly, and be able to confirm your suspicions. I can only go off scientific findings.'

'Yes, ma'am,' Steve began, before she interrupted him.

'Oh, please don't call me ma'am, I'm neither a serving police officer nor royalty. Professor is fine.'

Steve flushed and apologised hastily, before he went on, speaking rapidly, unsure of himself.

'I was wondering about the possibility that the mother was drugged. If everything is not as it seems at first glance, that might explain a few things. And I know testing for some drugs is time-critical, which is why I raised it with the DCI.'

'Again, despite what you might see on TV, I can't pinpoint the time of death with any precise accuracy. It's often easier to do it from other factors. How long ago was she found, for instance?'

'13.37, Professor,' Steve informed her.

She was wearing a wristwatch and consulted it at his words. 'Nearly four hours ago. Theoretically, traces of some drugs should still be eminently detectable. I can certainly take samples now, but I can't, of course, guarantee when it will be possible for the lab to analyse them.

'Tell me what makes you think that all is not as it seems, DC Ellis.'

Much more hesitantly, Steve went over what he'd told Ted earlier. The Professor didn't look at him, sensing his unease. She concentrated on examining the two bodies as he spoke. Once he'd finished, she said, 'Well, if anyone were to consult me to see if that would make a plausible basis for a television drama, I would tell them it was ludicrous.

'However, you are very observant, DC Ellis. At first glance – and I stress that this is in no way based on anything at all scientific – that initial wound to the wrist raises some questions in my mind. Ones to which I will only have the answers once I complete the autopsy and have the results of all the subsequent tests back from the lab, I'm afraid.

'All of which means, Chief Inspector, that the decision on what to do with the husband for the moment rests entirely on your shoulders.'

The husband was still sitting in the area car with PC Ron Hardy. Ted went over to the vehicle and slid into the back seat.

'I'm so sorry you've been kept waiting all this time. I'm Detective Chief Inspector Darling, the senior officer in attendance. We need to take a detailed statement from you as soon as possible, and I wondered if you would have any objection to that being done at the station? Once there, purely as a matter of procedure, we would ask to take the clothing you're currently wearing for forensic testing, largely for elimination purposes, in case it can help the investigation.

'Clearly you won't be able to go back into the house until further notice, so do you have somewhere you can stay, for tonight, at least? If there's anything at all you need from inside, I can get one of the officers to bring things out for you.'

'No, you're all right, I always keep an overnight bag in the boot of my car, in case ever I have to pull a double shift. I can go and get that.'

'I'd prefer it if you gave the keys to PC Hardy to get the bag for you. Again, it's purely routine.'

The man had turned to face Ted when he'd first spoken. There was a fleeting change in his expression, then he said smoothly, 'I just remembered. I took it out last night to sort out what was in it, and I don't think I put it back in. If you ask someone to grab stuff like my shaving kit and a change of clothes from in the house, that will be fine. Thank you.'

'And what about your car? Would you like an officer to put it into the garage for you, or the driveway, at least? For security?'

This time the answer was swift. Almost glib.

'No, you're fine. I locked it. I remember doing that. After I'd found my phone and called the police. Before I went to try to break in. I know I locked it.'

Chapter Eighteen

Ted's mobile rang as he drove back to the station. Jo Rodriguez, sounding mortified.

'Ted, I'm so sorry to have let you down ...'

'It's fine, Jo. How's Mateo?'

'Poor little sod. He was in so much pain. A really nasty fracture-dislocation, so it needed surgery and he's going to be in a few nights, at least. I didn't dare phone the mother of my children. Between you and me, she's not the greatest driver in the world at the best of times. The prospect of her driving back with the three girls in the car, in a hell of a state about Mateo, really didn't bear thinking about.

'But I am sorry I ruined your day off. Is Trev ever likely to forgive you?'

'He's threatening to have an affair with an architect. He reckons their hours may be a bit more reliable than mine. It's going to cost me an expensive dinner out one night this week, but a bottle of a decent red wine should smooth the way in the meantime.'

'So what have we got? Rob briefly mentioned a murder-suicide but then I had to rush off and sign forms of consent for surgery and such like.'

'I'm almost back at the nick, so I'm going to have to call you back later. Steve's doing a grand job at the scene. He's spotted some possible inconsistencies, so I'm going to talk to the husband to get a few details. A basic witness statement, to start with. We'll have a catch-up as soon as I've done that. You concentrate on Mateo for now.'

As instructed by Ted, the husband of the deceased woman had been given coveralls to replace his work clothes which had been taken for examination. Then he'd been shown into the vulnerable witness room, where PC Hardy had given him a drink and was waiting with him for the DCI to arrive. In response to Ted's nod, he stayed where he was.

'I'm sorry you've been kept waiting. All of this is merely routine which needs to be followed. Firstly, do you have somewhere you can stay for the time being, until the examination of your house is finished?'

The man was leaning forward, legs slightly apart, his elbows resting on his knees. He raised his hands to his face. Made a rubbing movement over his eyes and forehead, as if marshalling his thoughts.

'Yes, I have a brother in Denton, I can go there. I called him while I was waiting.'

'Once we've finished, I'll arrange for someone to drive you there,' Ted told him.

The man looked up sharply at that.

'I could go and get the car and take that.'

'I think perhaps for the moment, it might be better if you didn't visit the scene. Not until we finish everything we need to do there. I'm sorry for the inconvenience.'

The husband's expression was suspicious at that. Ted tried to keep his face neutral. He was thinking of how keen the man seemed to have been not to let anyone near his car.

Then the man slowly shook his head from side to side a few times, as if to clear it, and went on, 'Yes, sorry, of course. I understand. I've attended violent deaths before, as a paramedic. You never really expect it's going to happen to you. To your family. It's hard to get your head round.'

'First of all, let me stress that you're being interviewed purely as a witness. It's always very helpful to us if we can get an accurate statement as soon as possible after an incident like this. Would you have any objection to me recording what you say, and taking notes?'

'Whatever it takes. I just want it all to be over. Nothing's going to bring either of them back.'

'Thank you. First of all, was your son an only child?'

'Twins,' the man told him. 'He's … he was … a twin. It was a very difficult and protracted birth and the hospital totally screwed it up. I kept telling them something wasn't right but they wouldn't listen to me. Why would a mere paramedic know better than an Obs and Gynae consultant?

'Our son was born first. Slight hypoxia left him with minor brain damage. He has … had … frequent headaches, some lack of concentration, and some anger management issues. His sister was starved of oxygen for much longer. She has severe brain damage. Far beyond the state where my wife and I could look after her at home. She's been in full-time care since she was born and is likely to remain there for as long as she lives, which is, according to the experts, an indeterminate period.'

He paused to take a drink of the water the PC had provided for him. Ted sat in patient silence, waiting for him to be able to continue. When he seemed to have recovered his composure, Ted asked him, 'How did your wife cope with such a traumatic experience?'

'Not well, especially to start with,' the man told him. 'Neither of us did, really. You hear of people being badly let down by the system, of course. But you never imagine it affecting you. My wife was very ill for quite some time after the birth. Not just from the after-effects of such a bungled delivery, but she suffered from such severe post-natal depression that she was unable to do anything much.

'She missed the chance to bond with our son and she never saw our daughter. Couldn't at the time and has refused to ever since. I go, occasionally, although it's pretty pointless. She has no idea who I am. No cognitive abilities at all. Not quite vegetative, but not far off. They get her up every day at the home but she has no speech, no awareness. She simply … exists.

'My wife could never bring herself to see her. As if, in some sense, she blamed herself, although that was rubbish, of course. It wasn't her fault.

'I took action against the hospital. They admitted liability. There wasn't much they could say in their defence. They were negligent and they knew it. It's not what it was about, but we did win significant damages against them. It's invested to provide proper care for life for our daughter. But it also bought us a nice home, because I thought that might help the wife to get over it all a bit. A fresh start.'

'And how has your wife been recently? Did she ever talk about harming herself? Did her general state of mind give you any cause to be worried?'

'Do you honestly think I'd go out to work and leave her alone with the boy if I thought she might be thinking of harming herself, with him in the house? She didn't seem too bad, of late. The lad hadn't long started secondary school. He was struggling a bit. He was always going to struggle, because of what happened to him. But he was managing and she was so proud of him. She'd sit and help him with his homework. So patiently. He could get angry and frustrated when he couldn't understand things like other kids in his class could. But she was really good with him. It never even entered my head that she might harm him, not in any way.'

He stopped to drink more water. Ted's voice, when he posed his next question, was as gentle as he could make it.

'Do you have a theory as to what might have happened?'

'I can't get my head round it. Not any of it. My wife was never violent. Not to the lad, not to anyone. The boy wasn't either. Yes, he shouted a lot when he got frustrated. He'd throw things and slam doors. That kind of thing. But he was never violent towards anyone. Never. Not at school, not at home.

'I can't make any sense of it. The only thing I can think that could have happened is if for some reason he got so angry the wife might have been afraid of him and grabbed a knife to protect herself. It's never happened before. Not that I know of. Unless it had, and she was keeping it from me, for some reason. So perhaps he might have gone for her and she was afraid of him and trying to defend herself.'

'Was your wife on medication of any kind? Did she see a doctor regularly, and was she taking something to help her cope with what was clearly a difficult situation?'

'She wouldn't go near a doctor. Not after what happened. She'd lost all faith in the system.'

He paused for another drink before he went on.

'When can I ... you know, at some point I need to arrange funerals and things, I suppose. I've never had to do anything like that before. I'm not sure I know what to do.'

'I'm afraid funerals won't be possible for some time. There are various stages which need to be gone through in a case like this. It's complex and it all takes time. You'll be informed by the Coroner's office about things like that. There will, of course, need to be an inquest. That's standard procedure. But there is plenty of help available to you.'

'An inquest?' He looked surprised. 'I hadn't really thought about what happens next. I'm in a bit of a daze, to be honest. It's a lot to take in.'

'Don't be afraid to ask for help, whenever you need it. Meanwhile, that's all for now, and thank you for your cooperation. Hopefully an officer will have brought your change of clothes, then we can arrange to take you to your brother's house. We'll need to have your contact details, of course, so we can keep you up to date with any developments.'

Ted sprinted upstairs to the main office. He knew Rob O'Connell was back in now, slightly before him, and found him writing up his report. Ted was still in his walking clothes and boots, which made Rob look even more guilty.

'I'm really sorry, boss ...'

'It's fine, Rob. Seriously. You did the right thing. It was a difficult one to call. You were right to stay put with your case. That's all ended safely now, though? Is he in custody?'

'He is, boss. Something odd about it all, though. I've seen him bad a time or two before but never anything like that. Should I liaise with Drugs to see if there's a new supplier on our patch? And could it be connected to our blind dwarf, d'you think?'

'Do it discreetly, though. You know they're planning to try to move in on Data soon and they won't want to blow that op. So far he's the best lead any of us has to the dwarf.'

'Fair enough, I'll tread gently. How was the murder-suicide?'

'Steve was doing an excellent job when I arrived. He flagged up a few things which need looking at further, but he was well on top of everything. I've spoken to the husband, so I'm going to write up my notes then get off home, now you're back. Before Trev changes the locks.'

He phoned his partner while he was booting up his computer in his own office.

'I need to write up my notes but I'll try not to be too late back. If you want to book somewhere to eat out for Tuesday evening, I'll make sure I have cover. Come hell or high water.'

'Have you ever kept count of how many times you've said that? And how many times I've had to cancel?'

'I daren't.'

'One of these days I shall murder someone. It seems to be the only way to get your undivided attention. I'll cook something which won't be completely ruined if you're disgracefully late again today. And is there a budgetary limit as to where I can book for Tuesday?'

'None at all,' Ted assured him, trying not to wince. 'It's the least I can do. Anywhere you like.'

Trev was still laughing in delight when Ted ended the call. He'd heard Steve come into the main office and went outside to talk to him.

'Any updates, Steve?'

'The professor was great, sir. I thought she'd dismiss all my ideas as implausible, but she talked to me about them.'

'Good. Make sure you write everything up ready for the morning. There were one or two odd things about the husband's behaviour which jumped out at me. Particularly the fact that he didn't seem to want anyone going near his car.'

'If he had drugged her, could that be where he hid whatever it was he used?'

'Let's not get ahead of ourselves yet. We have absolutely nothing on which to base a request for a search warrant of the vehicle, but we can certainly do a thorough search of the house. The husband says she wasn't on any medication but we should check to see if she was taking something he was unaware of, which might explain her behaviour.'

'He wouldn't be stupid enough to leave anything in the house, surely? If he had given her something.'

'Doubtful, I grant you. But first we need the PM results to see if there's any trace of anything. If not, it's pointless searching for something which we can't link to the woman.'

As Steve opened his mouth to say more, Ted told him, 'I think you should attend the PM, though, Steve. You've earned that right. We've got a lot going on at the moment so we'll need to sort out who's working on what case. But you started with this one, so I'd like to see you take it further. You'll have Jo to help you, and Rob, once you've done the paperwork on yours, you can come on board, too.

'I'll see you both in the morning.'

Trev was in the kitchen, music turned up loud, singing tunelessly along to it at the top of his voice as he cooked. Even the cats had retreated to the sanctuary of the living room to escape the din.

Ted reached across to turn the radio down, planted a kiss

on Trev's proffered cheek then made a show of opening and closing the fridge and all the cupboard doors.

'What are you looking for?' Trev asked him.

'I'm just checking you haven't got an architect hidden away somewhere. I wondered if the noise was to stop me hearing whatever you were getting up to when I came in.'

'I did think about it, but then I found the perfect restaurant for you to take me to on Tuesday, and I was lucky enough to get a table at short notice as they'd had a cancellation. So I decided to inflict extreme pain on your credit card instead.'

The cats were venturing warily back into the kitchen now the noise had stopped. Adam made a beeline for Ted.

'Anyway, how was today? Was it a bad one?'

'On face value, a mother who killed her young son then committed suicide. That would be bad enough. But there's a slight possibility the husband killed both of them then staged a fake suicide. And if that's the case, it has to rank as one of the most cynical crimes I've ever come across.'

Oh, crap,' Trev paused in his preparations to give Ted a hug. 'That's going to be a tough one, whichever way it goes. And you've already got the other possible murder on. I know you. You'll want to be all over all the cases yourself. Just don't spread yourself too thin and not leave any time for yourself. For us. Especially not before Tuesday.'

The Ice Queen said much the same thing the following morning. She always wanted to be kept up to date on everything which was happening in her area. Ted caught up with her before he started briefing his own team. Like him, she was always an early bird.

'Have you got enough officers to cope with a second case of this complexity? We can look at bringing in more from other areas as and when necessary.'

'Sarah Jenkins has just about wrapped up her case, so I can poach some of her team. And Ashton aren't far behind. Their

CIO seems very on the ball so I'm sure she's up to tying up loose ends if I bring someone over from there.

'I'll put Jo in charge of yesterday's case and leave Mike on our earlier one. If we need more, I'll let you know. Jim Baker's itching for something to consult on, but I think we're on top of things. For now.'

'I can't imagine the sort of torment a mother would have to be in to kill their own child. Certainly not in such a brutal way as that. But as you said, the alternative doesn't bear thinking about either. What kind of a cynical, calculating mind would come up with such an idea?'

News of their latest case provoked a similar reaction from the rest of the team, when Ted called them to order for morning briefing. Although he expressed some sympathy with what the husband had been through, Maurice's language was the most colourful at the thought of what he might have done. Even Ted didn't pull him up on it. He was inclined to agree with him.

'Jo, can you lead on this latest one? I've forwarded you my notes from talking to the father. Steve, you should stick with this. You made a very good start. As I said, I think, too, that you should attend the post-mortem, when we get a date for it.'

'What did you make of the husband, boss?' Jo asked him. 'Gut feeling? You've had more experience than most of us with murders.'

'I don't like to go off the mythical intuition thing, really. Certainly some of what we saw at the scene, and a couple of things he said, flagged up questions in my mind. And Steve's.

'The big stumbling block we're going to come up against if we even consider him as a suspect is that he has the most solid alibi it's possible to have, unless the PM throws up something totally unexpected. And that is that at the time his wife seems to have died, he was outside the house in the company of two experienced police officers.'

Chapter Nineteen

'What I need to do first thing is to make sure that we have enough people on each case. So let's start with a round-up of who's on what, then I can see who I need to bring in.

'Rob, can you safely leave Uniform to process your man from Lancashire Hill yesterday for now? We'll need to talk to CPS about charges, but we've presumably got him on possession, for a start?'

'Yes, boss, he still had some of the stuff on him. Once he comes down off whatever it was, he may even start talking, hopefully about his suppliers. He has done in the past, in the hopes of a reduced sentence. I'll liaise with Drugs, as we discussed, and I'll see if I can get any idea on when they might be planning to move on Data.'

'Do it tactfully, though,' Ted told him. 'We really need the chance to talk to Data ourselves, to tie up that last case neatly. If, and it's a big one, he would cooperate, we could close the files on the Body in the Bowl and quite a few other elements of that whole affair. As soon as you've done that, though, switch to working with Jo on yesterday's case, please, from Damson Drive.'

'Are we treating it as a straightforward murder-suicide, or as two potential homicides?' Jo asked.

'Two suspicious deaths with no pre-conceptions, for now, I think is the best way forward. I'll find out what shifts Ron Hardy and Val Gabriel are on, then we should perhaps hear their own observations first-hand about yesterday.

'Mike, where are you up to with our other suspicious death case, Sandstone Street? When is the suspect coming back in for questioning and have you disclosed the findings about the drug yet?'

'He's coming this afternoon, with Ms Castle in tow, before he starts his evening shift. He's kept on working throughout. Says it's his way of coping, and we can't really judge him on that. I've not disclosed yet until I get all the paperwork together. I thought I'd do so as soon as they arrive, then give him half an hour or so with his solicitor before I start to question him.'

'Watch out for Ms Castle, though,' Ted warned him. 'She's a stickler for procedure, so don't give her the slightest opening or she'll exploit it to the hilt. If I'm not tied up elsewhere, I might watch part of the interview. I'll need to talk to CPS again once we hear what else he has to say for himself. At the moment, I would say we're a long way from being able to go for a murder charge.

'What's the situation now with the son?'

'Maurice and I are going to talk to him again later today, boss,' Jezza told him. 'I've been in touch with where he's being looked after, to confirm, and they say he's very gradually starting to open up to them and talk a bit more. None of it's favourable to the suspect.'

'Tread gently with him, please. He's the nearest we have to an eye witness, but we need to stay aware of the traumatic effect all of this is bound to be having on him.

'What about ordering the drug? Steve, where did you get to with comparing credit card statements with our suspect's shift patterns?'

Steve flushed, immediately on the defensive.

'I had started, sir, but I had to leave it to go to the incident yesterday ...'

'It's fine, Steve, it wasn't a criticism. You mentioned it was easy to get into his computer. What was the password?'

'The son's date of birth, sir. He even obligingly had it written down on a piece of paper.'

'So the defence will certainly argue robustly that with a password as obvious as that, it would be easy enough for the mother to have used the computer to order the drugs herself while her partner was out at any time. As long as she had access to his credit card.'

'Don't most sites have extra security now?' Jezza asked. 'Usually when you enter your credit card details, unless they're saved, don't they text a code to your mobile which you have to enter to complete the purchase? Which means she would have needed access to his phone, as well as his credit card, surely?'

'So far most of the orders I've been able to check were made when he wasn't at work,' Steve told them. 'Although that doesn't necessarily mean he was at home, of course.'

'And there's the gift to the defence, right there,' Ted said. 'No doubt he'll say that he might well have been at home but he was in bed asleep, leaving her alone with not only his credit card and his computer, but his mobile phone as well.'

'But then he must have seen what was happening, from his credit card statements, surely? Purchases being made by someone other than himself,' Jezza said. 'If he's as much of a control freak as it would appear from what I've heard of him so far, I can't imagine he would be someone who wouldn't go over things like his statements to check that everything was as it should be.'

Ted looked round the team then said, 'Virgil, can you take over from Steve on this one, please? See if there's a pattern there. See if he was always in the flat, or likely to have been, when the orders were placed. Can we trace where the phone was, too, when the codes were sent, if that's what happened, and if that's even possible? We need to show a balance of probability at the very least.'

'On it, boss.'

'Mike, I get the feeling that we know a fair bit about our

suspect but still not yet enough about the victim. Was she computer literate? Jezza, that might possibly be something the boy could reveal, if he does feel safe to talk to you. Would he have needed to use a computer, or have access to one, for his school work? And did she help him with it, or was it the step-father? If the defence do claim she was ordering the stuff herself online, we need to be in a position to counter that by showing whether or not she had the skills to do it.'

'It might be rather a lot for us realistically to get from him so soon, boss. We'll try, though, of course. But it may take more than one interview.'

'So what else do we actually know so far about our victim? Nick, Andy, what do the neighbours say about her?'

'Not a lot, in a word,' DC Nick Ross replied. 'They hardly ever saw her outside the flat, unless the Other Half was with her, and when they did, it was all she could manage to say hello. Quieter even than the boy, they all say. If they met her out with the other half, she hardly said a word unless someone asked her a direct question. And always looking to him, like for permission to speak.'

'Did she go out shopping by herself or anything like that? Did she work at all?'

'Never seen out without him in tow. Maybe that does lend weight to her not being in charge of the purse strings. And no, she didn't work. She seems to have spent most of her life in the flat.'

'Right, let's make it a priority today to find out much more about her. Have we got her medical records yet? If not, someone get them chased up. We're lacking anything concrete to make a murder charge stand up and I don't want him getting off on a technicality.

'Jo, can you go to our latest crime scene today and oversee a thorough search of the house? Basically anything out of the ordinary that turns up needs bagging and tagging. We're particularly interested in any type of medication, other than the usual packet of aspirins.'

'Sir, we need to do a thorough search of the garden, too,' Steve cut in, almost before Ted had finished speaking. 'By his own admission, the husband was shut outside for quite a few minutes waiting for the emergency services to arrive. He says he was trying to break back in, but it would have given him an ideal opportunity to hide anything he didn't want us to find. And him drawing attention to his car like he did might have been a distraction technique.'

'Ahead of me, as usual, Steve,' Ted told him. 'I want you to go with Jo and oversee a search of the garden. Because you're right, of course. If there was anything he didn't want us to see, he had plenty of time to put it in a safe place, out of sight.

'We'll need detailed statements from the ambulance crew, too. They might well have known him through work, so their input could be very useful.

'Claire, I've not forgotten you. Are you all right to tie up the loose ends on the Black Mould Scam? To free up Rob? Are we going to go with the case here and add yours on?'

The two of them had finally caught up with their scammers, arrested, charged and bailed them. A search of their properties had found enough of the missing property to give them a good case, and several of the victims had now identified the scammers from photos.

'Yes, all over bar the shouting, I think, and I'm happy to carry on with it.'

'Thank you. That will be a nice big tick on the crime figures. Right, let's all crack on with what we've got and we'll get together later.

'Jo, can I have a quick word, before you go to the scene, please?'

Jo followed him into his office and shut the door behind them.

'Are any of your family playing contact sports tomorrow?

Only I've promised to take Trev out for a special meal in the evening, somewhere posh and pricey to make up for spoiling his day out yesterday. So this time I definitely need you to cover for me, come what may. He's threatening to commit a murder if I'm a no-show again. He reckons it's the best way to get my undivided attention.'

'What are we like, eh, us coppers?' Jo said. 'We're not the easiest to live with, that's for sure. I feel as if I should offer to pay for the meal to make up for yesterday, but I fear it might be too rich for a humble DI's wallet, by the sound of it.'

'I've a feeling it may be too rich for mine,' Ted grumbled. 'Anyway, I wanted to flag up that, come what may, I need to leave at a decent time, and have my phone off all evening.

'Please do keep an eye on Steve over this case. He's getting the bit between his teeth already, and we both know he hates getting things wrong. I'd like to see him spend some time on it. If nothing else, it will focus his attention while Océane is away. But we need to be ready to pick up the pieces if he's barking up completely the wrong tree and sees it as total failure on his part.'

'Even with his alibis backing out as fast as they can, he's still claiming he didn't kill her,' Sarah Jenkins told Ted when he called her later for an update on the suspicious death her team were working on. 'He knows we can't physically place him in the house at the exact time of death. But he also knows now that he can't place himself anywhere else. And it doesn't go in his favour that he's deliberately tried to falsify an alibi.

'Then there's the boot print on the back door. Tests show it's a perfect match for his boots, which were found tucked away, and there's no evidence of anyone else having worn them. He denies trying to create the suspicion of third party involvement. He said he did it a few days prior to the incident because the door was sticking. But that doesn't hold water, and he knows it. It would have been impossible to close the door, let alone lock it, because of the damage.

'So again, balance of probabilities, why would he leave his property insecure like that, certainly not for a few days? Plus of course, we can show the print is more recent than that. The amount of heavy rain we've had would have made it much less clear than it was.

'I've spoken at length to CPS. They agree we've not a chance of making a murder charge stick, but I'm going to try to get him to plead guilty to manslaughter, in the hopes of leniency. As pleas in mitigation go, accidentally shoving her hard enough to kill her isn't right up there, but he might be able to persuade them there was no intent to do anything that serious.

'His previous form isn't going to weigh very heavily in his favour, and nor will the statements from his step-daughter and mother-in-law. Nor the boy, if he says anything. So with a bit of luck and a following breeze, we might possibly get him off our streets for a stretch, at least.'

'Good, an excellent result. Now, I need to poach an officer from you. We've two suspicious deaths, as of yesterday, so we're flat out. Who can you spare, and when can we have them?'

'Why not take Alan Burgess, now we've got him sharpened up a bit? I have a feeling it would do him good to keep away from Ashton for the time being. At least until Pete Ramsay remembers he's supposed to be a DS and starts exerting a bit of authority.'

Ted's mobile, on his desk, started to ring. He glanced away from the screen where he was talking to DS Jenkins. Gina Shaw, from Drugs, calling him.

'Great, thanks, send him as soon as possible, please. I have to take this call now.'

He picked up his mobile and asked, 'Gina, what's the news about Data?'

'I'm meeting him Thursday early evening, and we're planning to have a nice little reception committee waiting for him. I wondered if you wanted to come to the briefing to plan the op? You already have a lot of knowledge and experience to input which could be valuable.'

'Love to. When is it?'

Even as he asked, he had a premonition. A feeling of dread. She confirmed it as she said, 'Tomorrow, end of play.'

Tuesday. When he'd promised to take Trev out for a posh meal to make up for Sunday. When he'd agreed to him booking the table and had vowed to be there, come what may.

'What d'you call end of play?' he asked hopefully, busily doing some calculations. The briefing would be in Manchester, which was where the restaurant Trev had booked was situated. All was not yet lost.

'Six o'clock. Is that a problem for you? I'm afraid there's no leeway to move it.'

'I could come for half an hour right at the start, if that would help? As long as it starts on time.'

It would be tight. He was taking a risk. And Trev was going to go off the deep end when he heard. But Ted desperately wanted to be at that briefing. Data had slipped through their fingers once before and he was anxious to make sure it didn't happen again.

'Have you got Firearms back-up?'

'We weren't going to use them. I'm meeting Data somewhere fairly public so the risk was considered to be too high. He's seen and spoken to me often enough round the clubs not to be suspicious of me. I've bought from him before and met up in similar places. This time is meant to be not just to score from him but to arrange this supposed porn session through him for me and my fictitious boyfriend.

'I know Firearms is one of your areas of specialist knowledge, so are you saying you think we should use armed back-up? If so, I think we'd have to rethink the whole op and that might make him suspicious. We've probably only got one chance to lift him and I don't want to blow it. We've all in-

193

vested a lot in this.'

'I'm basing my advice on the man we arrested in the park in our case, when he was taking his dog for a walk. Ex-Special Forces and extremely high risk. If he's representative of the kind of men who protect our blind dwarf, you'll need to be extremely vigilant. After them losing one of their own, who's in the process of being deported back to where he came from, they're going to be even more wary than before. They'll no doubt be keeping close tabs on Data, ready to spirit him away at the first sniff of a reception committee, like they did to us.'

'It really would be an enormous help if you could come tomorrow to present all of this. Me passing along what you've said won't be the same at all.'

'One hour. Absolute tops. Seriously. And that's pushing it.'

'Oh, look, pussy cats. It's that strange person who sometimes graces us with their presence. Usually when he wants food or a clean shirt,' Trev commented to the assembled felines as Ted walked into the kitchen.

Ted was reasonably early. He thought he'd better not push it by turning up late and then having to explain about the change of plan for the next day. That was going to be hard enough, without starting from the back foot. He gave Trev a kiss, but his partner wasn't finished with him yet.

'And phone your mother. She's always telling me she never hears from you. She knows you're busy but you really should make time for her. She sounds a bit worried about something at the moment, but she won't say what. Whenever I ask she just says *popeth yn iawn* and I'm not at all convinced that everything is all right.'

'I will do. I'll call her when I go up to change in a minute. I need to tell you something first.'

Trev turned to face him, an ominously sharp-looking paring knife in one hand.

'Ted, if this is you building up to telling me we can't go out to dinner tomorrow night after you promised and I've booked it, you might want to think very carefully how you phrase that. Especially while I'm armed to the teeth.'

'No, no, we're definitely going, that's all sorted,' Ted bent to lift up young Adam as he spoke. He decided he might feel safer with the little cat as a shield. 'It's just that I need to attend a briefing first, so I'll have to meet you at the restaurant.'

'Ted ...'

'It's fine, honestly. I know you don't like doing it that way in case I don't show up, but I will be there, I promise. I'll leave you money for a taxi. You go straight there. I'll take a change of clothes with me, shower and change at the nick. The briefing's in Manchester, almost on the doorstep, and I only need to stay for the first hour, tops. It'll be fine. I won't let you down.'

'Honestly Ted, I've heard that so many times ...'

Ted sat Adam up in his arms and gently lifted his front right paw.

'I do solemnly, sincerely and truly declare and affirm that this promise I shall give shall be the truth the whole truth and nothing but the truth.'

Trev couldn't help himself. He was laughing before Ted had finished the affirmation. He put the knife down and moved closer to hug him, gently, being careful not to squash Adam.

'This is your last chance, though. I'll trust you one final time, although goodness knows why. I sometimes wonder why I put up with you.'

'Because you know I love you beyond reason,' Ted told him simply.

Chapter Twenty

'You've now had chance to go over, with your solicitor, our findings from your computer. I wonder if you can please explain to me the highlighted purchases on the documents.'

The team were watching the playback of Mike Hallam's interview the previous day with their suspect for the violent death in the flats on Sandstone Street. They were using the conference room downstairs and the large screen there. The team was bigger than usual, especially now Graham Winters was back with them, and Alan Burgess had been sent over from Ashton. He sat observing the rest of the team as much as looking at the screen, getting a feel for things. He'd already learned that no one got away with any slacking or sloppy procedure under DCI Darling.

The suspect looked relaxed and at ease so far in the interview. Sure of himself.

'Like I said before, I'd started getting medication online for the wife. To try to help her with the terrible mood swings. I got her some stuff I found which seemed like it would do the trick to get her back on an even keel. It seemed okay at first, but then she started to get hooked on it, like, and when it wore off, she got worse and worse, so I stopped buying it for her. Ages ago.'

'And yet you will have seen from the orders that several of them had been made quite recently. Can you explain that?'

'The wife must have been more hooked on it than I realised. I reckon she must have been using my credit card to order it herself on my computer, once I told her I wasn't going to order any more for her.'

'But you surely must have noticed, from your statements, that orders were still being made and paid for with your credit card?'

The man shrugged and spread his hands.

'You know what it's like, with the paperwork. You keep putting it to one side and telling yourself you'll get on top of it, one of these days. But somehow you never do.'

'Was she computer literate? Did she have access to your computer, or was it password protected?'

He shifted slightly in his seat as he answered that question with, 'I didn't think she was, but maybe I was wrong, or maybe the lad showed her. Kids these days know about such things, don't they? And the password were just his birthday. Not very secure, I know.'

'Pants on fire,' Jezza said distinctly. 'Lying through his teeth.'

Mike Hallam continued his questioning on the playback.

'Were you aware that this particular drug is not licensed for use at all in the UK? Certainly not for use on humans.'

He gave a look of feigned surprise.

'I didn't realise. I thought if you could buy it easy enough online then it was okay to use.'

'His nose just grew.'

Another aside from Jezza.

'And in fact the boy has told our officers that neither he nor his mother ever touched your computer. He was afraid to. Afraid of what would happen to him if he did. His mother was even more afraid, and he said she had no idea even how to turn it on.'

Jezza had made a quick phone call to Mike when she and Maurice had been to see the boy, to pass on the information he'd given to date to those who were looking after him.

The man's eyes narrowed and darkened at that.

'You shouldn't be talking to him. Not without me there. He'll be worried sick. He won't know what he's saying.'

'It's already been explained to you that as you're not a direct relative of his, various processes will need to be gone through before you're allowed contact with him. And for the moment, we need to talk to him first as he was a witness to what happened.'

'He didn't see anything,' the man said, rather too quickly, ignoring the raised hand of caution from his solicitor.

'You can't be sure of that, though, surely?' Mike asked, his tone reasonable. 'You've already said that inside the flat you were busy trying to fend off your wife as she attacked you. Even to the point of having to grab her by the throat to hold her at arm's length.'

'By the neck, sergeant,' Ms Castle corrected him. 'My client admitted to holding her by the neck, You are the one who says throat. That's inflammatory language.'

'Even so, that must have taken most of your concentration,' Mike went on, blanking the solicitor. 'And then you say your wife broke away and ran out towards the staircase, with you behind her to try to stop her from doing herself any harm. So can you be absolutely certain of where the boy was and what he was capable of seeing, all of the time?'

A brief hesitation, then, 'You know what it's like, when you have a kid in the house. You get like a sixth sense, to know where they are and to make sure they're safe at all times.'

Mike stopped the recording at that point as Jezza said, 'Excuse me while I throw up. Boss, is it all right if Maurice and I add our two penn'orth at this point? It might be useful. Because the boy is starting to make a connection with us now. Especially with Daddy Hen.'

'I got lucky,' Maurice told them all modestly. 'He was trying to put a puzzle together when we arrived, and not having a lot of success. He let me help him with it and we got it sorted between us. He talked to me a bit while we were doing it and seemed happy to carry on chatting after that.'

'Something interesting we both noticed,' Jezza went on. 'He never calls our suspect anything other than Him or That Man. So much for him trying to play the doting parent with concerns for the boy's welfare. The boy clearly doesn't see him as a father figure at all. More an object of fear.'

'Did you get anywhere about computer use? Other than what he's already told his carers?' Ted asked them.

'We did. I had a flash of inspiration so we did a quick detour to my place to get the tablet I let Tommy use. He has a basic one of his own but this one is much better and it's my bribery piece. His time on it is limited and strictly based on it being a reward for acceptable behaviour.

'I produced it to show the boy some of the apps Tommy enjoys playing with. He was fascinated by it all but it was clear he has only very limited computer skills of any sort. He was happy to talk to us while he was having a go with it. He says he's not allowed to touch That Man's computer at home and he seemed genuinely afraid of what the consequences might be if he did.

'I slipped in some questions about whether he uses a computer for his homework and if his mum helped him with it. Very definite no to both. He said his mum helped him with written work but she didn't know anything about computers, according to him.

'I assume tests on the computer might be able to show who used it. If the only traces on it are from him, then he's not going to be able to stick to his story of her ordering for herself.'

'Are you going back to talk to the boy today?' Ted asked them. 'And yes, the computer will be tested, but we don't yet have any results. Steve's been working on it but with a separate keyboard, of course.'

'We'll keep going back as long as it takes to hear what the boy might want to tell us,' Jezza replied. 'We'll only stop if it's clear that talking about it all is having more of a detrimental than a beneficial effect on him. We're also liaising each time with Children's Services to make sure they're happy we're acting in his best interests.'

'Mike, can you talk to CPS about what you've got so far. There should be enough to charge him with possession of the drug, if nothing else. We've nothing like enough yet to go for a murder charge and I'd really like to. So let's keep digging.

'Right, you'll have noticed we have PCs Ron Hardy and Val Gabriel with us to give us their observations from Sunday's suspected murder-suicide. We'll hear them now, as I don't want to delay them longer than we need to.'

The two of them exchanged a look, then Val spoke up first.

'Guv, on the surface, he behaved exactly as you would expect him to in the circumstances. He appeared distraught when we got there. Kicking at the front door and rattling it. He was bleeding from the knuckles of one hand where he told us he'd been thumping at windows, trying to get back into the house after the door slammed shut on him.'

'Did he offer that information, or did you ask him about it?'

Jezza pounced on the detail first, before Ted, who was thinking the same thing.

'He made a show of noticing the blood when he was telling us what had happened. As if he'd just seen it, at that moment.'

'Genuine, do you think?'

'Hard to tell, really. You know people can behave very strangely when they're in shock.'

'Was it only blood or did you see an injury?' Jezza again.

Val Gabriel had a lot more years of service than Jezza. She tried to keep her tone neutral as she replied, 'It wasn't really our main priority. We'd been told there was a dead child inside and a woman who had already made one attempt to kill herself, so we were more concerned about gaining entry than checking him for injury. He was a paramedic, after all, so he'd know better than us if it needed attention.'

Ted cut in before things had the chance to get heated.

'He'd just come off shift, I think. So was he planning to go out again? Only wasn't his car on the road, rather than in the driveway, or even in the garage.'

'We didn't ask about that specifically, guv,' Ron Hardy told him. 'I did wonder if he'd moved it, thinking about getting an ambulance there. Y'know, thinking like a paramedic, he might have wanted to leave the driveway clear for that. He might have been on autopilot and done that like by reflex. We didn't ask though, sorry.'

'It may not be important but Jo, can you make a note to check up on that. What was the husband's reaction when you gained entry?'

'He ran straight to the woman, then started wailing and shouting because she had the knife sticking out of her chest. We let him check her, because we thought he'd know what he was doing. He said she was dead, recently. He'd already told us that she'd been alive but unconscious, with only the superficial wound to her wrist, when he ran out of the house.'

Ted was thinking of the contamination of the crime scene. The transference of blood from the husband to the weapon and to the wife's body. It was going to present some problems for the post-mortem and the various forensic results. Not the fault of the first responders, though. They had no reason to suspect things were anything other than they appeared to be. They still might not be.

'Thank you. Did anything else strike you as out of the ordinary in any way?'

When they both said no, he let them go.

'Jo, still on Damson Drive. How did things go with the search of the property yesterday? And any news on when the PMs will be?'

'Nothing at all out of the ordinary so far, but me and Steve are going back again today, to make sure there's nothing at all we could have overlooked. And both PMs are tomorrow.'

'Steve, are you happy enough to cover them both? It will be the Professor doing them, for a case like this, so you should be able to put your questions to her as she works. She'll at least listen.

'Jo, while I remember, I'm going to a briefing late afternoon today about Thursday's attempt to round up Data.'

'Today? Are you sure that's wise?'

'I checked the timings carefully and it's doable. It'll be fine.'

'If you say so, boss,' Jo told him with a grin. 'On your head be it.'

The briefing was taking place in the office in a smart building which Gina Shaw used for her cover as an advertising and marketing consultant. Apart from a discreet nameplate on the door, the setting was anonymous. When Ted saw the half dozen officers who arrived one by one to join her, all male, he knew there would be a back way in. The way most of them were dressed, they would stand out as unlikely clients of such an enterprise. Her colleague Ian Bradley was not among them, but Gina had previously told Ted that he was currently working off the radar, in deep cover, so he was out of contact for the foreseeable future.

'This is DCI Ted Darling, from Stockport,' Gina told the others.

There weren't enough chairs in the room for all of them so they were variously perching where they could or leaning against walls.

Compared to the others, except for Gina, Ted was seriously overdressed; freshly showered and wearing his best suit with a shirt and tie. He was determined to get it right for the evening. Trev had told him the restaurant was posh and had insisted on sorting his wardrobe. Ted hadn't wanted to run the risk of not having enough time to change after the briefing. Gina had been complimentary of his outfit. The rest of the team members' looks told him their opinion of him.

'Ted's here because he and his team have already tried and failed once to get their hands on our boy Data, so I thought it might be useful to hear his experience first-hand.'

'Bit careless, that,' one of the officers said with a note of scorn.

'It was a well-planned op. As well as yours is doubtless going to be. We had every entrance of the park where it was happening covered. The one thing we weren't aware of is that the supposedly blind dwarf we believe is the supplier for the drugs Data sells, and the buyer for the porn films he produces, is protected by some Albanian ex-Special Forces types. We managed to arrest one of them shortly afterwards, but I can't emphasise enough to you how dangerous these people are.

'Their role will be to ensure that someone as valuable to them as Data never falls into the hands of the police and risks leading us straight to him.'

'Albanian Special Forces? For real, or is this some sort of a wind-up?' the same team member asked, not bothering to hide the scepticism in his voice.

'I'm completely serious, I assure you,' Ted told him. 'A mistake was made in our investigation – entirely my fault – so we didn't pick up on that connection as soon as we should have. Our interest in this gang was purely for the cuckooing, which included serious abuse and sexual exploitation of a young woman with learning disabilities. It was because of a sudden death in her flat that we found the connection to the drugs gang and passed the info on to you.

'The reason for my presence here today is to emphasise that these people are clever, highly trained, and ruthless. They spirited Data away from under our noses. If they get the slightest whiff of a police presence, they'll do the same again on Thursday. And don't overlook the possibility that they'll treat

Data as expendable, if it comes to protecting their operation. They'll do anything it takes to stop him being arrested and interviewed.'

'Couple of things there, Ted,' the same officer again, sounding increasingly truculent. 'First off, take a look at us. None of us in here looks remotely like most people's idea of a copper. We do this all the time. We know what we're doing. Second, this Data is a valuable asset. They're not going to want to lose him. So surely they won't be thinking of taking him out.'

'All I'm saying is that as a last resort, they might.'

The debate rumbled on, sometimes getting heated. Ted was trying hard not to step on any toes, but he was determined to make the rest of them consider all possible outcomes for the operation. He didn't realise how long they had been talking until the alarm he'd set on his mobile went off. He took it out of his pocket to cancel it then looked apologetically at Gina Shaw.

'That's my time up. Thank you for listening, at least, everyone. I hope you'll bear in mind what I've said, and I'll see some of you again on Thursday, hopefully for a positive outcome.'

Ted had allowed plenty of time. It should only take him ten minutes to drive to the restaurant, and he'd still left himself quarter of an hour to spare in case of difficulties in finding a parking space.

Even that was easier than he feared, so he found himself walking into the restaurant ahead of the appointed hour.

A waiter showed him to the table, presented him with a menu and asked if he wanted an aperitif. Ted settled for sparkling mineral water.

Trev wasn't there. For once, it was Ted who was left sitting on his own like Billy No Mates, wondering if this was going to be the ultimate revenge from his partner.

The taxi arrived five minutes early. A good start. Trev had been hovering in the window, looking out for it. He turned to the cats as it pulled up outside.

'Right, boys and girls, your other daddy has promised to take me out to a lovely restaurant and spoil me rotten. Which means, of course, that he won't turn up. I don't know why I even bother getting ready. But just in case, I'm off now, and I need you all to promise to behave yourselves. And if he does stand me up again, which is highly likely, I intend to get quite outrageously bladdered at his expense, so I apologise in advance if I return in a deplorable state.'

He went out to the taxi and slid into the front passenger seat next to the driver. The man checked the address with him as he pulled away then added, 'I've heard that's a nice restaurant. Special date? Some lucky young lady?'

'Actually, my husband's taking me out to dinner because he's always letting me down for such things. It's not his fault. His job's very demanding. He probably won't turn up, yet again, but I don't want to be late arriving or I'll never hear the end of it, if by some miracle he does make it.'

'Oh, sorry, mate, no offence intended. What time's your table booked for?'

'Seven-thirty, and none taken.'

'That should be no problem, we've plenty of time.'

Not very many minutes later, the driver was mumbling profound apologies and Trev was nearly climbing the side of the taxi when they found themselves stuck solid in heavy traffic at the scene of a collision, which had clearly happened moments before. With seemingly no way to go forwards or to get round the incident.

'I'm really sorry, mate, I usually get an early tip-off of anything like this but it looks like it's very recent. With a bit of luck, we'll get round it in a bit. Do you want to give your bloke a ring, to tell him what's happened?'

'It's fine, don't worry. He won't be there. Certainly not on time. And he's in a meeting, so there's no point phoning him, he won't answer the call anyway.'

They were stuck for a good twenty minutes before they were finally waved through. The driver used all his skills and local knowledge, helped by his sat nav, to take every shortcut he could find to make up lost time. Trev was still more than fashionably late by the time he got to the restaurant. He thrust the cash at the driver, generous tip included, brushing away his protests and saying he'd ask for him again if he needed collecting after the solitary well-oiled dinner he was anticipating.

As the waiter showed him to the table, Trev was stunned to find a rather smug-looking Ted sitting waiting patiently for him. Ted stood up to greet him and Trev smothered him in a hug.

'You came! I can't believe it. I'm late because we got stuck in traffic. But you're here. Thank you.'

'I said I would,' Ted smiled, taking his phone out of his pocket and putting it on the table. 'And look, phone switched off. I'm at your exclusive disposal for the whole evening.'

Trev's grin turned mischievous.

'In that case, let's gobble our food quickly. Or ask for a takeaway, and get home as soon as possible.'

Chapter Twenty-one

'Right, DC Ellis, first of all, thank you for arriving on time. This is your first PM with me. Have you done others previously?'

'No, Professor,' Steve told her, remembering not to call her ma'am.

'A quick run-down of my rules first, then. It's quite normal to puke, but please don't do it in my autopsy suite. Secondly, contrary to rumour, I don't bite, so don't be afraid to ask questions, even while we're working. I'm perfectly capable of multi-tasking. I know you have some doubts over this case, so it's my role to tell you if they have any foundation. But only based on forensic findings. I don't do speculation. Although I have been known, on occasion, to postulate hypotheses.

'As we have two autopsies to perform, my colleague, James, will be working on the young boy, whilst I work alongside on his mother. If you could manage to observe both of us without getting in the way, that would be very much appreciated.

'Like you, we are truth-seekers, James and I. It is our job to present you with factual evidence of what happened to these poor unfortunates.

'Now, I haven't yet had time to share your thoughts with James, DC Ellis, so perhaps you would be kind enough to go over them again for him? That way they will be recorded, along with my comments, which might be helpful to us in the future.'

Steve could feel himself instantly flushing behind the face mask he was wearing. He wished he could control it, but had never found a way to do so. He was always waiting to be jumped on and shot down in flames for everything he said.

'Before you start, DC Ellis, can we call you something other than that?' James asked him. 'It's a bit of a mouthful. I'm James, so what can I call you?'

'Steve. My name's Steve,' he began, then stumbled on, setting out his theory about the woman's death, painfully aware as he did so that it sounded implausible even to his own ears. At least both James and the Professor were giving the appearance of listening politely, apart from the odd aside they made for the voice recorders, with basic details about the victims they were examining.

'I see,' James said, when Steve had finished, keeping his tone neutral, so Steve had no way of judging what he was thinking. 'Well, I have to confess, if you're right, this is quite the most bizarre case I've ever heard of. Not to mention audacious. Because if the mother did kill herself while he was outside, whether or not he had somehow convinced her to do it, he surely has a cast iron alibi, being with the police at the time?'

'Unless we can show he killed the boy, not her,' Steve told him, a stubborn tilt to his chin now. 'Speaking of which, I don't know if the information is useful to you but the first responders said the husband was bleeding from one hand. He said he'd done it trying to break into the house when he got shut out. But I imagine that will mean that his blood will be on either or both bodies, and possibly on the knife too. And him drawing attention to it might simply be a way of him establishing a reason in advance to explain his traces on the bodies and on the weapon.'

'Deviouser and deviouser, said Alice,' James commented.

'Without realising how bad her grammar was,' the Professor responded, clearly finishing off an old joke between the two of them.

Then she went on, 'I have to confess to having been sceptical when DC Ellis outlined his theory to me at the scene. It still sounds implausible in the extreme. However, I do agree that the strange positioning of the woman's body in relation to the first superficial cut to her wrist had occurred to me, too. She was definitely lying down when that injury was inflicted, but with the arm which was injured stretched out to the side. And clear evidence that it had been in that position at the time the cut was made.

'Because I never take anything I see at face value, I decided to do some experimentation at home, to try to recreate how easy – or not – it would be to inflict that sort of an injury on oneself whilst lying on one's back on the floor.

'In one of those "don't try this at home" warnings, I should stress that this is definitely not something which should be attempted with an extremely randy young Staffy puppy in the house. Even after Spilsbury was removed to a place of safety, I found it a really counter-intuitive way of trying to inflict serious harm. I was using an extremely sharp kitchen knife, although I put the protector over the edge of the blade to be on the safe side.

'The most logical thing to do was to move my left arm across my chest in order to bring the knife down across it. But we know from the blood patterns at the scene and on the body that she didn't do that. Which begs the question, why not?'

'Could it be that, if she had been drugged with something, then she was still very weak from the effects? Perhaps dizzy? Might that have affected her actions?' James suggested.

'Dizzy would be a possible explanation. Weak I'm finding harder to accept as a factor, because either way would involve lifting one arm and moving it. You actually have to move yourself more to roll towards the arm, rather than to lift the arm towards the knife.

'You've checked, Steve, of course, which was her dominant hand, I take it?'

Steve felt himself flushing an even darker red than before as he mumbled, 'Not yet, Professor.'

'Please do so. It could prove pivotal to your theory. Sometimes I would be able to give you a suggestion based on a slight difference in muscle development between the two arms. This lady was so thin that it becomes more difficult to do so.'

'What if she didn't make that cut herself at all?' Steve suggested hesitantly. 'What if she was unconscious at the time, and she only came to later to find the boy dead next to her and her with a wound on her wrist?'

'We won't be able to address that hypothesis today, I'm afraid,' the Professor told him. 'For that we will need the results of the blood tests as well as having the information on what the knife can tell us, in terms of fingerprints.'

'From my initial observations at the scene, I believe that the knife was withdrawn immediately from the boy's chest. Had it been left in place, I would have expected to see far less external bleeding and subsequently to find more blood in the chest cavity. The knife would effectively form a damn, to an extent. I should be able to confirm that theory for you once we look inside.'

'I'm about to crack the boy's chest, Professor, if you're happy for me to do that now? Do you want to have a closer look externally before I do so?'

She paused in what she was doing and went to join James at the table he was working on. Steve also moved closer, fascinated by it all. Relieved, too, that he had so far not encountered mockery from either of the pathologists for his ideas. And that he was too enthralled to think of feeling ill.

She spoke aloud, both for the recording and for Steve's benefit.

'The body presents with a single, deep stab wound to the chest with what is likely to have been a steel kitchen knife, the same knife found in the mother which appears to have caused her fatal injury. I'm basing that assertion on there being no other apparent weapon at the scene, which I think you would confirm, Steve?'

'Yes, Professor. There appeared to be only the one knife in evidence. Unless another one was used and removed, but we haven't found it, despite searching the whole of the property, including the garden.'

She nodded, then continued, 'The knife has apparently gone deep into the thoracic cavity, so it would have required some force behind the blow. Based on the wound's location, and the likely depth of the injury, I would expect to find a penetrating wound to the heart. If that is the case, death would have been very rapid.

'I'm expecting to find something very similar on the mother, although as I said, the bleed pattern will be different as the weapon was left in place in her case. I'm reserving judgement pending further investigation, but again, based only on initial examinations, I doubt she would have been able to pull it back out again herself, had she wanted to for any reason.'

'Would the mother have been capable of inflicting a wound like that on her son, Professor?' Steve asked her. 'Given what you said about her being thin and lacking muscle?'

'Physically? As we observed at the scene, it appeared that the poor boy was taken completely by surprise and made no attempt to defend himself. If the knife was sharp and the blow unexpected, then there's no reason why she couldn't have done it. Psychologically, though, that's a different matter altogether. It's relatively unusual for a mother to kill her child. Babies, sadly, sometimes, but less common at this age. To stab one to death like this is very rare indeed, in my experience.'

'I'm curious, Steve. I imagine, in your line of work, unlike ours, you would need to show a motive for a crime like this. It's extreme enough if the mother killed the boy, then took her own life once she realised what she'd done. But what would motivate a father to do something as twisted as killing his son, convincing his wife to kill herself, then setting her up to take the blame?' James asked him.

Steve hesitated. This was the part where his theory really seemed off the wall. Especially when he had nothing at all, other than intuition, on which to base it.

'Well, the family haven't had an easy time of it. The boy apparently suffered some slight brain damage at birth and was prone to violent outbursts, but nothing physical. The mother has suffered from depressive illness since the birth. She had twins, but the daughter was severely affected and is in full-time care. That must take its toll.'

'I could understand him suddenly snapping with the weight of all of that,' James conceded. 'But that's not what we're looking at here, if your theory is even partly correct. It would have taken cold, calculating pre-meditation to carry it off. Could there, perhaps, be a financial motive? Life insurance? Or would that not pay out in the event of a certified suicide?'

'There's a suicide clause in most insurance policies,' Steve told him. 'I've not officially looked into that idea yet because we have nothing on which to make the husband a suspect. But it did cross my mind as a possible motive so I checked up on the current situation. Depending on the insurer, they will only pay out after a period of either twelve or twenty-four months from the date a policy was taken out, in the event of death by suicide. And you can usually add a child to your own life insurance policy, so there could potentially be a payout on both of them. Of course if the husband could be found to be responsible for both deaths, he wouldn't get anything. Other than a prison sentence, hopefully.'

'It's monstrous, if you're right, Steve. How could someone come up with something like that? Was there any history of anything? Domestic violence, perhaps?'

'Very possibly. You'd be surprised how much of it goes on, very often with no one outside the family unit being aware,' Steve told him. 'People might even say someone was a great bloke, they knew him well, he was kind and helped everyone. Then the police come along and find out the truth and it's nothing like the rosy picture that was painted.

'So many households have their dirty little secrets. That's why it's vital that you give us anything at all to prove or disprove the theory.'

His tone and his demeanour changed totally as he spoke. There was passion in his voice, almost desperation. Professor Nelson heard it and replied as gently as she could.

'Steve, it's important that you realise from the start that, even if you are absolutely right in your theory, there's a strong likelihood that despite our best intentions, James and I might not be able to supply you with the balance of probability you would need for any kind of action against the father. As I explained to you at the scene, if you are thinking he might have administered something like GHB to the woman, the likelihood of us being able to detect it is slim at best.

'I should be able to tell you, from my examination, if I find any evidence of significant brain damage in the boy. Even if I don't find anything obvious, his medical records should confirm or disprove that. I would imagine that if he was prone to violent outbursts, it is remotely possible that that's what happened and that his poor mother, perhaps afraid for her own life, picked up a knife to defend herself, with tragic consequences.

'I said I don't like to speculate and I don't. But on this occasion I will say that I'm fully expecting not to be able to give you any concrete answers today, let alone the ones you would like to hear. The prints on the knife should be pivotal but with the probability of contamination, I wouldn't set your hopes too much on them giving you enough to make the husband an official suspect. That would then mean waiting for a coroner's inquest before you could proceed further. And if pressed, I would have to say, unless we suddenly find something totally unexpected, the probable outcome of that would be a murder-suicide verdict, so case closed as far as further police action was concerned.'

There was a palpable buzz of anticipation about the team at the end of the day when they got together in the larger room downstairs once more. Ted went down to join them, glad of the excuse to escape from behind his desk where he seemed to have spent much of the day pushing papers.

'Boss, a significant development on the Sandstone Street flats case,' Mike told him. 'We've finally found an eye witness. Nick spoke to him today and he says he saw pretty much what happened. He definitely saw the partner holding the woman by the throat against the handrail.'

Ted frowned.

'And he's only just now come forward, more than two weeks after it happened? Did he see her fall?'

'I actually felt sorry for the poor bloke,' Nick Cross put in. 'I'd been knocking at his flat most days but not getting an answer. The neighbours didn't know where he was. They don't know him well. Poor bugger has been absolutely flattened by bad flu, in bed the whole time, only just about able to make himself the odd cup of tea then crawl back to his pit. He looks shocking. His clothes are hanging off him so he's clearly lost some weight.'

'Didn't he have someone he could call? Is his story genuine, do you think?'

'I would say so. If not, he should get an Oscar for his acting. And no, no one to call. He's new to the area. The flat's a temporary stop-gap. He'd left work early the day of the death because he had a splitting headache and was getting the hot and cold sweats. He lives two floors up from our crime scene and when he heard it all kick off, he went outside intending to ask whoever it was to shut up because he felt so rough.'

'He could see it was getting heated but he was having trouble staying upright himself so he went back inside and pretty much crashed out. He'd no idea it had ended in a fatality and he's mortified that he didn't do anything.'

'But he'd testify now? Even though it doesn't necessarily

show him in a particularly good light?'

'He will. He's given me an initial statement. He's happy to ID our suspect and to do anything he can to make it right, as far as he's able.'

'As ill as he was, how reliable will his testimony be, though?' Ted asked. 'Would he have had a clear enough view from where he was?'

'Bird's eye. Literally. Two floors up, on the other side, so looking directly at where it happened.'

'Pity he didn't do anything,' Maurice grumbled. 'He could maybe have saved the woman's life.'

'Maurice, mate, he doesn't need the guilts from any of us,' Nick Cross told him. 'He went out to ask them to keep the noise down but didn't have enough voice to do even that. And he was two floors up. There were neighbours much closer who told us they heard what was going on, and not for the first time, but none of them went out to take a look, even, let alone do anything.'

'I've been going through the drugs purchases compared to our suspect's shift patterns,' Virgil put in. 'Every single one now confirmed as having been made while he wasn't at work. As Steve pointed out before, that doesn't necessarily mean he was at home. But have we at least got enough now to requisition his phone, boss, to check his movements, and if a code was needed for each purchase, in case he's not yet deleted the history?'

Jezza was looking like the cat who got the cream.

'We've got two eyewitnesses now, boss. The boy's started to talk. He's now been told his mother's dead and he keeps asking his carers whether That Man killed her. They've been skilfully avoiding a direct answer because they don't want to risk putting words into his mouth before we talked to him again, so they've simply been telling him she had a fall and died.

'As soon as we got there he rushed up to Maurice, with another thing he wanted him to fix, and while he was doing that he asked him outright if That Man killed his mum when he pushed her down the stairs.

'We asked him very carefully, with the approval of his safeguarder, if he'd seen what had happened and he said he had. He was watching from just inside the door to the flat, he said.

'The room we see him in at the home has soft toys about for the younger children who go in there. Again, having made sure it was all right to ask him questions, I asked if he could show me what had happened.

'There's a big teddy bear there. It must be nearly the size of some of the little ones. He went and got that to show us. He got hold of the bear's throat with one hand then lifted up one of its legs with the other. We were sitting at a table and he made a show of hefting it up then pushing it over backwards so it fell to the floor.

'While he was doing that he was using some really foul language. Shouting it right in the bear's face. Now, my brother Tommy will often say words like that if he hears them, because he has no real social filter sometimes. But I wouldn't normally expect a boy of this one's age to use words like that in front of adults, especially ones he doesn't know well. It added a lot of weight to what he was saying.

'So have we got him now, boss? With two seemingly reliable eye witnesses, plus the evidence of the drugs purchase? Have we got enough to charge him with unlawful killing?'

Chapter Twenty-two

Once they'd finished, Ted hurried back upstairs to get his things. He hadn't said anything to Trev for fear of getting his hopes up, but he was planning to get to the dojo in time for both the self-defence club and his own judo session. He'd had excellent feedback from the ACC about his alert system idea and he was anxious to tell the young members how much he'd appreciated their input.

He also wanted to try, at least, to spend some quality time with Trev before the coming weekend, when his partner was going down to London to talk to other victims of the abuse he'd experienced as a boy. It was going to be doubly tough for him as he would be staying at the family flat which he hadn't visited in years and which was bound to awaken old memories and wounds.

Ted knew there would be no chance of him getting to karate the following evening, because of the operation in Manchester, and he'd no way of knowing what time he would finally get home after that. Trev was going straight from work on Friday to get the train to London, leaving his bike safely locked in the workshop. Ted hoped it would be a pleasant surprise for him if he made the effort to get to the dojo.

He heard footsteps on the stairs behind him, then Steve's hesitant voice saying, 'Sir? Have you got a minute?' and realised he may have been optimistic in his plans for an early getaway.

'Yes, Steve, of course. Come up to my office.'

He led the way, sat down at his desk and indicated for Steve to do the same. When the DC hesitated before speaking, he prompted him gently, hoping he wasn't in for a long session.

'What can I do for you?'

'Sir, would we be able to get a warrant to search the car, at Damson Drive? Only, we haven't found anything at all out of the ordinary searching the house and garden, so that's the next most likely place for anything to have been hidden.'

Ted hesitated, weighing up his reply carefully. The last thing he wanted to do was to quash Steve's enthusiasm for his work. But nor could he afford to indulge the DC's theories without something more solid to go on.

'At the moment, we have absolutely nothing on which to base even applying for one. Both deaths happened in the house, and so far there appears to be nothing at all to back up your theory of the husband's involvement.'

He saw Steve open his mouth to say more but interrupted him.

'I know it's frustrating, but unless and until the post-mortem results throw up something solid to allow us to take it any further, there's nothing much we can do.

'You know I'm not swayed by such things but I also have to consider that if we made such an open move against a grieving husband and father and got it completely wrong, the consequences could be disastrous. It could leave us open to legal action by him. There would need to be an inquiry, and the whole thing could seriously damage public confidence in the police in general.

'You may be absolutely right in your intuition. It's perfectly possible, although extremely unusual. All I can do is promise you that if there's the slightest doubt, the smallest loophole, in the reports which come back from the lab, we'll do whatever we can to see that justice is done.'

'But what if I'm right, sir? What if he's some sort of a sick monster who's plotted the whole thing? What if he's killed his own son in cold blood then callously set up the entire scene to frame his wife? And if he then walks away? He maybe does it with a load of cash from life insurance, and he gets away with the whole thing scot-free? Just because we didn't search his car.'

'Not didn't, Steve,' Ted told him, keeping his tone as quiet and patient as he could. 'Couldn't. We can't randomly request search warrants with no basis for doing so. You know the procedure as well as I do. We have the apparent weapon for both deaths. What we don't have, at this stage, is any indication of an unlawful substance having been used. We have no signs at all of third-party involvement. No indication of a break-in.

'More than that, we have two police witnesses to say it wasn't possible to break into the property without a lot of force.

'All I can do is to promise you that if anything at all shows up from the lab results, I'll get us a warrant as soon as humanly possible.'

'But it might be too late by then!' Steve's voice was rising, his frustration apparent from his tone and expression. 'He might reclaim the car in the meantime and dispose of anything in it.'

Ted paused for a moment before replying, aware that his response could potentially sound like a patronising brush-off.

'Steve, sometimes, even though we're sure we have the right person in our sights, we simply can't make a case against them. Or something gets in the way and we don't get the result we want. It's no reflection on us.

'Occasionally, whatever we do, we can't bring a case to its conclusion. Outside influences prevent it – *force majeure*. Tomorrow Drugs are having another crack at bringing Data in. You know that our op to get him was properly planned and well executed but we still lost him. It was no one's fault. Especially not yours.

'Why not talk to Bill this evening? Take him for a pint, maybe. He can tell you of the number of past cases which have slipped through our fingers at the last minute. Ones where we were sure we knew the guilty party, but we couldn't make any kind of a case against them. Others which got all the way to court and then collapsed. It happens.

'All we can do now is wait for the results and hope they give us some slim chance of going after the husband. But make sure you prepare yourself for the possibility that there's absolutely nothing we can do and we just have to accept the case as what it appears to be at first sight – a tragic murder-suicide.'

'Hey, you, this is a pleasant surprise. I wasn't expecting you.'

Trev was coming out of the changing rooms when Ted arrived. He was glad he'd put his kitbag in the car before he'd left home that morning. Having had to stop to talk to Steve would have made it tight to get there on time if he'd had to call at the house to collect it on his way. As it was, he was on the last minute.

'I didn't say anything, in case I couldn't make it after all. I'll definitely be late tomorrow, though. No karate.'

'That's fine, you're here now and that means a lot. I'll go and get started while you change.'

Ted had his usual magnetic effect on young Flip. As soon as he appeared in the main hall of the building where they trained, Flip lost all interest in what Trev was saying and rushed over to his hero, a beaming smile on his face.

'Wow, your boss, he were the Assistant Chief Constable, weren't he? That's nearly the top job. I looked up his uniform online. A wreath and them crossed staff things. What do you have to do to be an ACC?'

'Tipstaves,' Ted corrected him, 'And Trev's talking, so you need to go and join in and listen to his instructions. First important lesson for your career path. Be at the briefing.'

Ted smiled to himself as he watched Flip scuttle off to

where he was supposed to be. If ever a boy deserved to get into the force and make a decent career of it, it was Flip.

It was a good session. The youngsters were pleased to hear they'd helped and seemed to work better than ever as a result.

The lively judo session which followed was exactly what Ted needed to wind down.

Trev had walked down. When he got into the car with Ted to go home, he asked, 'This op you're going on tomorrow. Is it a dangerous one? Will there be an armed presence, and what exactly is your role in it all?'

'No firearms. And I'm strictly there to observe. No active involvement at all. In fact, I'll be sitting in my car drinking tea and eating a sticky bun, looking like a bloke who's just stopped for a quick sugar boost on his way somewhere.'

Trev was looking at him searchingly. He knew Ted would never deliberately lie to him about something serious. But he also knew that if anything suddenly kicked off, his partner would find it impossible to stay sitting in his car eating cake whilst the action was going on all around him.

'Promise me, Ted. Promise me that whatever happens, you won't put yourself in danger. This isn't your case, after all. Not your circus, not your monkeys. Repeat after me.'

Ted had to laugh at that.

'Honestly. I'm there for one reason only – to see Data get arrested at last, and to advise if I'm needed to. Plus to stake a claim on our rights to interview him about our case. That's all. Promise.'

Ted had chosen a jam doughnut from what was on offer, with a cup of tea. He was sitting in the front of his car, the driver's window partially down so the steam from his drink didn't risk misting up the windows at a crucial moment.

He was parked in a side street off the road where the meeting between Gina Shaw and the young man known only as

Data was set to take place. The road itself was relatively quiet, away from the busy city centre. The chosen venue was more small square than park, set back at the side of the road with neither fence nor entrance gates, so no bottleneck access. There were raised beds of flowers, some managing to survive the littering and vandalism they received, and benches which were popular for lunchtime customers of nearby food outlets. At this time of day, they were relatively empty.

From his position, Ted had a good line of sight to where Gina Shaw was sitting on a bench near to the front of the square, her mobile phone in hand, into which she was chatting away. The cover was good. She looked exactly what her undercover role made her, a businesswoman making endless calls to clients while she took a brief moment out from her busy schedule to take the weight off her feet, in her stylish, though no doubt uncomfortable, high-heeled shoes.

Ted knew that the rest of her team would be close by, and he knew they would be professional. He was still impressed that, even having seen them before, he didn't immediately spot any of them. The couple he did spot were purely because he was looking for them, not because they were drawing attention to themselves.

Ted was listening through his earpiece to any comments from the rest of the team. He heard a voice announce, 'IC4 male, alone, no tail in evidence, approaching from the south. Appears to be in the right age range for our target.'

Lifting his cup to his mouth, Ted turned his head to look towards the direction indicated. A natural enough movement. Someone who'd stopped for a refreshment break, simply looking idly around while he was enjoying his drink. He saw that Gina Shaw was also looking about her, still with the phone in her hand. To the casual observer, she looked like someone waiting for their next client, or perhaps for a boyfriend, husband or partner to pick them up. From where she was, she wouldn't have clear sight of the young man approaching unless she got up and took a few paces forward, which might look suspicious.

It was Ted's first look at Data in the flesh, the presumed leader of the cuckooing gang from his team's last major case. A good looking young man, well dressed, his stride bouncy and self-assured. He clearly had no hint of the reception committee waiting for him. Gina had met up with him several times before in different places. There should be nothing to alert him that things were in any way different this time.

Traffic was starting to slow and build up as lights further up the road turned to red. A motorbike with two people on board was finding its passage up the inside of the queue of cars, close to the kerb. Despite the traffic noise, with his window partially down, Ted heard the unmistakeable cough of a handgun with a silencer, saw the young man fall to the pavement. Knew instinctively, because he'd seen such things happen before, that he was dead.

In one swift movement, Ted dumped his snack, grabbed his photo ID from his jacket pocket to hang round his neck, leapt out of the car and sprinted across the road between vehicles. His eyes were still glued to the rear of the motorbike which had jumped the red light and disappeared off to the left.

'Target is down. Shot. Two persons on a motorbike,' he announced into his mouthpiece.

Because of living with Trev, he knew a bit about bikes and was able to give a make and probable model, as well as part of the number plate, although he knew it would be a false one. It would be replaced as soon as the bike could leave the road, heading as it no doubt was for a pre-planned secure place. It had all the hallmarks of a professional hit.

There weren't many pedestrians about to get in the way but people were beginning to get out of their cars, milling about, some pulling out mobile phones and starting to film. The ghoulish modern instinct to try to be the first to post something gory on social media.

Ted waved his ID then started ordering people to get back in their cars to clear a way for an ambulance, although he could see immediately that it was pointless. Gina Shaw came hurrying out of the garden area, her face pale and set in an anxious expression. Ted knew it was essential for her not to blow her cover so made sure not to show any sign of recognition.

'Can you keep back, please, miss,' he told her. 'More police and an ambulance have been called. If you saw anything, we'll need to get your statement. That's my car over there, the Renault. Would you like to go and sit in that and I'll come and talk to you very shortly.'

'I didn't see a lot, officer,' she told him. 'I don't know who this person is. I've never seen him before. I just saw him fall to the ground.'

She was looking at him hard, making sure he'd correctly interpreted the meaning of her words. Whoever the person was, lying in a pool of his own blood on the pavement, he was not their intended target, Data.

None of the other team members appeared from wherever they were watching and waiting. Ted understood. They couldn't afford for any of them to risk the identities they'd carefully created for themselves by appearing on the scene. They would make themselves scarce and there would be a pre-agreed place for all of them to meet up to debrief after the operation.

It would be up to Ted to stay in place and make sure that the first responders were made aware of the delicacy of the situation. He hoped they wouldn't be too long arriving. He wanted to hand over as soon as possible then go with Gina to find out what could have gone so catastrophically wrong.

He had so much to keep an eye on that he didn't spot the big black 4x4 which pulled out of another side street nearby and drove away from the scene before it was closed off.

There were two rear-seat passengers. One man was a dwarf, barely above four feet tall, mirrored shades hiding his

224

eyes, a white stick propped up next to him against the seat. The other was a young Asian man, slim, strikingly attractive, expensive clothes.

The man in the glasses moved his arm and put one of his small hands on his companion's thigh, giving it a squeeze.

'You see, young Data? You see how precious you are to the Big Man? He would never risk any harm coming to you. When he got wind that there was going to be a reception committee waiting for you, he wanted to check it out. The other boy was expendable. Pretty enough, but without your brains. Now you know you can trust him completely. Now you know the lengths to which he and the rest of us will go to protect you.'

Apart from directing Ted where to drive to, Gina Shaw was quiet on the short journey to the debriefing venue. They weren't going to her office this time. It turned out to be a back room in something like a warehouse. Anonymous and sparsely furnished. It did at least have a kettle. The rest of the team were already there and had brewed up. The mood was tense, angry.

'What the fuck happened back there?' the one who'd previously been aggressive now sounded more belligerent than ever. 'All those weeks planning this and we lose this Data lad at the last minute? How the hell did they know we were there waiting?'

Gina hadn't yet told them it was the wrong person. She did so now.

'That wasn't Data, Derek. At least not the Data I've been speaking to and buying from. He looked a lot like him. Same hairstyle, wore the same sort of clothes he does, but it wasn't him.'

'So who or what the fuck tipped them off?'

Derek was looking straight at Ted as he asked the question, the meaning behind his words clear.

Ted returned his look as he replied, keeping his tone as measured as he usually did.

'Think about it, Derek. Even if somehow someone had spotted me and ID'd me as a police officer – bearing in mind I didn't have any visible ID and I was in my own car – that still wouldn't make any sense. They clearly knew well in advance that something was going to happen, otherwise how did they have the time to sort a ringer to go to the RV in place of the real Data? They sent in someone who was expendable to them to check that the coast was clear.

'Somehow, and we don't yet know how, they got wind that it was a set-up. I'm not playing the "I told you so" card here, but I did mention that the sort of Specials we know operate with this gang will be fine-tuned to the slightest thing out of the ordinary.

'You'll need to have an inquiry into what went wrong, of course. But can I suggest you don't overlook any possibility, no matter how extreme, from hacking phone and radio frequencies to the presence of a mole within your team.'

It was late by the time Ted got home. Trev and the cats were still up, watching television together, sprawled on the sofa. Trev moved enough cats for Ted to sit down but from the look on his face Ted guessed there had been something on the news about the shooting.

'Ted, you promised. It wasn't supposed to be anything dangerous and it's been all over the local news about a shooting in Manchester. Was that what you were involved with?'

Ted leaned back against the cushions and closed his eyes. He picked up his partner's hand, kissed it and kept hold of it as he said, 'Can we not do this now? Please? It's been a totally crap end to the day. It was supposed to be a straightforward op with no firearms involved. It all went completely tits up and now I've got some of the Drugs team looking at me like I'm the enemy within and deliberately screwed their operation. So can we just talk meaningless rubbish like so many other married couples at the end of a hard day. Please?'

Chapter Twenty-three

Ted had an early-morning meeting with the Ice Queen. He'd phoned her briefly the previous evening to let her know of the failed operation. He wasn't surprised to hear she already knew. It wasn't her division, but she always seemed to have a handle on what was going on.

Trev had still been fast asleep when Ted was ready to leave, so he'd contented himself with planting a kiss on top of his black curls, which had provoked no reaction.

The coffee machine was on when Ted walked into Debra Caldwell's office, after a brief knock for form's sake. He'd not long had his morning brew, but the coffee she put in front of him had an inviting aroma.

He gave her a quick summary of what had happened and was anticipating her first remark. She was also firearms trained, an excellent shot with a hand gun.

'A single fatal body shot from the back of a moving motor-bike at a distance? That's impressive. And professional. Do you have a theory?'

Ted took a swallow of his coffee before he answered.

'This isn't about point scoring,' he began.

'I think I know you well enough by now to know that,' she interrupted him.

'I was concerned from the outset that not all of Gina Shaw's team seemed to take the potential threat of the Special Forces involvement seriously. You and I have both trained with some of those types, under Mr Green. We both know that it doesn't do to underestimate them. Ever. They must have been on to the set-up well in advance. They had to find someone who looked like Data as a decoy, for a start.'

'Why shoot him, before he even got to the meeting point?'

'They could have spotted something which alerted them, although the Drugs team were professional and not all that obvious. Gina Shaw, in particular, seems to have excellent cover in place. She's not just playing the marketing role, she clearly knows her stuff and does it well.

'They obviously couldn't risk the stand-in falling into police hands, on the off chance he might be able to tell them something which could lead back to them. That's highly unlikely, but they wouldn't want to run any risks.'

He paused to drink more coffee.

'A possible explanation, one none of us ever likes to consider, is a tip-off from inside the team. A bent copper somewhere along the chain. I'll give Gina a call at some point today to see what the latest is. I imagine she'll be in bits. That's her cover totally blown beyond redemption. I doubt she'll be able to work in the field in Manchester again. Certainly not for a long time.'

He drained his coffee and stood up to leave.

'I'd better go and tell the team. It's a disappointment for us too, of course. Without Data, we've nothing with which to wrap up our loose ends, and I can't see how we're going to get another chance for the foreseeable future.

'Oh, and I wanted to remind you that I've put in for some leave, coming up shortly. There's somewhere I need to be. For Trev.'

'We're all entitled to time away from the job, Ted. It's essential if we are to retain our sanity.'

She knew that Ted never liked talking much about his private life at work, so he surprised her when he smiled and said, 'That's good to hear. Because I have a feeling that if I let him down this time, he really might leave me.'

All of the team members were in the briefing room when Ted went in to join them from the Super's office. Even Alan Burgess, after a couple of late starts which he'd tried to blame on traffic, had cleaned up his act and begun making sure he arrived on time.

'Before we start with our own cases, an update from yesterday's op,' Ted told them. 'Not good news, I'm afraid. Once again, we didn't get Data. It went wrong in a big way. A switch was made. Another young man turned up and was shot dead by someone unidentified.

'Now, we don't know at this stage whether he was connected or was an unfortunate passer-by. A simple case of mistaken identity. The fact that he looked and dressed like the person Gina Shaw, the Drugs officer, has been in contact with as Data, is probably too much of a coincidence. But as of now, we are back to the starting block in our efforts to get any further with the case.

'So, Jo, Mike, have you got any good news of progress to share, please?'

'A bit of light on the horizon with Sandstone Street, boss,' Mike told him. 'Jezza, why don't you start?'

'Boss, since the boy started talking to us, it seems he's hardly stopped since. Dolly and Aileen, the ladies looking after him, say he's even talking to them about it now. Maurice and I are going to another meeting later this morning to discuss in detail, with the experts, if it would be in his best interests to allow him to testify.'

'And it's really rattled our suspect to hear that,' Mike continued. 'I spoke to him again at length late yesterday. You know Ms Castle of old, of course, boss, and she doesn't give much away. But it's still clear that she's concerned at the prospects for her client if there are two eyewitnesses, including the boy.

'It clearly never entered our suspect's head that the boy would say anything to anyone. It's almost as if he thought he had him so brainwashed and terrified of him that he would never dare. And he was stunned to hear of the upstairs witness. With it taking him so long to come forward, he must have thought he was in the clear as far as the neighbours are concerned.'

'I'm planning on some desk time today, so I'll talk to CPS. I agree with you, Mike, Ms Castle is never going to let him admit to premeditation because she knows we can't prove it. Let me have the up to date file, please. We've probably got enough for a manslaughter charge. It's certainly an unlawful act to throw someone down a stairwell. It's demonstrably dangerous and clearly any sober and reasonable person would recognise the danger. Don't get your hopes up too soon though, everyone, but this is looking good.

'Jo, any update from Damson Drive?'

'I'm filled with envy for Mike's success. Steve and I have been back there yet again, still with nothing to show for our efforts. We took Jan and Avril with us from Uniform and they went talking to the neighbours while Steve and I did one more sweep of the house and garden. Still nothing to be seen. We'll have one more go at door-to-door today, to cover all bases, but I think we need to free up the house now.

'The husband's been off work all week, staying with his brother, but I've spoken to him and he's anxious to get back to the job as soon as he can. I imagine it will be some comfort for him. And that's going to mean him needing his car, which has been parked there all week.'

'Can we search it first, sir? Or at least get dogs round it and in the garden?' Steve had a stubborn set to his jaw as he asked.

Ted really didn't want to have to put him down with not only the full team there, but also the officers from elsewhere. But he clearly needed to say something.

'If the forensic results come in today and if they indicate anything, I'll see what I can do, Steve. As regards dogs, I don't think that's even possible. As far as I know, from my limited experience of working with them, they're individually trained to a specific scent. I don't think there are any yet which are trained to detect things like GHB, for instance. So unless and until we know if any drugs were used at all, and specifically which they were, if so, I think we're out of luck on that score.'

Ted was on a video call with the CPS when his mobile phone rang. The screen showed him it was Gina Shaw calling him. He excused himself for long enough to take it and to promise to call her back as soon as he could, then returned to discussing his cases.

The files for the Sandstone Streets flats case had already gone through to the prosecutor he was speaking to. She'd only had time for a brief glance before they spoke, but her verdict was encouraging.

'I think you have enough there to charge him with manslaughter and bail him for now, Ted. Based on what we have so far, especially if the boy is a witness, I doubt there's a jury that wouldn't convict him, to be honest. I know you and your team will keep digging right up to trial, but I'm happy enough for him to be charged on what we have so far. Will you want to oppose bail?'

'I think that might be pushing it, Laura. We've no reason to suppose he might reoffend. I'd want reporting conditions, and we could ask for a residency requirement somewhere other than at the flat because of the risk to witnesses. He doesn't know where the boy is, so there should be no danger of him trying to approach and influence him.

'As far as the presumed murder-suicide at Damson Drive goes, that's still what it is, for now. A presumed case of a mother killing her child then taking her own life. One of my officers suspects there might be more to it than that, but at the moment we have no evidence at all to back up his theory. I'll keep you posted on any progress, though, although I appreciate it might not be you handling that case.'

He ended the call then phoned Gina back as promised. He couldn't begin to imagine how she was feeling after the total disaster of the day before. She sounded subdued as she answered his call.

'Thanks for calling back, Ted, I really appreciate it. I know you have your own cases to deal with but I was really in need of a friendly voice and yours always sounds nice.'

'Tough day?'

'The worst. I'm toast here. I clearly can't work undercover in Manchester again for the foreseeable future. Probably never again. Which means picking myself up and starting out afresh somewhere new. Goodness knows where. And we still have to find out what went wrong with it all. We were so careful. With the benefit of hindsight, we should have taken more notice of your warnings, though.

'My problem is my immediate boss is a real Neanderthal. He's a walking stereotype from crime fiction. Straight out of *Life on Mars*. The sort who should have disappeared years ago but he's managed to hang on, and I dread to think how.

'The training courses on "All police officers are equal, even the women"? He must have been at home with a sick note. Two failed marriages, kids who hate him, drinks like a fish, chain-smokes, bends every rule in the book, but somehow gets the results. He's been dying for me to come unstuck. To make it worse, he's pretending to be supportive, which makes me want to throw up. Luckily the next level up are more modern and more reasonable, so I might get the offer of a transfer somewhere else to start again.

'Anyway, I was phoning to ask a massive favour, and it's really presumptuous, as I barely know you.'

'If I can help you with anything, I will.'

'Have you got time after work to meet up for a drink? I could get the train down because I should warn you, I'm not planning to stop at one drink. Only I need to talk to another officer, one not directly involved in our case, but with specialist knowledge around it. I'm not allowed to talk to any of my team pending the various inquiries.'

'You're suspended?'

'No, not officially, but I have been told to claim some of my outstanding leave, for the time being. I know it's a big ask, but I'd be really grateful, if you're free.'

'You're in luck, as it happens. My partner's going to London this weekend so I'm on my own. I don't drink anyway so I'm happy to drive up there, if it makes it easier for you?'

'No, really, that's very kind of you, but Manchester doesn't feel like a good place for me to be at the moment, so I'd welcome the chance to get away.'

'There's a pub near the nick. The Grapes. I'll give the landlord a call. I can usually use the back room, if there's nothing on, for a quiet chat. And they do food, if you fancy something.'

'Thanks, Ted, it's really kind of you. I appreciate it. I'll see you later.'

Ted found Gina Shaw waiting for him in the bar of The Grapes, nursing a large gin and tonic. He was shocked by the change in her appearance. Not only the designer suit and high heels replaced by jeans and a baggy cardigan, the minimal make-up, and the hair pulled back into a casual pony tail. Her posture had lost all its former self-assurance. She looked younger, vulnerable. Defeated, even.

He could understand why she chose to talk to someone more on the outside of her team, and why it needed to be another copper. He'd no idea if she had a partner of any kind. If she did, no matter how supportive they might be, they couldn't begin to imagine how she was feeling right now.

'This is really kind of you, Ted, I appreciate it. I'm in the chair, so what are you having?'

Dave, the landlord, had come over when the door had opened. When he saw who it was, he asked, 'Usual, Ted?'

'Thanks, Dave. Are we still okay to use the back room?'

'Shop talk? Help yourselves, we're not exactly crowded out, as you can see. Will you be eating?'

Ted looked towards Gina.

'I suppose I should, if I'm planning on drinking. Are you sure I'm not keeping you from something more interesting than listening to me whinge about work?'

'Really, it's fine. I'll come and get the menu when we're ready, Dave.'

Ted waited for her to take a long swallow from her drink, once they were settled in the back room, before starting up the conversation she'd come to have.

'Do you have a theory, about what happened?'

'The only theory that makes any kind of sense is a mole on the team somewhere. But I don't even want to think about that. I've worked with all of them for ages. I would have said I knew them all well and they were sound. But like you pointed out, this wasn't a spur of the moment thing. It took some planning, so they knew in advance.'

Ted took a drink of his Gunner before he posed his next question. It was a tricky one to ask, especially to someone he hardly knew at all.

'And Ian Bradley? You said he was off the radar, out of contact. In deep. Is it possible it was him? The mole?'

'It's the logical thing to think, isn't it? Is he so deep in his cover he's gone over to the other side? But I've known Ian longer than anyone. I would have said I knew him better than anyone else. But someone clearly tipped them off that we were on to them and it was a set-up to bring Data in.

'If it was Ian, his info would still have had to come from within the team. I've not had contact with him for ages and I didn't think anyone else had. I'd really struggle to believe it was Ian, though I know we can't rule out any possibility.'

'It can happen, of course. We had something with a sergeant here. None of us would have believed what came out about him, but it turned out he had a really serious gambling addiction none of us knew about. It led to him doing all sorts of stuff none of us would every have believed him capable of.'

Gina Shaw was on the point of replying when Ted's phone rang. Trev calling.

'Sorry, it's my partner, I'd better take it.'

'Of course, I need to go to the ladies anyway. Shall I bring the menu? And are you ready for another drink?'

He nodded to the first but put his hand over his glass. He'd scarcely made a dent in it.

'Did you make the train all right?' he asked when he answered the call.

'Yes, and don't worry, officer, I'm in a quiet zone, I'm not breaching any regulations. But you'll never guess what. You might not have heard yet. There's been another shooting! Manchester is getting worse than Detroit, it seems. It was very close to the station. We were late leaving because of it and everywhere being in chaos. I think we were lucky to get away at all. There were police appearing everywhere.'

'But you're all right? Were there any injuries, any fatalities?'

'I haven't been able to find out any details yet. They're just talking about an exchange of gunfire near to the station but not much more than that so far. Are you at home yet? Can you put the telly on? They might have more info by now.'

'I'm in The Grapes. With a woman.'

'Ted Darling, you swine, I've not even got as far as Crewe and you're two-timing me!' Trev said teasingly. 'I'd better leave you to it, then. Let me know if you hear anything, though, I'm all agog. And don't be late home. The pussy cats will be starving. Love you.'

'They really won't, you know. And me too,' Ted said awkwardly, as Gina had come back into the room, carrying two menus and another drink for herself.

'There's been another shooting, up near Piccadilly,' he told her as she sat back down. 'Have you heard anything?'

She pulled her mobile out of the large shoulder bag she had with her, checked the screen and told him, 'Nothing from anybody. I suppose everyone's been told not to contact me.'

She was flicking deftly through the phone as she spoke until she found the site she was looking for.

'They're saying an exchange of gunfire near to the station, with not many further details. No signs of any bodies or of anyone injured and no arrests made to date. Unless they're not saying, for some reason.'

She looked up at Ted, frowning. 'You don't think it could in any way be connected with what happened yesterday, do you? It's not as if shootings are a daily occurrence in Manchester.'

'Too early to jump to any conclusions, until we have any more details. Now, if you tell me what you want to eat, I'll go and order. And do you want me to get you another drink while I'm going to the bar? Some wine with the meal, perhaps?'

It was a very much merrier Gina whom Ted drove back to the hotel she'd booked herself for the night, on the station approach. She'd insisted she was fit to walk there, but Ted didn't fancy her chances of getting there in one piece, left to her own devices. He even escorted her the short distance from the nearest parking into the hotel reception to make sure she got there safely. Once she was checked in, he put her into the lift and pressed the correct floor button, but he wasn't going to take the risk of going with her in case she got the wrong idea and he found himself in a compromising position.

It always felt strange walking into a dark and empty house, whenever Trev was away. Ted was met with accusing glances from the cats as soon as he put the lights on. He knew Trev would have left them with plenty of food to keep them going, but he still went to freshen their bowls and clean up after them. He knew he'd get no peace from them until he did so.

Then he took his jacket, tie and shoes off and went to sit on the sofa to put the TV on. He flicked through various news channels until he found one running a piece on the Manchester shooting. Details were still sketchy but it featured a senior police officer Ted knew doing a piece to camera, appealing for witnesses.

'In particular we're keen to hear from two people on a motorbike who were seen leaving the scene at speed shortly after the shooting.'

Chapter Twenty-four

It was shortly before five in the morning when Ted was jerked from a fitful sleep by the sound of his mobile phone on the bedside table. His mind had been churning most of the night, going over and over the failed Drugs operation, trying to identify anything he'd missed at the time.

The incoming call was masked so he answered it with a guarded, 'Hello?'

'I need you, Gayboy. Now.'

The familiar voice of Ted's special skills instructor, Mr Green. He rattled off a grid reference, said, 'And bring a first aid kit,' before he rang off abruptly.

Ted knew it was futile to ask questions, even if Green hadn't ended the call. The man's response to any such attempt was always the same: 'Ask me no questions, I'll tell you no lies.'

He dressed hurriedly, dumped some emergency rations into bowls for the cats, grabbed his car keys and was just about to open the front door when he spotted young Adam sitting halfway down the stairs, looking at him reproachfully. None of the other cats had stirred at his departure.

'I'm sorry. I won't be long, hopefully, but I have to go. Don't look at me like that.'

He checked where he was going with an app on his phone. His Renault didn't boast anything as sophisticated as a sat nav. He wasn't surprised to discover that his destination was on a remote road, one which wound over the moors above Glossop heading out towards Woodhead.

There wasn't much traffic at that time in the morning. Ted found the appointed spot easily enough; a stopping place set back from the road with plenty of tree cover close to. He parked as far from the road as he could, so his car wouldn't be immediately visible to anyone driving past.

There was no sign of a living soul about, nor of any other vehicle. He didn't expect there to be. Wherever Green was, he would be watching to make sure there was no one else in sight before he appeared.

Ted tried to stay as alert as possible, watching for Green, and for anyone else who might be about. He still jumped when a dark form slid soundlessly out of the shadows, opened the front passenger door and sat down with a wince of evident pain.

'Did you bring the first aid kit?' was Green's opening remark.

He was holding his right arm across his chest, the hand up on his left shoulder.

Ted could see fresh blood on his hand. He reached behind the seats for the green box with the white cross on it. As he pulled it forward it touched the back of Green's arm. Green spat a word in a language Ted didn't recognise, although he got the gist of it and hastily apologised.

'You're supposed to be here to render first aid, Gayboy, not finish me off.'

'What kind of an injury are we looking at? Apart from a bleed. Can you get your jacket off?'

'Gunshot. And you'll have to cut everything. Whenever I move, it bleeds like a bastard again. Have you got a knife?' he asked as if it were a thing anyone would carry in their car.

The best Ted could offer was a pair of scissors for dressings which he knew would struggle to cut sticking plaster.

Green did no more than give a tut of annoyance before reaching awkwardly behind himself with his left hand and producing a formidable bladed weapon, which must have been in a sheath on the back of his belt.

Ted managed cautiously to slide the top of Green's jacket down out of the way without cutting it. The knife was every bit as sharp as he'd feared it would be and he was worried about inflicting further injury with the wicked metal edge. It bit through the top layer of a sweatshirt and made short work of the wicking T-shirt underneath to reveal the site of the wound.

Now Ted was starting to get concerned. If a professional with Green's skills had got himself badly injured then, whatever he was up to back in the area, things were serious.

There was a field dressing of sorts in place but it was soaked through with blood. Ted didn't dare to try to lift it to assess the damage in case he made the bleeding worse. He knew he should simply apply another one over the top and try to contain the bleed as best he could. Not an easy task in the confines of a small Renault.

'How long ago did it happen?' Ted risked a question to help him with his assessment of the injury and the action needed.

'Ask me no questions ...' Green began to trot out the familiar phrase but Ted cut across him.

'This is me doing triage, not asking random questions. I need to know timings so I can do the right thing to sort it. To assess how much blood you've lost, for one thing.'

Green made a movement like half a shrug with his one good shoulder.

'A good few hours ago now. Look, Gayboy, stop yapping and slap a good tight dressing on it. I can't get it tight enough with one hand. Then I need you to find me a safe place to stay for a day or two until it starts to heal.'

'I can't take you to my place ...' Ted began.

'Don't be soft, Gayboy. They know where you live.'

His words sent an instant chill through Ted's blood.

His mind went into overdrive. He was thinking back to some time ago.

To Trev in tears. To a little cat laid to rest in the garden.

He wanted to ask who 'They' were. Part of him thought he might be better off not knowing. The analytical side of his brain was racing, examining the possibilities. Mr Green, the supposedly retired mercenary, suddenly back in the area. An exchange of gunfire the evening before, near to a main station in Manchester. The station from where Trev had set off in connection with a trial against a highly placed establishment figure.

Coincidence, he told himself firmly. Coincidences happened all the time in real life.

'Not like you to come off worse in anything,' he told Green, as he unwrapped several dressings and got bandages ready.

'You should see the other bloke,' Green responded in a rare moment of humour.

'This needs medical attention. It's soaking through the dressings as fast as I put them on.'

'No hospitals, no doctors. You should know the drill by now, Gayboy.'

'It might need blood vessels tying off or something. It's still bleeding like a good 'un. I know someone who might be able to help us. And she's likely to be awake this early, too.'

'No doctors,' Green repeated.

'She's not a doctor. She's a pathologist.'

Green made a sound which might have been amusement.

'That's a bit premature.'

'It won't be if it gets infected. Let me call her, at least.'

'Put it on speaker. I want to know what's being said. Can you vouch for her?'

'One hundred per cent.'

Ted got his phone out and did as he'd been instructed. He spoke the minute the call was answered. He didn't want Green to hear Bizzie call him by his full name, so he set the tone by addressing her formally.

'Professor? It's Ted. I need some help and it's probably highly unethical.'

'How very intriguing! What can I do for you?'

'I'm with a ...' he hesitated. Friend was certainly stretching things. '... an acquaintance who's been injured. There's a lot of bleeding and I can't get it under control with pressure. Shoulder wound. He needs someone who knows what they're doing to look at it, and he needs somewhere to crash until he can move on. It's a huge ask, I know.'

'What kind of a wound?' Bizzie asked.

Ted looked to Green to know how much to divulge over the phone. He spoke for himself.

'Green here. It's a gunshot wound. So this is strictly off the radar. Which is why I can't go to A&E.'

'I see,' she said, her tone neutral. 'Ted,' she was taking her lead from him, from the name he'd used when speaking to her first. 'Is this acquaintance of yours trustworthy?'

Ted was looking directly at Green as he replied, 'I would never turn my back on him. But he's house-trained. A good cook, too. And at the moment he's bleeding all over my car.'

'In which case, you'd better bring him here. Heaven knows there are plenty of empty rooms in a house this size. You know that I can even burn ready meals. Douglas does his best but his repertoire is limited, so the cooking sounds like a fair exchange, if he can manage it. I can't see him in any kind of official medical capacity of course, except as a humble first aider, you understand. But by the sounds of it, if you leave it too long, I would have the pleasure of his company in my autopsy suite unless you bring him here, so I'll see you shortly.'

'Half an hour, at least. And thank you.'

'Are you sure this is wise, Gayboy? You know I have trust issues.'

Ted had had to help Green on with the seat belt. Despite the amount of dressings he'd put on the wound, blood was already starting to soak through them.

'You can trust the Professor. She's very discreet. It's not like you to get hit, though. And I thought you'd retired for good. So what happened?' Ted risked another question, once they were on the way.

The movement of the car on the rough surface as they made their way back to the road clearly caused Green some pain.

'There was an urgent job. They needed someone skilled and expendable. Which is why they called me. I made them pay through the nose. The grandson wants a pony. He can now have a stableful if he wants, with what I charged. It was done in a rush and the intel was bad. I should have done my own recce. Should never have trusted them to get it right. Because of the time-frame, I did, and you can see the result. But the job was done.'

It was a long speech for him, and an unusually frank one. Ted was itching to ask more but didn't dare push it. They drove the rest of the way in silence.

Bizzie had clearly been anticipating their arrival. She'd opened up the gates to the driveway and was hovering, looking out for them. Ted drove straight in.

Green opened the car door and made to get out but was starting to look decidedly wobbly. Ted hurried to help him, knowing he would hate every moment of it.

'Professor Nelson, Mr Green,' he said by way of introduction.

'And not before time, by the looks of things. Let's get you into the house and see what we're looking at here. Then I think it would be a good idea for you to make yourself scarce, Ted,' she told him, again avoiding his full name in front of Green. 'This is clearly all highly irregular, so I think the fewer of us who are involved the better, don't you?'

It was still early, so Ted decided to go back to the house before heading into the station, as he had planned. He'd need a shower and a clean-up. So would the car seat. There was still blood on his clothes and his hands. He could also take the time to do some apologising to the cats. More than anything he wanted to phone Trev, to check that he was all right, as soon as it was a suitable hour to find him up and about.

The sudden appearance of Green on a mission had rattled Ted. It was perfectly possible that he'd been the person on the back of the motorbike on Thursday. The one who had shot the Data lookalike. Although the wound suggested that his injury had happened more recently than that incident. It may have been him at the shooting near the station the previous day. It could even be something which had not yet come to light.

Whatever had brought him out of retirement might have had nothing to do with either of the shootings in Manchester. But his mention of the mysterious 'They' and the timing of his presence made all sorts of thoughts start racing through Ted's mind. He'd only feel reassured once he'd spoken to his partner and made sure he was safe.

'Hi, I hope I didn't wake you,' he told Trev when, freshly showered and changed, and the right side of bacon sandwiches and a mug of tea, he phoned him in London.

'I've been awake for hours, or so it seems. Eirian is a total sadist and woke me up disgustingly early to make sure I'm not late. Teenagers today! How can she possibly be my sister? I don't think I ever surfaced before lunchtime when I was her age, except to do horsey things, but she wants to do all the shops while I'm tied up.'

'And is it okay? Are you okay? Being back in the flat?'

'It's the weirdest thing. Part of it is like I've never been away. Part of it is as if I'm somewhere I've never been before. I wouldn't sleep in my old room. Too many memories. I've got the guest room. I've never slept in there before. But it's fine. I'm fine.

'Are you all right? Any more excitement? Are you going in to work today?'

'Yes, I need some desk time to catch up with myself. And no, nothing exciting.

It wasn't a lie, Ted told himself. It was merely giving facts on a need to know basis. At least, that's how he squared it with his conscience.

'I hope it all goes well for you today. Take care of yourself in that big city.'

Jo and Steve were both in for the day and Ted wanted to take the opportunity of sitting down with them to go over everything they had so far for the Damson Drive case. There were still no forensic results in, but Ted hadn't yet had time to go over all the statements taken from neighbours concerning the family and what was known about them. If the blood tests revealed nothing they could act on, he wanted to see if there was anything else which would justify digging deeper into the case or whether it would be up to an inquest to determine what had happened.

They got together in Jo's office. Jo was collating everything they had, including the statements from neighbours. He gave Ted a summary.

'Most of the neighbours knew about the details of the boy's problems. Some invited the lad round to be with their children for things like birthday parties. The father had explained the situation to them, because the boy had those flare-ups of getting angry if he didn't understand things, although they all say he was never violent to the others. He might shout and throw things but knowing his history, they all seemed to be kind and helpful towards him. Not all of them knew anything about the twin daughter, the one in care, but the family only moved to Damson Drive when the money came through from their claim against the hospital trust.'

'I've been checking media reports, sir,' Steve told him.

'There was a lot about the case when the family made their claim. It was a big payout because the brain damage to the girl was catastrophic and the hospital was found to have been negligent in the care provided.'

'And the money is to provide for her ongoing care?' Ted queried. 'Is that not available to her free from the NHS?'

'There's different levels of care, sir. She could get basic care free, yes. According to everything I've read, there's virtually no chance of her ever improving from the state she's in. But the father has chosen to stay optimistic. He's put her in a special place where there's all kinds of therapy. Physio, aqua therapy, all sorts of stuff, which is where the money goes.'

'So that would be another difficulty in building a case against him. If he had a motive to kill any of his family, surely it would have been the daughter? She must take an emotional toll on them, as well as a financial one. And he appears to be a model parent, as far as she's concerned, at least. What else do the neighbours say about him?'

'We took Al Burgess with us this time, boss, and he proved to be surprisingly good at getting people to talk to him. It took a lot of cups of tea, though. Almost universal praise for the father. They see him as a hard-working essential service worker who does his best for his family in the face of considerable difficulties.

'The wife doesn't mix much at all, although is perfectly polite and civil when they see her. They all seem to know she suffers from some sort of depressive illness. There was nothing at all from any of the neighbours to suggest either she or the boy were in any way afraid of the husband and father.

'There was one neighbour who did say something which might possibly be an indicator of another side to him, though. She has a son, similar age to the boy, who they invited to their house for a party one time. They were playing some sort of game he didn't understand so he got angry and started shouting. She couldn't manage to calm him down and it was upsetting some of the other children, so she phoned his dad to come and collect him.

'He'd just come off a busy shift and she said he was a bit sharper than he usually was. He would normally speak quietly, the boy would calm down and he'd take him home, happily enough. That time he actually grabbed the lad by the arm, which made the boy react, and for a moment, she said it looked as if things might actually kick off between them. Then the father seemed to get a grip of himself, let go of the boy, and the two of them went off quietly together.

'So in summary, we have absolutely nothing to indicate any tension, let alone violence, in the household. A bit the reverse, in fact. The picture painted is more of someone with the patience of a saint in trying circumstances.'

'Sir, should we at least be asking questions about the man's character and behaviour where he works? For background? In particular, should I try to find out what sort of a shift he'd had at work on the day of the incident? In the absence of any other motive, if I could find out if it had been a particularly difficult shift, that might explain why he snapped, if that's what he did?'

'That would fit if he killed the boy in a sudden loss of control. But not with your theory of him setting his wife up to take the blame. Until we get those blood results back, we really can't do anything. Certainly not be seen to be treating him as a potential suspect at this point. All we can do is wait, for now, Steve.'

Ted stayed behind when Steve left the office. As soon as the door shut behind him, Jo said, 'He's getting totally obsessed, isn't he? Time to pull him off the case? Working closely with him on it, it's becoming obvious that he's not carrying out an impartial investigation. He's specifically looking for ways of making his theory fit. Is he going to fall apart at the seams when he finally finds out there's no case to be made?'

'You think the husband is innocent, then?'

'I wouldn't necessarily go that far. I haven't talked to him to form any sort of an opinion. What I would say is that, short of the bloods producing a miracle, we have absolutely nothing on which to build a case against him. And I'm seriously worried about how Steve will cope when that becomes clear to him.'

Chapter Twenty-five

Ted was surprised to find Steve working away at his desk when he walked into the main office on Sunday morning. Doubly so as he knew that he was not on the rota to work that day. It was still early. No one else was yet in.

'You're not down to work today, Steve.'

'Don't worry, sir, I'm not counting the hours. There was something I thought about last night and I wanted to come in and go over the notes again to see if I could pin down what it was.'

'Go home, Steve,' Ted told him. 'We're given days off for a reason. Once we get the test results through, it will be all systems go to work on the file, whichever way it turns out. Until then, there really is no point in you going over anything. Go home.'

'But, sir ...'

'I can make it an order if you want me to, Steve, but I'd rather not have to. Go and have a break. Why not take Bill out somewhere? Grumpy old bugger that he is, it would do him good. But go home.'

For a brief instant, Ted thought Steve was going to defy him and refuse to leave. But then, flushing dark red and clearly not happy, he shut down his computer, stood up, grabbed his things and left the office without another word.

Ted sighed. With everything else he had going on, the last thing he needed was the normally most compliant and timid member of his team to start playing the rebel. He got his mobile phone out as he went into his office.

'Bill? Ted. I need a favour. I've had to send Steve home. He's not meant to be in today but he's getting totally obsessed with this latest case. I told him to go home and take you out somewhere. I owe you a pint if you let him.'

'Bloody hell, Ted. Me, go out somewhere on a Sunday? When every man and his dog will be out clogging up the roads and getting in the way? That will take more than a pint. Where do you expect me to go, anyway?'

'I don't know. Anywhere that's not the nick or a crime scene. Certainly nowhere near Damson Drive. A park? A car boot? A garden centre?'

'With screaming kids running round everywhere out of control? Are you trying to get me arrested for losing it and slapping one of them?'

'A meal and as many pints as you like? A decent bottle of Scotch? Come on, Bill, don't make me beg. I'm worried about him. I actually had to pull rank to get him to go and you know that's not like our Steve.'

Bill gave a theatrical sigh.

'There's a special new food I want to try for Jack and only the garden centre up Otterspool stocks it. I don't feel like driving because the old leg injury is playing up, so perhaps Steve could take me there. He loves my bird almost as much as I do, so he might go for that. Does that sound convincing enough?'

Ted chuckled his relief.

'And the Oscar for the best actor in a dramatic role goes to … Thanks, Bill. I owe you, big time.'

'I won't let you forget it.'

Ted's next call was to Bizzie Nelson. He'd held off talking to her the evening before, not wanting to bother her. He was already so much in her debt for helping him out with Green.

She answered on the first ring, bright and breezy as ever.

'Edwin! And before you worry that your mysterious friend is listening, he's having some breakfast out in the garden with

Douglas. The two of them are getting on like a house on fire. In contrast, Spilsbury is very wary of him indeed, and you know how friendly he is normally. Although your friend does seem to eye the pup with a rather culinary interest.'

'Sensible dog. I don't blame him. I really can never thank you enough for helping out though, Bizzie. I couldn't think of anyone else to ask, but I really don't want to cause any trouble for you.'

'I doubt there will be any repercussions. There's no reason why anyone would know he's here.'

Ted hesitated. He wasn't entirely convinced. It would rather depend on who Green had rubbed up the wrong way this time.

'Be careful though, all the same. Especially of Mr Green. Sometimes he works for the good guys, but you can't always rely on that.'

'Oh, I'm under no illusions, believe me. But for the moment, he's being quite charming.'

Her description didn't quite tally with the Mr Green Ted knew, although he realised he was a chameleon who could change his colours to suit the company he was in.

'And is he all right?' he asked. 'The injury, I mean?'

'He will be, but not immediately. You were right to call on professional help when you did or things could have been much worse.'

'I really am in your debt for this, Bizzie. You must let me take you and Douglas out for a meal some time, with Trev, to show my gratitude.'

'That would be delightful. As long as our house guest doesn't murder us in our bed before he leaves, to guard his anonymity,' Bizzie said jokingly.

Ted wished she hadn't said that. He could guarantee nothing where Green was concerned.

He tried a quick call to Trev, to see if his sister had woken him early again. He knew he had another morning with the support group for the victims of his abuser, in preparation for the upcoming trial, but then he would catch a mid-afternoon train back home. He'd spoken to him at length the evening before but with Green's presence still playing on his mind, he couldn't shake off the feelings of anxiety.

'Are you all set for today? Did Eirian get you up at sparrow's fart again?'

'She slept like a baby. I plied her with wine at dinner, so I could sleep in.'

'She's under age.'

'Oh, Ted, stop being a boring policeman. It's very nearly legal, with a meal. And you know perfectly well she looks and acts as if she's in her twenties. Anyway, she's off shopping when she surfaces, we're having lunch together then catching our respective trains.'

'Leave the bike in Manchester tonight. Get off in Stockport. I'll sort you a taxi to work for the morning and if you let me know what time your train gets in today, I'll come and collect you from the station.'

'Ted, that's so sweet, but I can easily go and get the bike.'

'Humour me. Please. I've missed you.'

Ted had to end the call at that point before Trev's response made him blush. He'd heard Mike and Virgil's voices in the outer office so he went out to talk to them both. He hadn't yet caught up with Mike about his latest interview with the Sandstone Street suspect. Mike had spoken to the man late on Friday, when Ted was in The Grapes with Gina Shaw.

'Are we there yet, Mike? I'm not confident of a result for Damson Drive so I'd really like to tie up Sandstone Street if we can.'

'Charged and bailed him, boss. He's visibly shaken, especially with the update I was able to give him. Jezza and Maurice came back from their meeting to report that Children's Services are happy that, in the right conditions, not only would it be acceptable for the boy to testify, they now think it would be therapeutic for him to do so. They say that since he's started to talk, and to understand that he will be listened to and believed, he's really beginning to come out of his shell.

'Ms Castle was tight-lipped, as ever, but I can't see her advising her client to risk a not guilty plea now, with the amount of evidence that's building up against him. His best chance is to plead guilty but to say in mitigation that he had no intention of killing her. I doubt a jury would believe him, especially with what people have said about him and his character. But we both know that if he tries to deny it, shows no remorse and takes up a lot of the court's time, at great expense, he's likely to cop for a much heftier sentence if he is convicted, which seems likely.

'How's it going with Damson Drive, boss? I've been a bit out of the loop on that one.'

'Steve was in this morning, working on it.'

Mike frowned.

'He's not on the rota for today.'

'I know. I had to chase him out. With some difficulty. He's getting too bogged down in it. He almost refused to go.'

'The thought of Steve refusing to do anything you told him to is hard to imagine. Why is he so convinced the father is guilty?'

'To be honest, I don't know, but it's becoming worryingly close to an obsession. We need to keep a close eye on him because if the blood results come back negative, I'm not sure how he'll react. You know how stubborn he can be.'

It wasn't until late Monday morning that Ted received the lab results on samples taken from the bodies at Damson Drive. It was the news he had been both anticipating and dreading. There was nothing at all recordable to show the presence of any medication or drug in either body. The person doing the report had added a scribbled note on a Post-it to say they had tested for GHB as requested but that it was known for disappearing from the bloodstream rapidly. The note ended, 'Shame it happened on a Sunday. Made our job impossible'.

Ted decided to speak to CPS before he told the team. He was fairly sure what their advice would be, but he wanted chapter and verse to present to Steve if, as he suspected, he didn't want to let it drop. He'd never known him as fixated on a case before.

'He was determined to find the time to sit down quietly with him, somewhere away from work, and try to find out why this particular case had clearly affected him so badly. He must also buy Bill the first of the promised pints and see if he could shed any light on the current situation with Steve. He might simply be missing Océane but Ted had a feeling there was much more to it than that.

He sat for a moment, deep in thought, staring at the innocent enough little yellow sticker. He noticed he was tapping his pen against the desk, a repetitive sound which was starting to annoy him. He took hold of his phone to make a call.

'Jim, have you got five minutes for me to run something past you?'

'Ted! Good to hear from you.' Then, as an aside, 'It's Ted, dear. I'll go out into the garden to take it because it's shop talk.'

Ted heard the sound of a door opening then closing again, followed by Jim's voice once more.

'I can't tell you how glad I am to hear your voice, Ted. Bella has just this minute got all the maps and guide books out again to plan our next trip to a stately home or garden or something. I'd be even more pleased if you were phoning me to say you needed me to come in to consult on something. Even if I don't get paid for it.'

Ted had to laugh at that.

'You're painting a blissful picture of retirement. Glad I'm not heading towards my pension yet. I can't run to a visit, I'm afraid, I need to phone CPS next, but I wanted to run something past you, in case I'm missing anything obvious.

'Remember when I tell you all this that you know I don't drink, and I promise you I haven't fallen off the wagon.'

Jim listened without interruption while Ted set out succinctly what Steve was thinking about the Damson Drive case.

Then he said, 'Bloody hell, Ted, I've never heard anything as far-fetched in all my life! You don't drink, but what about Steve? Is he hitting the bottle? Or taking prohibited substances? I thought he was fairly level-headed.'

'He is, usually. I'm sure he's wrong – well, almost a hundred percent sure – but I keep thinking what if he's right? The thing about problems with blood tests on a weekend, and about GHB disappearing so quickly. A paramedic would possibly know that sort of information, after all.'

'And so might anyone with access to a computer,' Big Jim scoffed. 'Come on, Ted, this isn't like you. Section 2 of the Suicide Act 1961, encouraging or assisting suicide. I've come across it once before, in another division, so I know how hard it can be to prove. How the hell could you show that the man did either of those things, if he was outside the house at the time and apparently desperately trying to force his way back inside to prevent a second suicide attempt? And your two witnesses for that are coppers.

'Seriously, you need to have a long talk with CPS to be sure, but I don't see how you could remotely prove intent to assist. Nor prove any encouragement which may or may not have taken place. Not on what you've told me so far.

'I wish I could keep you talking for longer, to get me out of looking at more brochures. But it's CPS you need to be talking to, not me. I've never come across a case like this before and I'm glad I don't have to get involved in anything as complex as this any more. Even Jacobean architecture suddenly sounds appealing in contrast.

'Good luck with it all, and keep me posted. You're my get out of jail free card, after all.'

Ted decided he needed green tea before calling to speak to one of the Crown Prosecutors, to get their advice on how to proceed on the Damson Drive case. He spent the time it took him to drink it looking at the relevant Policy for Prosecutors in Respect of Cases of Encouraging or Assisting Suicide, so he'd at least have some idea of what they would be talking about.

All the information they had to date on the case had already been sent through via intranet, but that hadn't included anything about Steve's theory. That wasn't something Ted wanted to go outside the office in writing. At least not yet.

He phoned and asked to be put through to the prosecutor working on the file. He was pleased it was someone he got on well with. There were some he would hesitate about mentioning such an idea to.

'Hello, Pushpa, I don't know if you've had time to look at our file yet?'

'A very quick glance so far, that's all. Is there something new?'

'Nothing evidential, no. One of my officers has a theory, but we have nothing at all to back it up. I've had a quick look at the relevant legislation on the site but if you have a few minutes, I'd welcome your opinion on whether or not we could make a case.'

She listened in silence while Ted outlined Steve's theory. Occasionally she interrupted politely to ask a question for clarification. When he'd finished speaking, she was quiet for so long that for a moment, he wondered if she was either trying not to laugh or choosing her words carefully. Knowing her as he did, it was almost certainly the latter.

'The boring thing about us prosecutors is that we set a lot of store by the evidential stage. We have to consider that above all else, including the public interest. For background, as you probably know, the law has been tested and clarified specifically in assisted suicide, or voluntary euthanasia, which is often where we find such cases. It's also arisen because of some of

257

these terrible websites which incite people, often young people, to kill themselves.

'What you've mentioned here is something completely different, on the face of it. To clarify, your officer thinks the man first stabbed his son then somehow encouraged his wife to kill herself, but to do it whilst he was outside creating an alibi for himself. And there's nothing at all from the blood test results to indicate that either of the victims was drugged?'

'Nothing. A case like that, on a Sunday afternoon, inevitably led to delays. We were lucky to get a pathologist there at all. Ordinarily there wouldn't have been one available.'

'What about fingerprints on the knife? What do they show?'

'I'm still waiting on those results.'

'You've probably already studied the Act yourself, but if not, to get a successful prosecution we would need to show that the suspect performed an act capable of encouraging or assisting the suicide or attempted suicide of another person, and that the suspect's act was intended to encourage or assist suicide or an attempt at suicide.

'So in summary, Ted, as you have nothing showing up on the bloods, no witness, no fingerprints yet, and your potential suspect outside with the police at the time of death, you can see the difficulties, I'm sure. Are you absolutely certain about the timing of the death? Could the lady have killed herself, if indeed she did, earlier, when the husband was in the house? Before the police came to break in?'

'Both the first responders, who are experienced officers, say it looked as if she had died moments before they gained access. The body was still warm to the touch and the blood from the wound hadn't yet started to congeal.'

'And there's no way, for example – excuse me if I sound as if I'm telling you how to do your job, but I'm merely covering all bases on which to offer my advice – but could he possibly have stayed inside with the wife, making sure she did the deed, and only hurrying outside at the very last minute when he heard the police arrive?'

'He would have been taking one hell of a risk, cutting it fine like that. Timing would have been critical, if that really is what happened. I doubt the area car would have arrived on twos for something like this, although they might have had the lights on. I doubt they'd have used the siren on a Sunday afternoon in a quiet residential area. But that's something we can at least look into, and it gives us one more thing to check before we come back to you for a definite decision.'

'From all you've told me so far, and going on my initial scan read of the file, I'd be inclined to say this sounds like something which needs an inquest to determine. I certainly don't see you having the shadow of a case against the husband at present.

'Let's talk again tomorrow, see if either of us has anything further to add. If I had to second guess it, which I don't normally like to do, I would see this having a murder-suicide verdict returned by an inquest jury with no further action required from your side.'

Ted agreed with her. She was thinking along exactly the same lines as he was. Now all he had to do was to persuade Steve that there really was nothing more they could do with the case and he needed to let it go.

Chapter Twenty-six

Ted was about to go and see who was in, to report on his discussion with the prosecutor, when his computer pinged and he found the results of the fingerprint analysis on the knife recovered from the scene, where it had been found still in the woman's chest.

No surprises there. The last prints on the handle were those of the wife herself. The husband had willingly provided his for elimination purposes. There was a smudged one, most probably one of his, close to the hilt. Blurred, and not enough of a match to be of any evidential use. Unless he was never involved in any cooking or washing up in the house, it would be unusual not to find some indication that he had handled the knife at some point.

Without anything else to back it up, Ted knew that they stood no chance of making any kind of a case based on one partial smudged print.

He went to find Jo first. Steve was at his desk working but studiously ignoring Ted, although he had returned his greeting first thing. There were clearly some bridges to be built there, and the news Ted was going to have to give him wasn't going to help with that.

'NFA pending the inquest then? Do you want me to let the husband know that he can go back to the house whenever he wants to?' Jo asked him. 'Although I can't imagine him wanting to go back there to live. Perhaps he'll put it on the market and get somewhere else. Shall I tell Steve or will you do it?'

'Let's get everyone together at the end of the day and tell them all then. He's not going to be happy so we need to find him something else to start work on straight away to keep his mind off it.'

'Oh, I think we can rely on the local scallies not to leave us short of work.'

Steve listened to the news without comment, before they all finished for the day, his expression impossible to read. Ted had found time earlier to talk to Bill about him.

'There's not enough beer in any Stockport pub to compensate me for the horrors of a Sunday in a garden centre,' Bill had complained. 'I even put up with us having our dinner there because I thought Steve might talk to me a bit more over a meal. I should have known better. I've interviewed some hard cases, Ted, but Steve can be like a Trappist monk in comparison. I did try, though, I really did, so you still owe me that pint or three. And don't worry, I'll keep an eye on him, as best I can.'

* * *

'For god's sake, woman, it doesn't matter what you wear. It's not you he wants there. It's me. I'm the one he looks up to. The one he aspires to be like. What have you ever done for him, eh? He wouldn't even notice if you didn't turn up. Again. You've been letting him down all his life. You're nothing but one big disappointment to him. And to me.'

She kept her eyes averted from him. Not simply to save herself from looking at the scorn and contempt in his face, but so as not to give him any reason to kick off. If she wasn't looking at him, he couldn't accuse her of defying him.

Could he?

'I just want to be there. To see him in his uniform. I won't embarrass him. Or you. I promise. I won't even say

261

anything. I'll sit quietly. I won't show either of you up, honestly I won't.

'Which of these do you think I should wear?'

She was fiddling with two outfits she'd laid out on the bed. One he'd bought for her for a rare occasion he'd wanted to take her out to show her off to work colleagues, when it suited his agenda. The other was one her son liked. He always said it brought out the colour in her eyes, which surprised her. She'd always thought of her eyes as a dull, lifeless, grey colour. Like everything else about her. Dull and drab.

Perhaps he was right. Maybe her son wouldn't want her there, now he had new friends, and a promising new career beckoning.

The man was shouting now. Mimicking the whine of her voice, like he did.

'*Which one should I wear?* You don't need either of them. Are you deaf as well as stupid? He doesn't want you there. Neither of us does. Why can't you get that through your thick head?'

'I just want to see him ...' she began, repeating herself. Remembering, too late, how much it annoyed him when she did that.

This time he gripped her, painfully, by the upper arms, his fingernails digging into her soft flesh. He shook her so hard that she felt her teeth clacking together. Then he flung her backwards onto the bed, on top of the clothes lying in readiness. Her head whipped back and connected with the wooden headboard.

He jumped onto the bed on top of her, straddling her with powerful thighs. Grabbed her by the hair and shook her some more.

'I'll show you the fucking photographs if it will stop you whingeing. But what have you ever done to earn the right to be there? You tried to take him away from me, don't forget. I'll never forget that. God knows where you thought you were going, or how either of you was going to survive without me.'

He was poking a finger into her breast as he spoke, each jabbing movement sending pain lancing through her body.

'Where d'you think he'd be now if I'd let you get away with that? Eh? Do you think he'd have got to go to university, living with a single parent in some sordid refuge somewhere? Got through selection? Got into training school? Of course he wouldn't. It's me who put him where he is today. It's me who's earned the right to see the results of all that hard work I've done with him. Not you. He doesn't want you.

'All you did was push him out into the world. You've never done a thing for him since, except embarrass him and stand in his way. And give him your pathetically weak genes, making him a target for the bullies.

'But at last he's getting somewhere, learning to stand up for himself. The only way you'll ever be any use to him is dead. At least that way I could give him the insurance money to start out in his new life.'

The hand which had been stabbing at her now moved to grip her round the throat. She started to panic, thrashing about, her legs kicking the carefully prepared clothes on the bed, crumpling them up.

She saw the familiar gleam in his eyes as he noticed her fear. Tried desperately to pull herself back from the brink. Not to show him the terror which was building inside her. His lips twisted in a sick smile.

His voice was much quieter now. Hoarse.

'You whore. You never could resist a bit of rough, could you? It turns you on, doesn't it? The pain. You pretend you don't like it. But I can see it in your eyes. Every time. You love it. You're gagging for it.'

263

She tried to shake her head in denial but he was gripping her too tightly, his other hand tearing at her clothing.

'If you're very good – very, very good – I might take a video of him to show you. It's up to you. But you're going to have to work for the privilege. Hard.'

* * *

Probationer Steve Ellis was sitting close to the front of the large room, waiting eagerly for the proceedings to start. He kept unconsciously tugging at his carefully brushed uniform. Flicking at imaginary specks on shoulders and sleeves.

Every few minutes he turned his head to look again at where the parents of all the other probationers were sitting proudly in smiling rows. There was no sign yet of his mother and father and that surprised him.

His mum wasn't a good timekeeper. She always got so nervous and flustered if she had to be anywhere at a certain time. He was sure she would have made an effort, though. Today, of all days.

She'd been so bitterly disappointed to have missed his graduation. Another of her so-called accidents. Another time for his father to haul her off to Casualty with some plausible story about what had happened, so it was carefully documented but nothing was ever flagged up.

He'd been there, though. Basking in reflected glory.

They were now very late. By the look of it, the last of the parents and relatives to arrive. His father was paranoid about punctuality. A certain trigger to make him flare up if anyone was ever late for anything.

Steve looked down at his shoes. Checking they still had the mirror shine he'd spent ages the night before putting onto them. The old traditional spit and polish. His dad had taught him how to do that. Then he looked round the

room once more. Perhaps his parents were there somewhere and he hadn't spotted them yet. He knew his
mother would want to wave to him, as soon as she
caught sight of him. Knew, too, how much that would enrage his father.

But they weren't there. Not even standing at the back,
having arrived late, and not wanting to draw attention to
themselves by finding seats amid the stares of all those
other proud parents present.

Now the Chief Constable was walking out onto the
platform to address them and Steve was confronted with
the reality. The proudest moment of his life, and his parents hadn't come to witness it.

* * *

'I'm really sorry to disturb you, inspector. I know how busy
Passing Out day is. I'm Steve Ellis's father and I'm afraid
I have some very bad news for him. I can't get there at
the moment so I wondered if you'd be very kind and pass
it on for me?

'Me and his mother were so looking forward to being
there today, of course, but I'm afraid ...' his voice broke
for a moment.

He gave a cough, cleared his throat, and carried on.
'Steve's mum has suffered a lot with depression over the
years and it all ... well, it got a bit much for her today.

'She's killed herself.'

'I'm sorry to hear that. What a terrible thing for you.'

'Thank you, inspector. It's really shaken me up, I can
tell you. I wasn't expecting anything like this. And certainly not today, of all days. She'd been so looking forward to seeing our Steve in his uniform for his Passing
Out. She missed his graduation because she'd had one
of her accidents. But it was the usual thing with her today.

265

She had very low self-esteem. She couldn't decide what to wear. She was worried she'd let Steve down if she wasn't dressed exactly right.

'I tried to help, of course. To tell her she looked lovely and Steve would be so proud to have her there. I thought I'd succeeded, too. She'd chosen her outfit, went off to have a bath and get herself dolled up. She was ages, but you know what women can be like, getting ready for a special occasion. I called to her but she didn't reply. So I went in.'

This time there was no mistaking the sob in his voice as he took a pause to regain control.

'She'd slit her wrists. There was nothing I could do, although I tried. She was already cold. Since then I've had the police here, the works. You know yourself how it goes. You think you know it all off by heart, but when it happens to you for the first time, it knocks you sideways.

'I'll talk to Steve myself, of course, when I've had the chance to come to a bit. To take it all in. But I know he'll be fretting that we weren't there, so I wondered if you could kindly tell him what's happened? Not too much detail, though, of course, I'd rather do that myself. But if you could please let him know that his mum's passed away. Give him my love and tell him I'll call him as soon as I can.

'Oh, and if you wouldn't mind telling him how proud I am of him, and how much I wished I could have been there. Both of us. Me and his mother. Thank you, if you wouldn't mind doing it.'

'Of course, that's no problem at all. You can safely leave it with me. And I'm very sorry for your loss, Sergeant Ellis.'

* * *

Ted and Trev were sitting together on the sofa, half watching the television, piled underneath purring cats. Trev's resolve to economise by sticking to one glass of wine a day with a meal had somehow slipped to one with supper then a second one afterwards, when they adjourned to the sitting room. He cradled the glass in one hand. His other arm was draped around Ted's shoulders.

'I'm glad I went, in the end. To London,' he began. 'To meet the other victims. That in itself was a bit of an eye-opener. I was so blind to the reality I honestly thought I was the only one. Harvey's special chosen one. The love of his life. Like I thought he was the love of mine. I didn't even consider myself as a victim in a way because I really thought it was a love affair. The stuff of fairy tales and soppy films.'

He paused and turned to smile at Ted.

'I realise how naive that sounds now. Even after all these years, I hadn't quite come to terms with it. No wonder Jono thought I wouldn't make a good witness. I must have sounded like a lovesick puppy, talking to him about it.'

'That's understandable. Abusers, especially paedophiles, are highly manipulative. It's how they get to do what they do.'

'Yes, but I should know better by now. I've been living with a cynical old copper for years.'

Ted turned to him with a suggestive expression on his face.

'Hey, less of the old, please. Or I might have to prove to you that I'm not past it yet.'

Trev's delighted laugh was cut short by the sound of Ted's mobile phone.

Bill calling.

'Ted, get round here. Now. Steve's slit his wrists.'

Ted let out an expletive and shot to his feet, scattering indignant cats. He made an apologetic face at Trev, mouthed, 'Sorry, got to go', then rushed out into the hallway to shove his feet into shoes, grab a jacket, the car keys and his photo ID. He wasn't planning on obeying any speed limits on the way. The

267

sight of that round his neck might help to prevent any hold-ups.

'Is he still alive? Have you called an ambulance?' he asked Bill, rushing to open the garage doors, hoping Trev would think to come out and close them again before someone nicked his bike.

He left the call connected to Bill, now on speaker-phone, while he drove as fast as he dared.

'Of course I've bloody called them. What d'you think? They're warning of a delay, though. And yes, he's still alive, but he's not responding. More like shut down than unconscious, if you know what I mean. Like he's embarrassed that I found him before he succeeded, or something.

'Come in round the back. You know how to. The front door's locked so make sure you open it so the ambulance crew can come straight in. We're in the bathroom. He's slit his wrists in the bath, the silly little sod. I've let the water go. I thought that might help. If he's cold he might not bleed as much. As long as it doesn't send him into shock.

'But I'm struggling to get enough pressure on both wrists at the same time by myself and my bloody bad leg isn't liking the position I'm in. So get yourself here as fast as you can, whatever it takes. He's hanging in there, for now, but only just. It's like he's given up. Wants it all to be over.'

Ted shot through one traffic light that was nearer to red than to amber, overtook wherever it was remotely possible, and no doubt frightened the life out of some other drivers on his way. At least he arrived outside Bill's house in record time.

He carefully squeezed down the side of the garage, climbing on top of the rickety fence to do so. He'd insisted on being shown the back way into the house after Bill had made an attempt on his own life with pills and booze some time ago, then had done nothing but grumble that the first responders Ted had called had had to break the front door down to gain entry. Ted had enjoyed teasing him about an ex-copper living in a house which was so easy to burgle. He was grateful now for the ease of entry.

Father Jack, Bill's irascible cockatoo, raised his crest and started squawking angrily at the site of an intruder coming in through the back door, but calmed down somewhat when Ted spoke to him. The bird had lived at Ted's house while Bill had been in hospital, much to the disgust of the cats and of Trev, who had a phobia when it came to anything feathered and flappy.

Bill had also heard him come in and called out, 'Top of the stairs, turn left, Ted, and shift yourself.'

Ted opened the front door slightly then sprinted upstairs, first aid case in hand, thankful he'd remembered to replenish the dressings he'd used on Mr Green. Force of habit, learned on one of Green's survival training courses, about never getting into danger by running out of anything vital.

Steve was limp and unresponsive, but there was eye movement behind his closed lids and he was breathing. Bill had wrapped towels round each wrist and was holding both arms, clamped together as firmly as he could, high up, in an effort to reduce the bleeding. Ted could see from his grimaces of pain that staying immobile in that position was causing pain to his old leg injury.

Ted went into autopilot mode, remembering every bit of first aid training he'd ever done, starting with trying to reassure the casualty.

'Steve, it's going to be all right. Bill and I are going to look after you, and the ambulance is on its way. Come on, Steve, stay with us.

'Bill, I think we should perhaps put a light cover over him so he doesn't go into shock. I'll take over here while you go and find something. We should leave the towels in place but I've got bandages. I could put those over them to get some even pressure on to try to stop the bleeding.'

Bill got up from his crouching position with some diffi-culty. There was no mistaking the genuine affection in his expression as he looked down at Steve, who was naked in the bathtub. Bill had previously told Ted that Steve always kept his T-shirt on in the shower. They could both now clearly see the reason for it. Both upper arms and his chest were criss-crossed with a web of fine white scars, long healed. The razor blade Steve had used on his wrists was lying in the bottom of the bath tub.

'This lad's been to hell and back, Ted, and we've all missed it. All of us. When he gets through this, we need to do a lot more for him.'

'He's right, Steve,' Ted said quietly as Bill stumped off to find a cover. 'We've let you down badly. It should never have come to this. But you're going to be okay. We're not going to let you go.'

From downstairs, he heard a knock on the partially open front door and heard a woman's voice call out, 'Ambulance crew. Somebody called us?'

There was no mistaking the relief in Bill's voice as he called out, 'Up here, love, top of the stairs on the left.'

Then he shouted, 'Shut up, Jack,' as his bird started screeching and swearing horribly at the intruders.

'You hear that, Steve?' Ted said, his voice still soft. 'Cavalry's here. You're going to be all right. You are. Everything's going to be all right.'

Chapter Twenty-seven

'He's in there, in the bath. Steve, he's called. Steve Ellis,' Bill told the ambulance crew as they came up the stairs. 'I'm Bill, he lodges with me. I was looking for a cover to put over him.'

'That's fine, Bill, you can safely leave him to us now. Thank you,' the first woman up the stairs told him, as she and her colleague headed the way Bill indicated.

'Steve? Can you hear me, Steve? I'm Amanda, this is Jayne. We're paramedics. We're just going to have a look at you, if that's all right?'

She barely glanced at Ted until he held up his photo ID and introduced himself, briefly explaining the first aid he and Bill had applied.

'You've done all the right things, by the sound of it. We'll need to get him to hospital as soon as we can, but we'll get him stabilised first. I might need to put a line in. Was he unconscious when he was found? And do you know roughly how long ago this happened?'

Bill gave her the details whilst she was assessing Steve. She sent her colleague to get what was needed from the ambulance while she worked.

'I imagine it's an awkward lift out of a bath, so I'm happy to help in any way I can,' Ted told her.

Amanda smiled her thanks but said, 'That's kind, but as you can probably imagine, it's a bit of a paperwork nightmare if I let you. You probably know all about that in your line of work. Risk assessments and all that stuff. It's fine. Jayne and I are trained for it.'

She turned her attention back to her casualty.

'Steve? Can you open your eyes for me? We're going to get you sorted then we'll take you to A&E.'

Still no reaction from Steve, although once again Ted saw eye movement behind the closed lids.

'He lives here, you said. Are you his next of kin, Bill, or does he have any family?' Jayne asked Bill when she came back with the equipment. 'Someone you need to call? And does one of you want to come with him in the ambulance, so he's with someone he knows?'

'I'll go with him,' Bill said immediately. 'I don't know about any family. He never mentions any. Ted, d'you know?'

'I don't. I'd need to get the details from his file. You go with him, Bill, I'll follow on in the car, then I can at least bring you home afterwards.'

Bill's chin jutted stubbornly at that.

'I'm staying with him as long as he needs me.'

Amanda and Jayne had been working efficiently while they spoke. They'd got Steve out of the bath and into the transfer chair Jayne had brought back with her. They'd put a cover over him and additional pressure bandages over what was already in place. They were now good to go, still explaining to Steve what was happening, although he remained unresponsive.

They put the blue lights on the ambulance as they pulled away, to give them a clear run to the hospital. Ted followed behind, taking the chance to put the phone on speaker and call Trev.

'Hey, you, are you all right? Was it another body?' Trev asked, sounding anxious, as soon as he answered the call.

'I sincerely hope not,' Ted replied with feeling. 'Bill and I are on our way to hospital at the moment, with Steve. He's ...' he paused, not yet ready to put into words what had happened. 'He's been injured. I've no idea what time I'll be home. I need to stay until I know he's going to be all right, then to run Bill home. He's in the ambulance with him.'

'Oh, god, Ted, I'm so sorry. Is he going to be all right? Are you?'

'I won't know about Steve until he's been seen in A&E. Bill hopefully got to him in time. I'll try to keep you posted when I can but like I said, I've no idea how long I'm going to be.'

Ted found Bill sitting with a morose and worried expression on his face in a waiting area, his eyes flicking towards the doors whenever anyone appeared. There was clearly no news but Ted asked anyway, for confirmation.

'Nothing yet. It seems like a bloody long time I've been sat here, but I don't suppose it is really. Ted, d'you think he was conscious all that time? He seemed to react to what was happening, I thought. Did he mean to kill himself, or was it just the proverbial cry for help? What tipped him over the edge? What is it about this latest case?'

'Honestly, Bill? I don't know. I should have seen it coming, but I didn't. Look, it's no point us sitting here speculating until we know if he's going to be all right, and we have some more details. Do you want a cup of tea or something?'

Maurice Brown would have suggested hot chocolate. Ted somehow felt Bill was not a hot chocolate sort of a person. And even if he was, now was not the moment.

'I'd prefer a bloody Scotch, but I don't suppose there's any chance of that here. Aye, go on, a tea. I'll wait here, in case there's any news while you're gone.'

There wasn't. They had to wait more than an hour, sipping endless cups of tasteless tea from a machine, before a registrar came to find them.

Bill started to talk while they waited.

'He was acting strange when he got home from work. Moody, like. He gets like that sometimes. Very closed. He usually goes up to his room and gets on his computer to talk to that

273

lass of his. She's good for him and it's clear how much he misses her. Sometimes he puts his music on. Not that I would call it that. Just noise, to me. He's considerate, though. Doesn't often put it on too loud.

'Today was different. He put some bloody soppy song on. On a loop, like. Over and over. Summat about wishing on a star. Proper got on my nerves, so I shouted up to see if he were going to have a shower before we had our tea. He turned it off and went to run a bath. He was still humming that tune, while he was in the bathroom. I should have realised sooner that summat were wrong. It's my bloody fault, Ted.'

'If anyone's at fault here it's me. I'm his senior officer.'

Bill snorted.

'Don't be so bloody soft, man. You've more than enough on your plate. You've got a DI and two DSs who should be keeping a closer eye than you.'

They were interrupted in their blame game by the appearance of a doctor walking towards them.

'I'm told you're here for Steve Ellis. Is that right?' she asked. 'Are you family?'

'Work colleagues,' Ted told her, holding up his ID. 'I'm his boss. Sergeant Baxter here is his landlord. How is he? Is there any news?'

'We have the bleeding under control so he's considered to be out of danger now. It's routine to want to keep him in at least overnight after something like this. We would normally suggest that he talks to one of our colleagues from the Psychiatric unit before he leaves. If he'll allow us to help him, that is.'

Bill opened his mouth to ask when they could see him but the doctor cut in, sensing the question he was about to pose.

'I'm afraid he's made it clear he doesn't want to see anyone for the moment. Again that's fairly normal behaviour with something like this. I've given him something to settle him, so the best thing I can suggest is for you to give him a bit of time to rest. You might as well go home, then phone in the morning for an update.

'I know it's a dreadful cliché but he really is in the best possible hands.'

It was late by the time Ted got back home. He'd had a long and sometimes heated discussion with Bill on the drive back about how Steve had managed to slip through the net without anyone noticing how much he was being affected by the current case.

Ted was anxious not to leave Bill on his own until he was as confident as he could be that he wasn't about to do something similar, because he was still busily beating himself up about Steve. He sat with him while he drank a couple of large glasses of Scotch, then saw him safely upstairs and settled before he felt happy to leave him.

Trev had clearly been waiting up for him but had fallen asleep in front of the television with the cats. Adam woke as soon as Ted entered the room, then jumped down from the sofa and went to wind himself in and out of his legs. He was purring his contentment to see his favourite human back home safely.

Ted picked him up, to Adam's delight, and held the squirming, purring cat against his chest as he stood for a moment, watching Trev sleep. It usually took loud noise and a fair amount of shaking to wake him when he was deeply asleep. He seemed to sense Ted's gaze on him, though, as he stirred, stretched like one of the felines surrounding him and opened his eyes.

'Hey, you. I was trying to stay awake for when you got home but I must have dropped off. Are you all right? How's Steve? And how long have you been standing there staring at me? From anyone else, that would be a bit pervy.'

Ted smiled and sat down as Trev made room for him by re-arranging cats.

'You looked too peaceful to wake. Steve's out of danger for now, but he still has a long way to go before he's okay.'

'What happened? Did he get assaulted again? Poor sod.'

'I can't really talk about it.'

Trev looked at him shrewdly, reading the unsaid meaning behind his words.

'Oh, crap, Ted. A suicide attempt? Is that it? It is, isn't it? I can tell by your face. Poor Steve. Is he going to be all right? What drove him to that? Is he going to be able to go back to work? Always assuming he wants to, of course.'

Ted leaned his head back against the cushions, exhausted and emotionally drained. He was still cradling the little cat in his arms.

'Physically, he's out of danger, they told us. But he's got a long and difficult road ahead of him, if he wants to come back to Serious Crime, after something like this. He perhaps doesn't yet realise quite how difficult.'

Superintendent Debra Caldwell echoed Ted's words from the night before when he went to her office first thing the following morning, to tell her about Steve. Even before he spoke, she sensed it was not going to be good news, so she put a cup of coffee in front of him without asking, then sat down to listen.

She didn't interrupt Ted as he gave her all the details, ending up with, 'Steve's been on this case since it started, because he was the only one available when the call came in. He has been getting a bit obsessed with it, and with his theory of what might have happened. I should probably have pulled him off it sooner, but he's been working on it with Jo, so I thought that might be all right.'

'There's no point in recriminations at this stage, Ted. Certainly not any self-blaming. Let me have a full detailed report as soon as you can, please. We'll certainly have to look into any possible failures in the system, and what we need to do about them in future.

'We both know that when he's ready to come back to work, it can't be straight back to CID. Certainly not to Serious Crime. He'll need to be seen by Occupational Health, of course, and there's a long road ahead of him before he rejoins the team. Assuming he even wants to do that, after something like this.'

'I had an idea about that. I didn't sleep well last night, going over it all in my mind. I'd like to see Steve come back to us one day, if it's what he wants to do and he's up to it. I wondered, in the short-term, if he could fill in for Océane while she's away. I know it's a civilian post and they may have filled it already. But Steve's almost as good as she is and it might be exactly what he needs, when he's ready to come back.'

'We may be jumping the gun, of course,' the Ice Queen told him, scribbling herself a note on the pad on her desk. 'But I'll certainly look into that possibility. I think it would be important to have a route back to offer to DC Ellis, if and when he feels ready to return.'

Ted opened his mouth to speak but she interrupted him, 'And yes, before you say anything, I know the situation leaves you one team member down. The ideal solution is to second someone on a temporary basis from another division. Let me know if that's not possible, for any reason, and I'll look at bringing someone in from outside.'

Ted drained his coffee and stood up.

'Now I need to go and tell the team as much as I can about what's happened. And I don't expect that will be easy.'

Ted took Maurice and Jezza to one side before the morning briefing. They were closest to Steve of any of the team. Jezza in particular. He wouldn't disclose confidential information, not even to them, but he knew Jezza was bright enough to join up the dots for both of them.

'I'll tell the others shortly but I wanted you two to hear it first. Sergeant Baxter and I had to take Steve to hospital last night. He'd injured himself. He had serious injuries to both his wrists.'

He was looking at Jezza as he said it. He could see straight away that she understood.

'Oh, shit. Is he all right?'

'Hopefully he will be. He didn't want to see either of us last night, but they said he was out of danger.'

Maurice was a few seconds behind catching on. He was frowning his concern.

'You mean Steve tried to ...'

'He was injured, Maurice,' Ted repeated. 'That's all anyone needs to know at this stage.'

'Can he come back from this, boss?' Jezza asked him. 'If he even wants to, I mean?'

'It wouldn't be up to me alone to decide, Jezza, and it's not something I've had first-hand experience of before. So I simply don't know. If he wants to do it and it can be done, you know he'll have my backing.'

Friday afternoon, and the team members were starting to wind down for the weekend. Steve was out of hospital and back home with Bill who, when he wasn't at work, was doing his best to look after him and to get him to talk. Steve was still refusing visits from any of his close colleagues, even Jezza, but apart from being even quieter than usual, Bill reported he seemed to be improving and was even talking about getting back to work in a desk job, away from Serious Crime for now.

The Ice Queen had pulled some strings behind the scenes – something she was good at – and Steve had been offered the opportunity to fill in for Océane whilst she was in the States. There was also talk of him taking some accumulated leave and going to visit her there before returning to work, on the first rung of the long ladder back to his previous post.

Ted had spent most of the day in his office, sorting paperwork. The trial in London was due to start the following week and he had promised to go down with Trev the day before it began. Trev would be one of the first prosecution witnesses scheduled to be called. They wouldn't be staying in the family flat this time as, to Trev's astonishment, his father was also being called as a witness for the prosecution, so he would be using his flat.

The prosecution were anticipating the not guilty plea would go ahead and had warned Trev that the trial could, in that event, prove to be a lengthy affair. Now they had Sir Gethin on side, and were also calling him early, they remained optimistic of a slight chance the defendant's legal team would advise him to change his plea to guilty and make a plea in mitigation.

Ted had booked enough time off to allow for the trial running on. He'd told Trev, much to his delight, that if it should finish earlier than expected, they'd use the time to go and visit Ted's mother, Annie, in Wales. Trev was still expressing concern about her, about something clearly bothering her, although she was always dismissive if either of them tried to press her on it.

Ted's door opened after the briefest of knocks and Jo came in, his expression puzzled.

'Have you got a minute, Ted? Something a bit odd here on the Damson Drive case, so I'd like your opinion on it.'

'Take a pew,' he invited. 'What have you got?'

'Well, I've been keeping in touch with the husband, to make sure he knows what's happening every step of the way, both with the case and the inquest arrangements. I couldn't get hold of him today, so I phoned the brother, in Denton. He says he's gone to stay with their sister for the time being, but he never mentioned anything about it to me when I spoke to him.'

'Spur of the moment decision?' Ted suggested. 'Maybe he's closer to the sister? Had a falling out with the brother? He should have let you know, of course, but I wouldn't say it's odd, exactly.'

'Except that she lives in Australia.'

'Australia? Do you not need some sort of visitor visa to go there?'

'Not these days, apparently,' Jo told him. You can fill in an Electronic Travel Authorisation online, get it within the hour, and you're good to go for ninety days.'

'So it could still be a spur of the moment thing, despite the distance involved.'

'Why not mention it though? I've been speaking to him most days. Liaising with him so he has no cause at a future date to complain that he wasn't kept informed of the progress on the case.

'There's more, too. The brother says his house is on the market. And he says their sister has been saying for ages what a wonderful country Australia is and how there are plenty of job opportunities for paramedics where she lives.'

'Selling the house is understandable, though. He surely wouldn't want to go back there to live, after what happened?'

'In estate agent speak, it's on at "an attractive price for a quick sale". Ted, you don't think Steve might possibly have been onto something, do you? That the husband somehow pulled this whole thing off in a way we can never prove, just to get away and start a new life Down Under?'

'What about the daughter, though? Would he up sticks to move to another country and never visit her again?'

'By all accounts she doesn't know who anyone is, so she would hardly miss him. And her financial needs are all taken care of. He could have been planning this all along. He might even have applied for a visa, or whatever you need, to settle there and look for work.

'If Steve was right the whole time and we didn't take him seriously, it's little wonder he did what he did.'

Jo was the only one of the team members to whom Ted had divulged all the details of what Steve had done.

'It's worse, I'm afraid,' Ted told him. 'I checked Steve's files before I did my report for the Super, to see if there was anything relevant there. Steve's mother committed suicide. On the day of his Passing Out. He started self-harming because of it. As soon as he could, he put in for a transfer up to Manchester. His scars were noticed when he had another medical to change forces, but he seems to have convinced them that it was connected to losing his mother like he did, and especially because of the day it happened, and that it was now all in the past.

'His father gets a brief mention on his file, but not as his next of kin, and he seems to have no contact with him. He's a serving police officer. A Uniform sergeant.'

Jo switched to Spanish to do the swearing, knowing that the boss didn't appreciate strong language.

'Have we got this wrong on every single level, Ted? Have we let a guilty man fly off out of reach, and have we put Steve through hell because of it?'

'We had no evidence, Jo,' Ted told him. 'You know that as well as I do. No forensics, nothing usable from the post-mortem. Only Steve's hunch. And we can't go off intuition alone, no matter how good it might be. There's still the inquest, and an outside chance that the coroner and jury might not accept it as a simple murder-suicide. And still a slim possibility we may uncover something we haven't turned up before, despite all our best efforts.

'And ninety days, you say, for the travel document, if it's the temporary one and he has to come back? Then let's spend every spare minute we have before the inquest to see if there's anything at all that's been overlooked. Put Maurice onto it. You know he's good at things like that, especially if he thinks it might help Steve. And if the husband doesn't return for the inquest if he's summonsed to appear, he could risk being in contempt of court for that, which doesn't help his case.

'It's not over yet, Jo.'

Chapter Twenty-eight

Ted's mobile phone rang as he and Trev stood waiting on the station platform for their train down to London for the trial.

Trev frowned his disapproval as Ted reached automatically in his pocket to answer it.

'Ted Darling, if that is work and you're going to abandon me, this will end in divorce.'

'Sorry. It's not work. I better take it.

The number was withheld so Ted simply replied with, 'Hello?'

'Don't look now like the total bloody amateur you are, because you've clearly forgotten all of your training. You didn't even know I was behind you. And to prove that I am, you should wear that shade of green more often. The colour suits you.'

Ted felt the hairs on the back of his neck prickle and a strange chill run through him. The proverbial goose walking over his grave. Except that on this occasion, the goose in question was Mr Green. And he definitely had eyes on him, as he said, because Ted was wearing his favourite sage green polo shirt.

He knew Green had left Bizzie's several days ago. She'd phoned him at work one morning to report that when she and Douglas had got up that day, the room Green had been using was empty, the bed stripped, the sheets in the washing machine and a brief but grateful note left for them on the breakfast table, which was laid ready for them.

Ted assumed he would have headed straight back to his remote Scottish island, as soon as he was fit to travel. It seemed not.

'Everything should be all right now. It's all sorted. But only if you keep your dull wits about you and watch your back, for god's sake.'

If Ted had been surprised to hear from him, he was completely gobsmacked by Green's next words.

'Your Professor did a good job, and neither of them asked awkward questions. So I owe you, Gayboy. You got me out of a fix and I never forget a favour. Call me if ever you need me. But for god's sake buck up and keep your eyes open.'

Then he was gone.

When Ted turned to look around him, there was no sign of the man anywhere.

The courtroom was packed with press and public. Media cameras and microphones were being wielded on every square foot of space outside the precincts of the court, their operators jostling for position to get the best images and interviews.

It was a high profile trial. A senior diplomat with a knighthood, often seen in public, facing numerous charges of grooming and sexual assault of young boys, mostly the sons of colleagues and even close friends. The red tops had been falling over themselves throughout the case to come up with ever more lurid headlines.

Ted had seen Jono, the Met officer in charge of the case, when they'd first arrived and had exchanged a handshake and a few words with him. Jono was there to give his evidence early on but would then go back to work, although he would no doubt return for the verdict and sentence. He'd want to see a positive outcome for all the hard work he and his team had put into the case.

Ted had been sitting in the public gallery throughout the trial. He'd given Trev a smile of encouragement when he'd taken his place on the witness stand. He was surprised when Trev opted for the oath rather than making an affirmation, as Ted himself always did when giving evidence. He thought Trev had left all trappings of his early Catholic upbringing behind him long since. Perhaps he was seeking some comfort from the familiarity of the words.

Trev's time spent with the other witnesses and advisors had paid off in spades. The factual content of what he said hadn't changed from what he had always maintained. But his delivery was totally different. When Jono had visited their house, both he and Ted had been worried that Trev made it sound like a romantic affair when talking about it. Still illegal, but definitely leaving room for the defence to go to town on the question as to whether or not the defendant, Harvey Warboys, could have reasonably been expected to know that the boy he seduced was under the age of consent.

Listening to Trev give his evidence now left little doubt. Ted could see that the jury members were following intently everything he said, one or two faces occasionally registering shock and revulsion at the breach of trust the words revealed.

The defence didn't have an easy job ahead of them. A character assassination of victims in abuse trials, apparently ones who were under age at the time of the alleged crimes, was always a risky strategy. The best they could try to do was to show that Trev was mistaken about dates and that he was, in fact, sixteen, the age of consent, at the time of his relationship with Warboys. Still morally wrong, in some eyes, given Warboys' close friendship with Trev's father, but not a criminal offence.

All those watching and listening could sense the jury members' reactions as Trev gave his reply, looking directly at Warboys in the dock. The accused was looking more mildly irritated by the whole procedure rather than worried about his future.

'I'm not mistaken about my age at the time. Harvey had

convinced me that ours was a special relationship. A love affair, if you like. I was naive enough to think that we had a future together. I wanted to tell my parents. He said we should wait and do it together. I was too impatient.

'Harvey and I had spent most of one particular afternoon together at his London town-house. Very much together. In bed, most of the time, in fact. My parents were also in London at the time. I had an exeat from school so I could visit them. I decided to tell them myself, which I did.'

Trev turned to look towards the jury for a moment, then looked at the judge as he continued.

'I told my parents all about my relationship with Harvey Warboys, and our supposed plans for our future together. I said he'd helped me to understand that I was gay.

'They were horrified. Revolted. And they didn't believe me.

'A lot of things were said that day. Hateful, unforgettable things. It ended with me being thrown out. My father gave me enough cash to get myself to Manchester where I had an aunt, who took me in. I lost everything. My family, my home, my education, the horse I loved. I was fifteen. I had to finish my schooling at a place in Manchester. The records of my time there are on file.'

The defence team must have known this was the one big weakness in their attempt at discrediting a key witness, but had perhaps been praying it would somehow not come up. Their counsel made a valiant attempt to recover, suggesting that Trev had perhaps not severed all ties with his parents after moving away, as he had said, but had continued to visit them after moving. That if, indeed, any relationship had taken place with their client, it had been during holiday visits to his parents in London, after he had turned sixteen. And that nothing improper had taken place between him and the defendant before his sixteenth birthday.

Trev was unshakeable in his testimony. Ted was used to

weighing up juries, getting a feel for how a trial was going. He could sense how much the jury believed Trev. He'd even seen one of them dab their eyes when he told of being thrown out by his parents at the age of fifteen.

Ted had kept the seat next to him reserved so that once Trev had finished testifying, he could sit beside him for the rest of the proceedings. As soon as Trev took his seat, he got hold of Ted's hand, fingers interlaced, and leaned close to him to ask quietly, 'Was that all right?'

'Perfect,' Ted told him, squeezing his hand.

Trev's testimony had been damaging to the defence. That of his father, Sir Gethin Armstrong, which followed immediately afterwards, was devastating.

Armstrong was brutally frank, making no attempt to defend his own actions. He stuck to factual accounts of the reasons why Warboys would know perfectly well that Trevor Armstrong was under age when he seduced him. Attending as a guest at his christening and his first communion. Taking his place with the family in church for Trev's confirmation. Being present to see him collect prizes from various schools he'd attended. Having been invited to most of his birthdays, when they were all in the same country at the same time, particularly his fifteenth, not long before the news came out about their liaison.

The defence were quick to pounce on his own admission that he had chosen to believe Warboys' word over that of his son. That, their counsel suggested, spoke to the high esteem in which Warboys was held by his friends and colleagues, and indicated how improbable the allegations were.

Armstrong's words, addressed directly to the judge, reduced more than one of the jury to tears.

'Your Honour, I did what no father should ever do. I chose to accept the word of someone I considered to be a trusted friend above that of my own son. I have never forgiven myself for that and I doubt I ever shall.'

Ted reached in his jacket pocket for his clean hanky which he passed to Trev who was unashamedly crying at his father's words.

Jono was waiting outside for Ted and Trev to come out when court rose at the end of the first day. He greeted them both with a handshake, then slapped Trev on the back.

'Bloody well done, Trev. Really good. I'm reading that as prosecution ten, defence team nil at the end of the first day. What d'you reckon, Ted?'

Ted was more guarded in his reaction.

'I'd like to think so. But we both know juries can be hard to read and very fickle.'

'I'm going for a pint before I get off home to my silly little dog. Fancy joining me?'

One pint turned into several for Jono, a bottle of wine for Trev and curries all round to follow. Jono turned out to be good company, the life and soul of the party. Ted hoped his dog had a strong bladder as it was much later than planned when Jono finally called himself a taxi to head home.

Ted had changed the usual arrangements he made for their cats while they were away. Instead of contacting the regular pet sitters he used, on a whim he'd phoned his old office cleaner, Mrs Skinner. He'd remembered her telling him one time how much she liked cats but could no longer have one because of where she lived. She'd been so delighted to be made to feel needed once more she had offered to visit twice a day without charge, although Ted had insisted on paying her. At least he knew he could trust her in his personal space.

Trev was quiet and thoughtful on the short taxi ride back to the hotel where they were staying for the duration of the trial. He only spoke when they got back to their room.

'Is that what he wanted to say to me, when he tried to get back in touch? I will never, ever, forgive my mother. No mother should ever throw their child out, no matter what. My father was always under her thumb. But what he said in court today? I could forgive him, after hearing him say all of that in public. I can imagine the effort it must have cost him.'

The defence team were now paddling a canoe with several holes in the hull and they knew it. Each subsequent witness only added to the damage. It was no surprise to anyone present when, after a short adjournment to consider, the jury returned a unanimous guilty verdict on the fourth day. It was approaching time for the lunchtime break so no sentence was expected before the afternoon.

Ted and Trev joined others who had given evidence during the trial at a nearby pub for lunch. The mood was jubilant. Ted had to suggest that Trev should limit himself to one glass of wine before returning to court, but he could imagine that whatever celebration was planned for the evening was going to be a lively one.

The courtroom was filling up rapidly ahead of sentencing. Ted stood aside to allow Trev to take a seat on a row which was already nearly full. Ted sat next to him, leaving one spare place at the end. He looked up in surprise as Sir Gethin appeared and stood next to the empty seat.

'Would you mind if I sat here?'

Trev blanked him. Ted, feeling compromised, simply gave a brief nod, then everyone was being instructed to stand for the return of the judge to pass sentence.

She spoke little, except to describe the crimes of which Warboys had been convicted as abhorrent and a heinous breach of the trust of friends. Then she announced the sentence as a total of twenty years imprisonment and the courtroom erupted, despite repeated calls for order and silence.

Trev jumped to his feet, pulling Ted with him and engulfing him in the biggest of bear hugs. Once he slackened his grip, Ted could see Sir Gethin was also on his feet, holding out a hesitant hand.

Ted turned to shake his hand. Then Trev was pushing past

him, putting his arms round his father, pulling him close and hugging him tightly, for what Ted knew was the first time in his life. He could see tears running down his partner's face as he buried it against his father's shoulder.

Sir Gethin looked directly at Ted over the top of his son's head. His lips moved silently.

'Thank you.'

The End

Printed in Great Britain
by Amazon

76345974R00180